THE VIGILANTE:
WHO KNOWS
THE
STORM

TERE MICHAELS

Dreamspinner Press

Published by

DREAMSPINNER PRESS

5032 Capital Circle SW, Suite 2, PMB# 279, Tallahassee, FL 32305-7886 USA
http://www.dreamspinnerpress.com/

ISBN: 978-1-63216-216-8
Digital ISBN: 978-1-63216-217-5
Library of Congress Control Number: 2014945929
First Edition October 2014

Printed in the United States of America
(∞)
This paper meets the requirements of
ANSI/NISO Z39.48-1992 (Permanence of Paper).

Someone I loved once gave me a box of darkness. It took me years to understand that this too was a gift.

—Unknown

You need chaos in your soul to give birth to a dancing star.

—Friedrich Nietzsche

PROLOGUE

New York City
Before

SEPTEMBER

NOX BOYET is fifteen and his only problems in the world are his upcoming physics test and the tiny shorts Patrick Mullens insists on wearing to lacrosse practice every damn day.

His father is traveling to parts unknown—again. He talks to the man's assistant more than he talks to his father, by a ratio of about ten to one. His mother has been at the hospital for four months due to "exhaustion"—again. Exhaustion means relapse and hospital means sanitarium, and he stopped needing codes when he was ten. Mrs. Grimes from across the street checks in on him every day, brings leftovers from the family dinners, and Nox uses the emergency credit card to eat a lot of pizza.

Then it starts raining.

OCTOBER

NOX BOYET is a few weeks away from turning sixteen. He desperately wants two things: for Patrick Mullens to stop being a cock tease (five minutes into a mutual hand job in the shower stall after practice and suddenly he remembered a piano lesson? Bullshit.) and for his father to let him have the old Beemer they leave at the house upstate.

He's getting A's in everything at Trinity, and the headmaster referred to him as a "fine young man, like your father" after assembly.

He'd tell his parents this in another attempt to get the Beemer, but his father hasn't been home in over a month. His mother? Five.

Mrs. Grimes said the LaMontes are leaving Manhattan because of the weather. She's staying to "watch the house," and Nox is secretly glad.

And it hasn't stopped raining for almost three weeks.

NOVEMBER

NOX BOYET is in hell.

Most of the neighborhood is deserted. Residents have fled for drier climes—some have moved temporarily to winter bungalows and summer residences outside the city. Every day there's another solemn story of people drowning and residents of the city and outlying areas being rescued by boaters. The subways and trains aren't running due to flooding. The tunnels in and out of the city are closed. Buildings have collapsed under the strain of the torrential downpours and ministorms sweeping in from the ocean. Nowhere on the island seems safe—and no one is making ark jokes anymore.

Mrs. Grimes has her nephew Roy staying with her at the house "for protection." She still comes across the street, splashing through the muddy river that is Ninety-Second Street, to check on him. He wants to tell her it's okay and he's fine, but honestly—he's not.

Trinity, like all the other schools in Manhattan, has cancelled classes. Most of his friends have left the city with their families. Patrick called him twenty minutes ago to say they're going to stay with his grandmother in Chicago. There are rumors the bridges will be shut down, like the tunnels already have. He's trying to be brave, but his father's assistant says she can't reach him and the lady who answers the phone at his mother's hospital says she isn't taking calls. She's in "isolation."

So is he.

He stays in his room, trying not to jump at every little sound. The power has been going on and off for almost two weeks, and if it weren't for all the crazy survivalist stuff his mother has hoarded in the basement, things would be way worse. He's never been so grateful for her paranoia and his father's black AmEx.

He's only a kid and he's not ready for this much responsibility.

ON HIS *sixteenth birthday, a policeman comes to the door as National Guardsmen roll down the street in jeeps, using a loudspeaker to tell people to be prepared to evacuate. He asks if Nox's mother is home, or another adult, but no, Nox is alone.*

Very alone.

The policeman tells him he's very sorry, but Nox's father is dead. His body was found at his office building near the stock exchange—a mugging, most likely. His assistant identified the body.

So sorry for his loss.

Nox doesn't cry. He walks around the house in a fog, the loudspeaker announcements of urgency fading to background noise. His father is dead. His mother is lost in a land of her own.

There are no grandparents, no aunts or uncles. All of the people considered "family friends" have fled, and really, it was mostly social, the connection from the Boyets to the movers and shakers of old money on the Upper West Side. They were hidden away in this house, shamed by his mother's illness and his father's workaholic ways.

He has no one.

A DAY *later, the National Guard goes door to door telling people they have to evacuate in twelve hours. The ferries will be departing from the Seventy-Ninth Street Boat Basin. Nox, curled up on his bed, looking at pictures of his mother on the wall, makes a decision.*

He fills his waterproof backpack with some food and water and all the money he can find in the house. He layers on the ski clothes he got last Christmas and prints out a map that will direct him all the way up to Inwood, where his mother's sanitarium, Morningside, is.

He's going to get her, and then they're getting the hell out of Manhattan.

HE HAD no idea what he was walking into—and no idea he wasn't coming back.

Now

SOMETIMES PATROL took Nox down past what used to be the Seventy-Ninth Street Boat Basin on the West Side. There was a memorial to the people who died when the ferries sank on Evacuation Day—a block of stone engraved with 1,957 names, the date. "Unknowns" tacked on the bottom for those who were never identified brought the number well over 2000. No bother of sentiment, no solemn saying emblazoned on a bronze plaque.

Only two names on that list mattered—he knew the location by touch, knew the curve of each hammered-out vowel. They were the reason he couldn't ever leave this place—they were the reason he walked fifty blocks a night to make sure the neighborhood was safe.

There were other memorials, other tributes to those who died during the storms. The floods downtown and on the Island, the fires in the Bronx and Queens, the building collapses on the East Side. But Mayor Freck's legacy was an administration that liked to remind the survivors their loved ones would want them to move on—they would have wanted the city to rise again.

Plaques said, *We remember.* The enormous hotels and casinos that cluttered inhabitable parts of the island said, *We've moved on.*

THE DISTRICT—blocks and blocks of Central Park West, Times Square, and Midtown real estate converted into casinos and hotels, built up and beautifully maintained, with a thriving clientele of wealthy jet-setters and a well-staffed security force that kept it as calm and orderly as a debutante ball. The New City.

After the storms, the city was left a hollow shell. So many uninhabitable buildings, so many residents forced into shelters in New Jersey, Connecticut, even Pennsylvania. Wait for the water to recede, wait for inspectors to check the buildings, wait for insurance companies. Real estate prices went from millions to pennies as abandoned buildings continued to sit dark and empty, molding as months passed with no one to tend to the mess. People, museums, and businesses relocated, with vague talks of "going back" when things got fixed.

When the federal money was slow to trickle in, the "going back" became "moving away permanently." With no commuters and no tourists, New York was a ghost town within five years of the evacuation. The wealthy business owners and their boards collected insurance checks and moved elsewhere—other states offered incentives to relocating businesses and the bottom line was simple. Cheaper to be elsewhere, cheaper than trying to rebuild. Cheaper to take tax breaks and move the headquarters of your company to Chicago or Dallas. Even better, most of your employees followed, because there wasn't anything to tie them to a rapidly declining city.

The middle and lower classes just couldn't survive. Many stayed as long as they could but in the end, six years after the storms, the population of New York dwindled to the lowest numbers since the turn of the century.

Three years later, as the remaining citizens complained of war-zone-like conditions and the rest of the country wondered why nothing was being done besides organized looting—Broadway in Las Vegas, museums around the world dividing up the great works of art, pro sports teams lured to nearby cities—a mayoral candidate named Louis Freck swept in like Hannibal on the elephant's back.

He demanded more aid from the federal government while at the same time preaching the resiliency of New Yorkers. He called for a radical plan to save the city: bring money in by lining the streets with gold and hookers.

Oh, he put it in a much nicer way. Playgrounds for the rich and richer. There were dioramas and beautifully rendered sketches for presentations, followed by minimovies and simulations as Freck's popularity grew. Worthless real estate revitalized by investment—all from the pockets of developers, not the citizens. The desperate New Yorkers attended rallies, cheering at the chance to have some hope. Rebuild the industry and the rest of the city would grow around it.

Freck won. No one even remembered who ran against him.

Things happened quickly after that. Dump trucks and backhoes from private companies cleared away the rubble; construction cranes once against dotted the streets. After two years, the skyline began to rise again.

Freck made an impassioned plea, and legalized gambling came to Manhattan Island.

Casinos.

Luxury hotels.

Boutiques.

Five-star restaurants.

The people in the outer neighborhoods waited for the trickle-down effect as time ticked by. One year, two years. Three years—so many promises, but the District needed time to grow, to make back their investments. It would happen—just be patient. Surely all of the money being poured into the District by visitors—surely it would reach their desperately empty pockets. Jobs would be plentiful.

Freck kept a few promises. He left some neighborhoods alone, zoned for residential rather than commercial use. They had power, fresh water. Crews removed debris from roadways, sometimes even repaved. A newly visible police force—as in, people actually saw black-and-whites cruising the streets.

It was a start, so no one questioned the curfew in the Old City. And now? Seventeen years since the Evacuation? No one bothered to complain about it. They'd grown used to the restrictions, the "doing without"—grown accustomed to the division of the city and abandoned their hopes that one day the largesse of the District would visit them as well.

Nox walked through Old Riverside Park, crossing up toward Ninety-First Street as he headed home. It was quiet. Curfew kept citizens inside after dark; the police didn't bother to patrol this far north, and the dealers generally stayed downtown near the underground clubs.

Generally.

These days they were growing bolder. Money was finally trickling out of the District, as whores and gambling bored the tourists after a while, and the "classy" joints couldn't keep patrons entirely satisfied. Visitors wanted something else, something thrilling and dangerous. Something they couldn't get anywhere else.

The secret of Dead Bolt: You could only get it here. A few hits of the pool-blue powder and the euphoria beat anything sold in those shiny casinos.

The movement of crime into residential areas worried him. For years he'd taken care of the stray criminal that ventured into his territory. He kept an eye on the street trade—he knew who had which neighborhood in their sights, which of the street gangs that had popped up over the years were an actual threat and which were just overgrown clubs for the bored and underemployed. The visitors could take care of themselves—he didn't care what they stuck into their veins or how many of them kicked it in alleys downtown. They were part of the problem, bankrolling the festering wound of corruption strangling his city.

Nothing would change so long as more money could be made on strangers with itches to scratch than on those carving out livings amongst the ruins.

THE COLD October air smelled like more snow—winter seemed to start earlier and earlier with each passing year, a double-edged sword of less crime and less food mixing together in five months of desperation. Junkies and dealers, workers and citizens, all trapped inside and trying to survive until spring.

It was crazy to stay—he knew that. It was just… still home to the ones who couldn't force themselves to leave. They'd survived the hell of the Storms; they'd made it when so many others perished. Maybe it was a badge of honor to scrape out an existence here.

He was a different story.

Where would he go? There were no fresh starts in the world for him. If he left the city, he'd leave behind all the tricks and lies he used to stay hidden. Here, money talked and laws were loose—he could play the system on the island. Off it? He'd be just another penniless drifter with no education, no plan, no real identity.

So he stayed. And he wondered if one day this city would be anything like the one he remembered.

A few blocks from home, movement caught his eye: two dark shadows hovering in the doorway of a long-abandoned store near the corner. A sliver of moonlight illuminated only their general shapes— men, most likely, darting together and pulling away but too tense, too sharp for it to be a romantic encounter.

A deal.

He blended with the darkness, stealthy and slow as he gained ground on the spot of transaction. The crisp, cold air was still, the icy sting pulling into his lungs with every breath. His clothes kept him warm; the black color let him blend into the shadows. The breathable fabric across the lower half of his face left him anonymous. A blackjack in his hand kept him safe.

Murmurings of the conversation caught his ears. He paused, listened.

How much can you get me tomorrow?

A pound.

He ducked and dodged the piles of bricks—buildings had come down on this street, destroyed by storms and fire, ignored by the city— until he reached the doorway one away from theirs.

Black-gloved hand tight on the weapon, breath held, eyes steady.

He exhaled and stepped out into the open.

They were unprepared for him. One lethargic and drunk on his own smug power—no police, people hidden away, no one to challenge him. The other's brain a mess from Dead Bolt and neglect, no idea how to defend himself.

It was over in a few seconds; the dealer lay unconscious, the junkie cowering in the corner.

"Stay out of my neighborhood," he said simply. He took the bag of poison and dumped it out into the dirty, slushy snow that lingered from the last storm. With the heel of his boot, he crushed it down to unusable dust. "If I see you here again, I'll kill you," he said, quieter now.

The man nodded, frantic and jerky in his movements.

He searched the dealer, taking his gun, credit cards, and identification pass before rolling him onto his back. A check of his pulse—alive and well—reassured him that his work was almost done.

His gaze on the wide-eyed junkie, he tugged the dealer's right arm away from his body until it was straight. Unfurled the fingers. A perfect target.

This was his signature, how they knew he meant business. He raised his foot, then brought it down onto the man's palm with his full weight behind it.

The dealer jolted awake, then passed out again from the pain.

Practice meant he knew exactly where to connect to break bones.

The junkie swallowed a scream; he scrambled away, tripping and falling in his haste.

Spoils in his pocket—and no backward glance—he continued his journey home.

At the corner of his block, he paused. Once upon a time it had been prime real estate—million-dollar brownstones, homes of the old moneyed elite who sent their children to Trinity, Dalton, or Spence. Pure class.

His mother's family had roots in the city that went back to when it was New Amsterdam. His father's people came later but in time to fight in the Revolutionary War.

He was a child of this city, generations of architects and bankers who believed this to be their legacy to the world.

They would hate it now.

The shadows cloaked his path to the doorway. Inside lay the world of another man, a man who worked a job and was responsible for another life, who paid his bills and lent a hand when his neighbors asked. He kept a low profile because he—more than anyone—knew that danger lay everywhere. And in everyone.

Nox dropped the gun down into an open grate; below, he could hear the rush of water that flowed under the city. Sewers, long-abandoned subway tunnels—the water lapped at the shores of Manhattan Island and crept up underneath them, a few more inches every year. The water would sweep the gun out to the Hudson. The credit cards followed, disappearing into the darkness.

The identification pass might get him into places he needed to be—that he kept.

When his knees finally creaked under the pressure, he stood up slowly, working out the kinks in his back as he twisted side to side. He had three hours before the alarm would sound on his other life—the Vigilante's night was over, and it was time to go home.

CHAPTER ONE

CADE CREEL liked to keep his clients happy and satisfied, so when Mr. White laid one pale, blue-veined hand on his knee and said, "I need you to do me a favor," Cade didn't hesitate with his yes.

"My favorite," Mr. White said, almost tender as he patted Cade's cheek. "This is our little secret."

Mr. White, at seventy-five, didn't ask for much from Cade—conversation and cocktails by the fireplace in the Monarch Suite, some pats on the shoulder and thigh now and again. A chaste kiss, once. He only wanted to spend time with Cade, tell his stories of a lost New York City and his glory days of privilege and excess, and be rewarded with dimpled smiles and smooth compliments.

For Cade, every Thursday night was three hours of civilized bliss. He got to keep his clothes on; he was treated like a person.

So when Mr. White asked a favor—just a quick run uptown to deliver a letter—how could he say no?

At the Iron Butterfly, the customer was always right, always entitled to whatever they wanted (as dictated by their credit rating and initial deposit, of course), and should always leave an employee's company smiling and satisfied.

"Of course," he said. "Whatever you need."

His need, apparently, was to have a private letter delivered to the Old City. He didn't trust the messenger services that handled all the mail, nor was he able to travel there himself.

All Cade had to do was place the letter in the hands of one Sam Mullens and he would earn Mr. White's undying gratitude.

Easy enough.

Which was how Cade—a minor celebrity in the District and the highest-paid "model" at the Iron Butterfly Casino—found himself trudging up what used to be Broadway, headed for Ninety-First Street.

He woke up early on Friday, determined to run his errands before lunchtime and take care of the favor well before curfew, but nothing went right with his morning or afternoon—the approaching Anniversary Weekend had thrown the entire place into a tizzy—and so now he was racing against the setting sun.

Caught in the Old City after curfew? He didn't want to have to explain that to the police. Or his manager.

Cade tucked his chin into the collar of his trench coat, arranging his cashmere scarf so everything below his eyes was slightly warmer. The wind off the Hudson River nipped at his heels as if reminding him to hurry the hell up. He'd walked all the way from the District, skirting around burned-out blocks and torn-up streets as he made his way north. Keeping the river on his left, Cade gave the old section of Central Park a wide berth.

He'd heard the horror stories.

District cabs refused fares up here—if you wanted to convince a driver, you'd better have a pile of cash on hand. He couldn't request a car from the service they used; this wasn't a job.

Following the grid pattern in the old part of the city wasn't easy— too many things up here were destroyed and demolished, streets covered in rubble and fallen high-rises, almost two decades of neglect wiping out the orderly function of numbered streets and avenues.

Normally, Cade stayed far away.

*Follow the river. As long as you see the red writing on the walls—*portus tutus—*you'll be safe. At marker 91, take a left. You'll see the gray house from there.*

Seriously—he'd played video games as a kid that started like that and usually ended with zombies and someone getting their brain eaten.

But what was the harm in a little adventure? So it was the Old City. So it was still touched by the ruin of seventeen years ago. So what if no one knew Cade was up here except a wealthy and slightly scattered millionaire who liked it when Cade wore white gloves to dinner.

Cade swallowed his nerves, felt the brick-heavy weight of the slender envelope in his pocket. He didn't know what was inside, but it might as well be a ticking time bomb given his jumpiness.

He wasn't cut out for this spy shit.

Sometimes the Iron Butterfly's manager, Rachel, imagined herself to be Mata Hari, keeping life interesting by playing with fire. He knew she dabbled in "information sales"—taking things picked up from scotch-soaked officials in dark corners of the casino and turning the murmured secrets into cash.

Sometimes she framed it as "doing good"—helping the little people who didn't have enough cash to bribe a cop or city employee like the rest of them. "Information should be free," Rachel would say, and maybe in other places it was. Here? Not so much.

Other times she drank too much and told him it was a good way to fuck with the bastards that ruined the city.

Did Mr. White fill his quiet days with the same sort of real-person chess? Was that what this was?

Up ahead, the path he was walking opened up a bit. Past the mess, he found a sudden expanse of space. Normality. Neat brownstones— bricks scarred and ivy covered—lined each street. A grocery store, open for business, showed off neatly lettered handmade signs in the window.

Milk—$10/qt

Homemade Bread—$6

Local tomatoes—$17 a bushel

We have REAL coffee! Only $35 a pound

A few people walked along the streets, most likely on their way home from the thousands of construction sites around the city—and all of them noticed Cade as soon as he emerged into the midst, their gazes like lasers.

Not one of them. Not a face they knew. Stranger.

Head down, Cade hurried on his way. There were signs here; like the grocery store, they were handmade. Red paint on black wood, fastened to buildings—or at least piles of bricks—on the corner.

89.

90.

91.

With the eyes of the neighborhood burning into his back, Cade strode down the third street he passed. The sidewalks were a mess, the streets torn up by weather and a lack of recent repair. Most of the buildings had clearly burned, hollowed-out shells with collapsed ceilings and walls. But the few houses seemed well kept, with many sporting flowers in window boxes along their top floors.

And bars on every window. Steel security doors marring the classic architecture. Gates lined each occupied home, sharp spikes deterring climbers.

In the middle of the burned-out block sat a slender gray townhouse that at first glance reminded Cade of a church. It stood defiantly in the ruins of that side of the street—at least half of it was nothing but overgrown rubble, the black char of fire giving the reason for its destruction. Only six homes remained standing on this street, a place Cade could imagine once housed the wealthy in this city.

He wasn't a native—home was the family farm back in South Carolina—but like every person in America, he knew what New York City used to look like.

For years after the evacuation, cable channels had run movie marathons and documentaries, detailing over and over the destruction of the world's most famous city. Storms and fires and freak events that erased everything it had taken hundreds of years to create. Tens of thousands dead. Landmarks and history reduced to nothing.

He was eight when it happened, and he didn't remember much—Mom made him and his brother get on their knees and pray for all the dead and missing. She stayed up late, crying over the pictures of death and destruction until Daddy made her go to bed.

Cade dropped his hand into his pocket as he skirted around a pothole that could have swallowed a delivery van. A huge tree, its roots erupting through the concrete, sat just in front of the stone steps, leaving barely a foot between its weathered gray trunk and the steel bars of the gate.

Cade took a huge breath, filling his lungs with the cold, crisp air. The insanity suddenly became more than just a hum in the back of his head; he was miles outside the District, with no protection, with no weapon, with no reason to be here he could possibly explain without getting in a shit ton of trouble.

The people back on the Avenue were dressed like what they were—the poor working class who built new hotels and casinos and cleared debris and delivered packages. They weren't even good enough to be hired to clean in the District—businesses imported people from the mainland for that. These were the idiots who'd never left, who'd never bothered to find better lives on safer shores.

This was where the crime was.

Creels aren't cowards, his dad would say with a shade of sarcasm, as if he didn't entirely believe the statement to be true in Cade's case.

So Cade walked, feet pounding against the concrete until he reached the front gate.

There was a latch, simple to unhinge. Leather gloves holding slightly trembling hands, he reached out, worrying all the time that it was electrified or triggered a silent alarm or….

Nothing. No bolts or jolts. Cade unhooked the latch and then pushed the gate open. It creaked, but no machine gun turrets appeared. No snipers with rifles. He took a deep breath.

He stepped over the threshold.

Still nothing.

Cade tucked his hands in his pockets, pinching his thighs through the fabric to try to control his anxiety. *Knock on the door, hand off the message. Get the hell out of there.*

A thin layer of sweat began to form between his body and the sweater/jeans combo he'd donned for this foolhardy trip. His boots clacked on the stairs. How was he so noisy? People would peek out their windows; everyone would see him. And those window boxes would turn out to be diversions when these people came out of their houses and killed him.

He pulled back his hand, whispered "fuck" under his breath, and knocked three times on the gray metal security door.

Nothing stirred inside the house. The curtains—dove gray and heavy—didn't move. No sounds could be heard.

Cade tried again, battering his gloved knuckles against the door.

This time a rattling followed, as if locks were being disengaged. Cade sucked in some air, stepping back slightly.

Hand over the envelope. Get the hell out of there.

After what seemed like forever, the sound of metal scraping signaled someone had heard his knocking. It pulled open only about six inches, then a young man's face appeared in the opening.

"Hey, hi. I have a delivery to make?" Cade tried to smile as warmly as he could.

The dark-haired kid didn't blink, amber eyes behind thick-rimmed black glasses, the collar and logo of a District messenger uniform visible and hanging loosely on his slender frame.

Ironic—he was delivering a letter to a messenger.

"We—we didn't order anything," he stuttered out. The door started to shut.

"No, wait. Um, it's for Sam? Are you him?" Cade asked quickly, trying to stop the door closing in his face. "It's from a friend of mine— Mr. White?"

No sign of recognition on the Mr. White part, but his eyes widened at "Sam."

"Yeah, that's me." Sam opened the door another few inches, still wary, from the look on his face.

"Great." Cade reached into his pocket slowly, then pulled out the letter. "I'm supposed to make sure you get this."

The kid reached out tentatively, like Cade was offering a snake. Or a snake offering an apple. He touched the corner, then snatched it away.

"Thanks. I think you should leave now," Sam said, his voice shaking. The door slammed a second later, almost knocking Cade backward off the stairs.

"You're welcome," Cade yelled before turning to leave. Seriously? All this effort to be treated like a delivery man?

"Not even a tip," he groused, jogging down the stairs. If he hurried, he'd be early for the staff meeting and could actually get something to eat before he had to get ready for his shift.

He walked back the way he came, the wind picking up as he got closer to the river. The people he'd seen before were gone, he assumed due to the approaching curfew. He *hoped* it was because of curfew, and not because they knew something he did not.

No, he wasn't doing that again. He would not see shadows or hear noises in the rapidly approaching twilight. After all, the worry he worked up on the way here turned out to be so much bullshit. His brother would probably count this as a "two punches for flinching" situation.

Next time he went for a visit (for the holidays... some holiday... at some point), Cade would bring this up to get a laugh from his family. Maybe a slight headshake from his father.

Of course you were scared, he'd think. *Pretty boy in a bad neighborhood.*

And then Cade would brush it off with a brag about his gorgeous apartment or latest electronics purchase, because that was how he and his father communicated.

Ah, home. Maybe he'd just call his mother for Christmas.

Something caught Cade's vision—a fleeting shadow on his left. He didn't slow down or move his head because he wasn't giving in to paranoia.

So what if he walked a bit faster. So what if he tried to remember the last time he ran for speed and not just to keep his body looking good.

Up ahead, shadows were moving, and Cade's hands tightened into fists. Paranoid or not, he couldn't explain away what was clearly a group of youths in matching jackets trying to stay hidden—and failing—a few hundred yards from his path.

Should he go back? Maybe the kid would open the door for money—Cade had some in his pocket, and he liked the odds of that over dealing with whatever was happening up ahead.

A particularly hard gust of wind knocked him a few steps to the right; Cade stopped to pull his collar up a bit higher. He regretted the lack of a hat right now. And maybe a gun. He should turn around now and make a run for the gray house.

In the middle of the fussing, he heard footsteps behind him.

CHAPTER TWO

NOX BOYET followed the man for five blocks, far enough away not to alert him to his presence. It was twilight, not his usual patrol time because the dealers wouldn't be out yet, but then it wasn't normal to find a stranger on his doorstep, talking to his son.

The jaw-clenching anger coursing through his body got him into his leathers and heavy boots before he could register what he was doing. He pulled his hood on, stuck the blackjack in his pocket, and waited for Sam to go into his room. Then he set off from the back entrance of the brownstone.

The man's expensive coat and shoes said "District." The neat shave, perfectly styled short hair, and pretty-boy face said "model."

Nox tried to reason out why he was there and why or how he knew Sam. Overly suspicious, Nox sheltered Sam to an almost obsessive level—homeschooling and hiding him away from the city until he couldn't justify the isolation to an ever-curious teenager. Reluctantly, he allowed him to take a very part-time job in the District, delivering documents to casinos and hotels.

The innocent answer to all this was that the guy wanted to sleep with his kid. The paranoia-induced alternative of someone knowing who Sam—or he—was made Nox walk faster, his soft-soled boots quiet against the uneven pavement.

They were nearing the narrowing of the street; damage, time, and neglect had turned everything between Seventieth and Fifty-Ninth into a concrete jungle, ignored by the city and useless to the residents because of the mess. It signaled the netherworld between the neighborhoods—and Nox's territory—and the edges of the District, where no one lived or worked except the junkies and their dealers.

Up ahead, the guy began to speed up. The darkness gathered in each corner of the sky, dropping shadows all around them. The curfew siren would sound in less than twenty minutes—but more pressing than that? Out of the corner of his eye, Nox could see some youth gang members loitering up ahead. Lying in wait.

Sam's mysterious visitor was about to get into trouble.

When he stopped near a partially collapsed building, Nox made his move.

Nox didn't blink—he crossed the twenty feet that separated them with a few quick strides and grabbed the man's shoulders. He shoved him into the small space between the remaining wall and a pile of broken concrete, deep in the shadows, slamming him against the wall.

The man froze—from fear, from shock—for a moment and then kneed Nox in the groin.

"Wearing a cup, but nice move," Nox grated out. He spun the kid around, then pushed him face-first against the wall, keeping his head down as he used his weight to hold him still.

"You want money? You want my watch?" the kid snapped, all indignant fury under that pretty-boy exterior. "Take it and get the fuck off me."

"Calm down—I just want to talk," Nox said smoothly, his voice modeled low and raspy, head bowed so the kid couldn't get a good look at his face. "What's your name?"

"Fuck you."

"Seriously? Must've been rough for you in kindergarten."

Nox adjusted as the kid moved continuously, like a prizefighter, trying to find the right angle to break Nox's grip. If he wasn't getting so damn annoyed, Nox would have been impressed.

"I'm going to scream this place down until the cops show up!" The kid was stronger than he looked, shoving back and squirming as Nox held him pressed against the wall.

"Stay still," he muttered, throwing his body weight into it and pressing his captive against the wall, molding their bodies together in a mockery of a lover's intimate cradling. "And shut up."

Close up, Nox finally recognized his little captive—every visit to the District meant seeing his face on the wall of the Iron Butterfly. A model, and a semifamous one at that. So what the hell was a fancy hooker doing chatting up his son?

"Cade, right?" he asked—which immediately stopped the struggling as the kid looked over his shoulder in surprise.

"How the hell...." Cade twisted, but he was clearly tiring out. "Let me go."

"Believe me, you're better off here than out there."

"Fuck you. The cops are gonna come up here and arrest you and I'm pressing charges," Cade spit out, struggling valiantly. Nox had a brief moment of nearly pitching over, so he dug his knee against the kid's balls until he grunted.

"The cops haven't been up here since the mayor's dog got kidnapped, which shows their priorities," Nox said, chatting casually as Mr. Creel turned redder and redder beneath him, one cheek pressed against the wall. "Take a breath before you pass out, sweetheart."

Pretty boy held his breath—out of spite, Nox suspected, and he shifted his weight the tiniest bit. He'd raised a toddler when he was seventeen years old—nothing this kid could throw at him would elicit a reaction.

"What are you doing up here, young Cade? This isn't really your territory unless you're trying to score something...."

The kid finally let out a breath, coughing a little at the end of the exhale. He shook his head. "I just came to—to see the area. I've heard things and I, uh—I just wanted to see it. I'm not from around here."

Nox cocked an eyebrow down at him. "That's your story? It's nearly curfew and you decided to take a walk to the Old City? You lived here long?"

Mr. Creel flinched, but his voice stayed perfectly convincing. "Three years."

"And after three years you decided to come see how the other half lives?"

"Yeah."

"Okay, then. I better let you get on your way."

Big blue eyes blinked up at him, surprised. Nox slowly slid off, letting Cade's hands go last. "Just be aware there are, like, five or six gang members about two hundred yards down the path. They probably won't be as understanding as I am."

The pretty boy turned and swung a haymaker in Nox's direction, missing a quickly dodging Nox by a hair. He nearly fell forward into Nox's arms.

"Fuck you," Cade wheezed.

"You keep saying that." Nox put his hands up in surrender. "Tell you what—you give me some information, and I'll make sure you get back where you belong."

The look he got in return was withering. Cade fixed his coat collar and scarf with shaking hands, then smoothed his disheveled hair. "I told you. I was just looking around up here and now I'm going home," he said breathlessly. "And I'm telling the cops you accosted me."

"As we discussed, the cops aren't interested in this part of town, so I handle things on my own." Nox gave him a quick salute, for which he received a serious scowl in return. "Those baby gangbangers probably aren't armed, but one look at your expensive clothes and they're gonna fall on you like wolves on a lamb."

Actual fear crossed Mr. Creel's expression. "Go fuck yourself."

"You really need a new insult," Nox drawled.

Cade stormed out of the alleyway but only got about twenty feet before stopping. He looked from side to side then ran a few more steps.

"Jesus Christ." Nox huffed out annoyance as he followed Cade, a few yards behind. In the distance, the shiny jackets of the Habanos were flickering in the setting sun's last rays. Their attention was focused on the young man frantically run/walking toward safety.

It was like watching an old nature documentary as a pride of lions stalked a gazelle.

Nox adjusted his pack, increased his walk to a trot. He veered off the path Cade was on and put himself in the sightline of the Habanos.

Their attention snapped to him, fear blooming in their eyes.

"This isn't your turf," the leader said, all gangly arms and legs and a shock of bright red hair.

"Turf? Seriously?" Nox took a step toward the youngster, using every bit of his broad-shouldered frame to intimidate. "Unless you want me to make it mine," he said, low and intense, "I suggest you let my friend pass without any problems."

No one said anything to that. They were all looking at the redhead, but he just shrugged.

"Don't let me see you around here anymore," the kid said, all bravado and a false sense of power.

"Deal." Nox refrained from laughing in his face.

Nox stepped back, his gaze never leaving the redhead's face. When the kid looked away, Nox knew he had won.

When he turned around, Cade was just a dot in the distance, well on his way to the District.

Now to go home and deal with Sam.

CHAPTER THREE

CADE DIDN'T have time to go back to his apartment and shower the fucking terror off his body, so he stomped and bitched under his breath until he reached the service entrance of the Iron Butterfly. There was a staff meeting this evening, and so what if he was a little bit early? It was just him being a gold-star employee.

Courteous Cade. Workaholic Cade. Cade, who was almost entirely booked up for the next six weeks with clients who couldn't get enough.

Cade, who just got tackled by a lunatic and menaced by some adolescents who thought they were Bloods or Crips.

Jesus Christ.

At least he delivered the letter. He would tell Mr. White things had gone perfectly well—the rest of it didn't matter, right?—and that lie might get him a few more hours a week of easy money.

He tried not to think too hard about what he'd just done, ducking around the puddles of melting snow, dirty from the wheels of hand trucks and the boots of workmen. Unlike the front of the casino, which boasted daily shining of the brass fixtures and glass front, no one bothered with the underbelly of day-to-day operations. A double door—black, battered, and bulletproof—kept out everyone not doing business with the Iron Butterfly.

After pulling off one leather glove, Cade lifted the cover off the keypad and pressed the eleven-digit code to get the security guard's attention. Two beeps answered him, and he keyed in another fifteen numbers.

The heavy door rumbled and buzzed, shaking slightly before creaking open a crack.

One dark eye and a bushy eyebrow appeared.

"Hey, Billy," Cade said, the epitome of laid-back casual, even as his heart thumped triple time. He didn't say why he was there early, didn't mention his dressed-down look in older clothing, didn't explain away the scrapes on his cheek.

Why start a lie when attitude would work just as easily?

"Mr. Creel." The door rattled open and the wide girth of their security guard greeted him. The black uniform—top to bottom, from cap to steel-toe boots—stretched out over Billy's pro-wrestling form. "You here for the meeting?"

An hour early went unspoken.

"Yeah. And I have some paperwork to fill out." He sighed dramatically. "Damian's on me about getting everything done before the Anniversary Gala." When in doubt, blame his bosses' attack poodle/money guy.

Billy nodded. His muscles bunched under the tight black fabric but then relaxed. And the door slid open entirely so Cade could get through.

"Go on up. I'll let Mr. Z know you're here."

Cade smiled thinly; of course Zed was up already. Of course. Hopefully he'd be busy with tonight's event and not in the mood for a… naked chat.

They didn't keep normal hours around here—you slept all day, woke up when the sun set, and then worked until dawn. Vampire hours here at the classiest casino-slash-whorehouse in the District. He ducked past Billy, his own height dwarfed by the guard's shadow.

Cade felt the warmth of the hallway in his face, blood rushing to his cheeks as he breathed deeply. Now that he was—relatively—safe, he felt like he could relax.

"Damn, I need some coffee," he said, turning to give Billy a two-finger salute. "Can I bring you back anything?"

Billy shook his massive head. "No, sir, Mr. Creel. I'm fine." He pulled the door shut behind him, the echo shaking through the narrow hallway. "You have a good day," he said, slow and careful. Cade could feel Billy's gaze crawling over his body, not because he wanted some action but because Cade's face, coat, and pants were caked with dirt.

"You too." Cade forced himself to walk up the staircase slowly, taking his other glove and scarf off, tucking things in the pocket of his overcoat. He opened the red door at the top, another quick glance at Billy.

Who watched him with curious eyes.

He disappeared through the doorway, hurrying into the brightly lit catacomb of hallways.

CADE HAD lived at the Iron Butterfly for three years, an "original cast member," as Zed liked to say, which made what they did sound like Disney World and not a high-class whorehouse. They were the first of the big-money places to open ten years ago and so held a bit of cachet—classy and elegant, where you spent your money when you wanted a bit of high society mixed with your scotch and a piece of ass. The piece of ass part was relatively new, and only if you felt it was worth it—that was Zed's thing. Putting out for anyone who asked or even offered to pay? A waste of your time. Cultivating clientele and escalating the "treats" for each visit? Then you are mining, not doing a smash-and-grab.

Zed's criminal past wasn't exactly a secret, but even less so when he used examples like that.

Cade made excellent money—most of which he sent home, much to his father and brother's annoyance—and had achieved some notoriety on the circuit. The New City was packed with entertainment, from the visual to the physical, casinos and sex and light shows and gourmet meals. Everything was calibrated to entice the few with enough money to pay the high cost of pleasure. And make everyone else so damned envious they counted their dollars until they could come too.

Cade was a star, like the people who used to make movies and television in the Big Apple or perform on Broadway, a few blocks away. His face flashed in advertisements, his body broadcast around the world to sell a masculine, polished look. *You, too, could look like me—a well-coiffed sex worker with a brain and a whole lot of brawn.*

Here's what I eat for breakfast. Here's how many sit-ups I do. This is my checklist for the perfect blowjob.

Clients paid money to see him model beautiful clothing. To be a charming and articulate companion for dinner and drinks and dancing and blackjack. They could also establish a visit schedule that enabled them to see what was underneath—and with each passing year, Zed could charge a bit more and Cade could ensure the family farm was safe.

A heartwarming tale, his manager, Rachel, would say dryly, and toss her long auburn hair as she mocked his bitching and whining when he felt like he was being overworked.

Poor you, she'd say. *Safe and warm and clothed, earning a living to support your entire family and doing it from luxury. I'm sure there are thousands of people living in shitty neighborhoods a few miles away who wish they were beautiful enough to do the same.*

Rachel was right, of course. She knew this business, and he stuck close, did what he had to do to stay her favorite.

Staying Mr. White's favorite put extra money in his pocket—even if that meant breaking a few of Cade's own rules.

Keep your head down, do your work, and never—ever—ask questions.

After depositing his outerwear and damp boots in the slim lockers of the "talent" lounge and washing off as best he could in the men's room (it took a thin layer of makeup to cover the scratches on his cheek), Cade walked the corridors of the Iron Butterfly from the sterile white of the service areas to the tenth floor, where the staff had their offices.

The cleaning staff lugged their equipment up the back stairs; Cade politely waited for the crew of black-suited men and women to maneuver up three flights until they reached the casino floor. Their day started hours before opening, but that was scarcely enough time to meet Zed's approval.

"Good day, Mr. Creel," a few of them murmured as he continued on.

The steel was cold under his stocking feet as he jogged up. At the tenth-floor doorway, he pressed his personal code onto the keypad and waited for the whir and click as the lock disengaged. He slipped in, alert for Zed or his mercurial assistant, Damian. Questions from either of them would force Cade to lie, and while he was a good actor, he was shit without a script.

The industrial feel of the building changed entirely; steel-gray carpeting and mauve walls greeted visitors to this floor. Doors painted the midnight black of the Iron Butterfly's logo lined the wide hallway, with silver sconces to light the way. Soft, serene.

At the end of the hallway, Cade paused. To the left was the suite of offices Zed used. The heavy double doors were usually guarded by security, but their absence signaled the boss was elsewhere.

Entertaining talent in his private rooms, one might imagine.

Cade took it as a good sign, turning to the right and hurrying to Rachel's door. A thin silver nameplate was its only decoration.

Rachel Moon, Talent Manager

He knocked twice, deciding to use a visit with Rachel to cover his sudden timeliness for the meeting.

The knob turned and Cade pushed in, sliding into the office and then shutting the door as quickly as he could.

"Stealth," Rachel said. She looked up at him, smirking, as she petted his stomach, wrinkling her nose at his plain gray sweater. "No need to sneak around, honey. Zed's not even here. And you better change before the meeting. You look like a homeless person." Her outfit was her usual prefloor uniform—a pale pink dressing gown over a set of white silk pajamas, her auburn hair perfectly smooth and falling over her shoulders in neat waves.

Rachel turned and walked back to her desk, a monstrosity of carved birds and flowers in heavy oak, utterly at odds with the delicate French boudoir scheme of the rest of the floor. She perched behind in a chair rumored to have come from a castle in Belgium, red velvet and ridiculous.

"To what do I owe this honor?" She shuffled around some green folders on her desk. Damian's demands for numbers, most likely. At some point they would end up in his wastebasket.

On fire.

Cade threw himself in the pewter wing chair that was set aside for visitors. "Just wondering if you have me booked for the Anniversary Weekend," he said casually, crossing his legs. The mud streaks were obvious, but Rachel didn't react beyond a flicker of her gaze.

"If you think you can convince me to pawn the Germans off on someone else…." She gave him a look that reminded him far too much of his mother—disapproval, affection, and the sure knowledge of complete control over his actions.

"No, it's fine. They're big tippers." They were also rough and a little nasty; Cade usually ended up staying in bed for two days after they left, in a state of painful melancholy.

"That's the spirit," she said approvingly. "Besides them, you have Mr. Valdez, Mr. White's regular, and a double session with Mr. and Mrs. Torres."

Cade's eyes went wide. "Double?"

"Yes." She looked pleased. "They've upgraded their weekly appointment to Tuesdays and Saturdays." The weekends cost more, and that meant their commitment had nearly tripled in price.

Cade didn't know whether to be excited or nervous. Mr. and Mrs. Torres weren't quite at the level of the Germans, but they were a double handful nonetheless. Lately things had been getting a little rough as Mr. Torres came to terms with some of his particular… appetites. Appetites his lovely wife had no interest in satisfying. Cade let himself go boneless in the chair, tipping his head back so he could stare at the ornate ceiling. Kissing cherubs, looking dirty and innocent at once.

"I'm not really supposed to handle the rough stuff," Cade said, not trusting his ability to say this while looking at Rachel. "And they seem to be headed in that direction…."

Rachel made a disapproving sound. "Cade."

He tamped down his whining and excuses for why he couldn't. "I'll handle it."

Rachel smiled. "Thank you." She opened her mouth as if to say something else, but just as quickly gave a shake of her head and turned her attention to her tablet.

THE STAFF meeting took thirty-four minutes—Cade counted every second of it, tired and itching for a shower. The lack of sleep was catching up with him, the crash of adrenaline burning through his blood and empty stomach. He still had a full evening ahead of him, one that would most likely end in the wee hours of the morning with his two-thousand-dollar suit on the floor of the high rollers' suite upstairs.

Zed—all thick black tattoos peeking out from the corners of a tight short-sleeved shiny suit—commanded their attention, stressing the importance of their upcoming Anniversary Weekend, the original two hundred guests when the doors opened, and how their continued patronage at the Iron Butterfly would keep them all very comfortable. He gestured with his hands, his mouth running a mile a minute; a Cockney lilt that might not be real, furious curse words and slurs that absolutely were, and a gentle threat under it all.

Pull your weight, make them spend more, or find out just how brutal five months of winter can be out on the street without a plane ticket home.

Rachel sat slightly behind where Zed stood, a smirk on her lips. She found their boss entertaining, even when he was furious, screaming and throwing things in the hallway.

Damian Oh—Zed's business manager, keeper of the money and details Zed didn't want to bother with—sat on the other side, perched at the edge of his chair. Every time Zed raised his voice to air another point, Damian scrunched up his face and nodded. He squinted at each of them from beneath a shaggy styled haircut, fierce like a tiny purse dog that thought it was a Doberman, silently willing (Cade assumed) their continued moneymaking ability.

"And before anyone asks, security will continue to be doubled." He paused to scowl. "Tripled, until the police find the prankster calling in bomb threats," Zed finished. This was an ongoing headache for him and all the other owners in the District. Bomb threats every few days, without follow through. Without even a random demand. Just— nuisances. Much like the fires and vandalism reported from job sites north of the city.

The police were no further in finding the culprits than they were when it started a few months before, and the moneyed District movers and shakers were furious their bribes and protection money got them no closer to the truth.

Cade found the girls in the massage room were terrible gossips.

As the meeting went on, all attention turned to Anniversary Weekend and the level of service expected of the models.

"What?" Zed said, stopping in the middle of a point about the add-ons to the various "acts" they were allowed to perform. Behind Cade, Alec had raised his hand.

A collective groan went up.

"Curious about a thing," Alec said sweetly, kicking his legs out to tangle with Cade's chair. "I'm assuming Herr Volder is one of the guests for the Anniversary Weekend."

Zed didn't even turn in Alec's direction, he just indicated to Damian he should answer.

"Yes, he was part of the original two hundred," Damian said, scowling. He didn't like Alec, for many reasons—mostly centering around Alec's refusal to do his time sheet properly.

"Marvelous. And can I ask who is assigned to keep Herr Volder company?"

A second groan, and Zed narrowed his eyes. "Rachel?" He threw it over to her; Cade knew how much she loved insulting the talent in front of large groups.

"He knows the answer." She toyed with the hem of her sleeve, the epitome of bored. "And he knows why."

Alec kicked Cade's chair. "Ah, of course. Well, then, I offer my protest at not being considered. I do speak German, after all," he said, all politeness and an accent like an action movie Euro-villain.

"He's not really interested in my conversation skills," Cade drawled, rocking his chair back suddenly, so Alec had to pull his feet away.

A titter of laughter.

Rachel clapped and then stood up, apparently unwilling to grant Alec the floor for his regular attention-seeking song and dance. "Do what you're told and make your money, Alec. You know the goddamn drill," she said with finality. "Improve your cocksucking skills and I'll see if I can't upgrade your skinny ass."

She said it with the sweetness of a kindergarten teacher, and someone in the back snorted loudly.

The meeting was over—which Zed realized a second later.

"All right. See you on the floor at nine," he said. Rachel was halfway toward the door. No one else moved a muscle until Zed turned around.

They were dismissed.

Zed, with Damian, left in a flurry of murmurs, no doubt Damian giving a rundown of how much money they were expecting to take in over the next three days. Long weekends were good for business, and the advertising cycles were pushing the glamor and glitz of the upcoming Anniversary Weekend like crazy.

The staff filed out, headed for the coiffing that would fill the time before they were due upstairs. On-site they enjoyed a salon and specialists catering to them looking their best. Half a floor was just wardrobe.

But Cade didn't move, and neither did Alec.

"Don't you get tired of repeating yourself?" Cade asked, tangling his fingers over his stomach. He didn't bother to turn around.

"Don't you get tired of being the shiniest whore in Whoreville?"

"You need new insults." He sat up and turned around to see Alec grinning delightedly.

"You love them." Alec elongated the *l* sound and batted his long eyelashes. He made most of his money off their female clients—wives and girlfriends who kept busy while their men were otherwise occupied. Female executives and politicians who wanted all the trappings of their stature, including paying for sex. The occasional threesome for their more bicurious guests. He and Cade performed together now and again, but Cade—well, he was primarily a solo act, and his prices reflected that.

The mixing of a Costa Rican mother and a French father produced Alec's exotic look, which initially turned heads—and the constant work he did on his body caught their second glances and their money.

The competition between them had started in their first days together—both young and beautiful, both anxious to find job security in a world that chewed up and spit out models on a daily basis. And oh, the pretty boys and girls who couldn't cut it in the first year, who didn't earn enough to cover the four grand for their plane tickets home—money wasn't easy to come up with when you were out on the street, and beggars got jail quicker than they got spare change.

"Come on, Farm Boy—I'll buy you some coffee before we get rouged up." Alec winked, tucking a line of black hair behind his ear. "You need a little extra help today. What the hell did you do to your face?"

"Sweet-talker." Cade stretched out, hearing his spine crackle and pop as he ignored Alec's comment. "I need a nap."

"Mmmm… is that an offer?"

He shook his head, standing up quickly. "Get your juices running with someone else. I'm saving my dick for someone who pays me."

Alec followed, crowding their bodies close together, Cade's back against his front. "You're no fun."

Cade allowed a moment—just a single second of an embrace. Alec was big and warm, breathing against the back of his neck in a gentle way. Wouldn't it be nice to do this with someone where money wasn't exchanged? Wouldn't it be lovely to be with someone just for the experience?

He'd never had that.

But that wasn't his life. He had a job to do.

CHAPTER FOUR

NOX FINISHED off the last of his coffee and a plate of toast and sausage. When he got home from his little confrontation with the pretty boy, Sam was holed up in his room, and all the knocking and requests for him to come out went ignored. His temper rose, and once again he remembered how out of his league he still was, still winging this parenting thing after all these years.

With a sigh, he cleaned the dishes, leaving a covered plate for Sam at the table.

Outside, night had fallen. The warning sirens sounded on the hour until eight, and then this part of town fell under a tense hush. No one went outside; no cars or people could be found. Once upon a time, people had walked on the street—taking their dogs to Riverside Park or going to dinner, coming home from work, or running out to the theater. On the rare occasion of his father being in town and his mother feeling well, Nox and his parents might walk down to Columbus and have dinner at the little Italian place with the great garlic bread. Nox would sit on the stoop of the townhouse and talk to Lidia, his neighbor and fellow classmate at Trinity. Or he'd go to his room and listen to music while playing video games with his friends.

Simple life, beautiful city.

Sometimes it occurred to him that Sam had never experienced that. He didn't know the simple pleasures of life. He had no memories of indulgent Christmases or vacations to St. Bart's.

He'd never been off the Island.

He didn't know his parents.

Aside from Nox, everyone who'd ever cared for him was gone now.

Well, that was something they had in common.

Nox sat in the recliner, rereading *The Art of War* as the grandfather clock ticked behind him like an ancient sentry. It had survived everything—storms and looters and violence. Every click reminded Nox of the slow and steady road of life. You couldn't let anything throw you off-balance.

Soft footsteps caught his attention; he looked up to see Sam in the archway of the study, his face drawn and pale.

"I need to tell you something," he murmured. His glasses were sliding down to the end of his nose, dark curls a mess, like he had been pulling at his hair in frustration. He was still dressed in his uniform, wrinkled and untidy in a way he never was.

"Okay." Nox closed the book, taking his time to put it on the side table.

"I…." Sam swallowed, fists clenching and releasing over and over at his side. "Someone came to the house today and gave me a letter."

"I know. I saw him." Nox waited a beat, folding his hands in his lap. "Who is he?"

"I don't know," Sam said, shaking his head. He looked genuinely surprised by the entire situation. "He knew my name and gave me this letter." A white square materialized from behind Sam's back.

Sam looked rattled, which made Nox's heart thump dramatically in his chest.

"What did it say?" He kept his voice even.

Tears sprang to Sam's amber eyes; he extended the letter as if to give it to Nox but pulled it back at the last second. "It says… it says that they might be able to help me find my parents."

The room tilted. Nox tripped out of the chair, the furniture crashing and falling around him. It had to be real, not a figment of his imagination, because Sam's words were amongst the worst he could have heard.

Because he knew that that was impossible. No one could find Sam's parents because they were dead.

The anvil dropped between them.

Tick, tick, tick.

Nox stood up slowly. He didn't like to use his size against Sam; the boy was slim and small, and Nox stood a head taller, his wide shoulders casting a shadow over Sam's form.

Finding his real parents—a quest Sam had become fixated on in recent years. He'd starting asking when he was seven and realized that babies came out of ladies and there weren't any of them in his life.

"Sam, I've told you all I know," he lied. "There isn't anything else. That night was pure chaos...." Nox poured every ounce of sincerity into his words. "So many people were killed...."

"I know—and I'm so grateful for everything you've done for me, Dad. You saved me, but I just—I just want to know what happened to them," Sam said, words chasing and tripping over each other, ending with a choked sound. "Or just their names, okay? Like, if I could just have that... I just want to know."

Nox felt like someone had ripped his chest open, exposing heart and lungs to the cool air. He nodded, though, just a small movement to show he was listening. "What else did the letter say?" Nox asked, his voice measured. "Was there any other information?"

Sam shook his head. "Nothing else. The person just told me he could help me find them."

"You know this could be a trick."

"Who would do something like this? I only see the people at work and people here in our neighborhood—and none of them know what happened, right?"

Nox tried to maintain his cool. He tucked his hands deeper in his pockets, glanced at the faded Persian rug under his feet. "They could make an assumption—I'm not that much older than you are."

"But who do we know that would do something like this? I know people at work, but I've never told them anything about me. And you don't see anyone except for at the jobsite. We don't have friends! Who would do something like this?"

"Sam, I know how much you want this. But you have to be prepared...."

"Prepared for what?" Sam snapped, annoyance clearly rising. "Prepared to be disappointed? Seriously, I've got that covered with the rest of my life."

Another anvil, hitting so hard between them Sam actually winced as soon as the words were out of his mouth.

Misery crept over his face. "I'm sorry."

"I know this isn't an easy way to live," Nox said softly. "I wish things could be different."

Sam stared down at the floor.

Nox couldn't offer platitudes. He couldn't tell Sam someday he could leave the city, go to college, live somewhere else. Sam existed in New York City. Outside? He was a kid without a birth record or certificate or anything else to prove who he was. He had a father who was still a child himself when he took responsibility for him. He was a secret no one else could know.

It was what it was, and Sam had no power over any of it.

"Just be careful. And—if you get another letter, I need to see it immediately," he said, finishing with a hint of reprimand. "People shouldn't be coming to the house."

His son nodded almost imperceptibly.

"Thank you." Nox couldn't resist the urge—he opened his arms and let Sam trudge into his embrace. For a long time it terrified him, this easy affection his son gave him. His own father had not been a demonstrative soul. His mother had her moments, but when the paranoia and fear came in angry waves, she retreated.

Nox had learned to do this—hugging and soothing and gentle touches to his son's back as he shook with unshed tears.

"I'm sorry," Sam murmured again, face pressed against Nox's shoulder.

"We're past that. Now you know—rules are important, Sam. They keep us safe."

Sam nodded, tightening his arms around Nox's middle.

He believed the lie, and that was all that mattered.

NOX GOT Sam to eat, then sent him to shower. He needed to get ready, but he wanted Sam asleep first—this wasn't a usual night's patrol. His skin buzzed with nerves—Nox didn't like being in the casinos, where surveillance cameras recorded every move you made from the time you set foot in their gilded halls until you walked out, poorer and wrung-out.

The trick was to obscure your looks and keep moving, stick to blind spots and never—*never*—draw attention to yourself.

The Iron Butterfly wasn't his usual haunt—too shiny, too involved with paying attention to the customers. He played roulette at the Bourbon Street Casino and blackjack at 21. The smaller places generally catered to those with lower credit limits and left you alone to drink and gamble in peace.

The crown jewel of the District was all about personal service.

In his father's study, he used his tablet to call up specs for the various hotels and casinos in the District. Being an electrician had its perks beyond decent wages—he could get whatever he needed from the city planner's computer and read the plans with ease. His other work— well, that had the benefit of shaking down folks for codes and access to whatever he might need.

Like an ID to get him into anyplace he wanted in the District....

THE DEALER'S name had been Brownigan, and he'd cried when Nox got him down on the ground one night the previous summer. He wasn't in physical danger—not of death, anyway—but Brownigan didn't know that. And he was frightened enough of the looming man in the black hoodie to offer his other services.

City identification. Worker passes. Stuff that looked so real no one even blinked. Wireless that didn't get routed through the city's computers like everyone else's—he could do that too. Passes that got him wherever he needed to be. Access to bank accounts filled with money siphoned from tourists.

A boot to his thick neck and some whispered threats were all it took to realign Brownigan's priorities in life. He swore off selling Dead Bolt and devoted his crafty brain and nimble fingers to making it easier for people to rip off the casinos and steal from the hotels. That was something Nox could get behind.

When Nox needed favors from him, he tripped over himself to fulfill the order. He made Patrick Mullens come alive via plastic and fake accounts—he allowed Nox to move about The District.

NOX POCKETED the all-access white square as he assessed himself in the mirror. From the deep recesses of his father's closet, he'd pulled out a vintage double-breasted Valentino tux, a remnant of his parents' old life, when they spent his mother's inheritance on globe-trotting adventures.

Then he was born and his mother's precarious mental state became impossible to ignore.

It felt strange to look at his reflection when he dressed up to be "Patrick Mullens"—trimmed beard, styled hair, the cut of the black tuxedo almost a perfect match to his body. He looked like his father, a humbling and confusing visual, because nothing about his life said "successful investment banker."

He might accept "workaholic" and "loner," though.

Or even "stand-offish."

He had a moment of guilt—his father was dead and couldn't defend himself or give his reasons for being away so much. He couldn't take back the missed holidays or birthdays. Everything had been swept away in the storms and the violence no one had expected, and Nox wouldn't hold it against the memory of a man whose life had been cut short.

"I think you'd be proud," he murmured, and then he slipped from the room, leaving the ghosts behind.

He used Patrick's name when he went to the casinos for information gathering or earning money. He used it when he chatted up the models, paid money for a blowjob here or there to make it look legit. It was ironic, in a way, pretending to be the kid who had been well on his way to being Nox's "first"—something he never did get around to having, not in any sort of meaningful way.

The real Patrick died during the storms in a small plane accident with his family—they made it to Teterboro, made it on the private plane. Made it to somewhere over a mountain in Pennsylvania before they crashed. Nox didn't hear the news until almost a year after it happened; he was a father by then, surviving as best he could, living in fear. Later, when Brownigan asked for a name for the fake ID, Patrick immediately came to mind. A recollection of a better time, an innocent mindset—when he could have grown up to be dashing and debonair and a high roller.

With Sam asleep and the security system engaged, Nox left at a quarter to midnight. He wore his black jacket and hood as he left the neighborhood—his shadow known enough to keep him from being stopped—and reached the edge of The District. What used to be Columbus Circle had been transformed into a gateway into another world: The District—welcome to Las Vegas's sluttier cousin.

Nox rolled his overclothes into a tight ball and zipped them into his backpack. He tucked everything into a slight opening created when several trees and stone walls collapsed near the edge of Central Park. It was a common hiding place of his, someplace to leave supplies and extra ammo on those busier nights.

Warm weather, the summer holidays. Higher body counts.

Central Park West—now just called West Street—began just past the old circle; it looped in from the Freck Memorial Highway, which was commonly traveled by cabs bringing visitors in from the ferry station. Planes landed at the newly built Manhattan Memorial Airport on what was left of Staten Island; tourists took the rest of their trip by boat, an ironic mode of transportation considering how many people had died trying to escape on them.

It made locals crazy: one bridge to ferry goods in and out, boats to cater to the tourists. The rest of the people? Stranded as much as they were seventeen years ago.

Sticking to the shadows, Nox walked along the road. It was newly repaved and a slick black, well lit for the most part, but Nox knew how to avoid the light. A cab—its top flashing green, which meant it was free—approached, most likely heading for downtown to see if it could pick up random fares.

Nox stepped onto the thick white line delineating the road from the shoulder and raised his hand as the cab's headlights fell on him.

The driver slowed, then stopped as Nox came into view. He opened his window as he coasted to the side.

"You lost?" the man asked, his dark suit and tight tie the standard uniform for drivers in this town.

"My date didn't show—I'd be upset, but it was a favor to my sister, you know? I was going to head to the casinos for a little consoling." Nox let his face relax into a friendly smile as he winked.

The guy's gaze narrowed; he was fifty, maybe older. His inflection told Nox he wasn't from around here originally—maybe another Midwesterner come to make a buck amongst the ruins.

Nox broadened his smile, willing the man to trust him. "I have cash, if that's okay...."

Most people didn't bother with it, but a few enterprising individuals were trying to bring it back into fashion. Easier to keep the government from tracking it. Or you.

A quick nod and the driver gestured to the backseat, disengaging the automatic lock. "Get in."

Twenty minutes later, Nox stared out the window at the blinding lights of the District. Hotels took up four or five city blocks. Casinos sprawled like small cities across eight or nine more. In the center, a slender tower of glass and steel—only thirty stories, but the oldest and most exclusive of all the establishments.

The Iron Butterfly.

The first. The best, or so their advertising claimed. Electronic billboards flashed all around the hotels, reflected back in their dark mirrored windows.

Gambling.

Dancers.

Shows.

Food.

Sex.

No such flair for The Butterfly—no. They simply unveiled their wares in brief bright pictures on their very walls.

Blackjack.

The most beautiful company in all of New City.

Faces illuminated as if by magic, each more attractive than the next. Nox watched them change and flicker until—

There he was—the lying piece of talent he'd had under him just a few hours before.

Cade Creel read the flowery script a second later.

"Stop here," Nox said to the driver, who eased the vehicle to the nearest median. Traffic crept past them as Nox slid over a wad of neatly pressed bills through the opening in the Plexiglas divider.

"You have a good night, now," the driver said as Nox slid out of the cab.

Nox straightened up, smoothing his tux as he looked up at the Iron Butterfly. As if by design, Cade's face appeared once again.

"Let's find out more about you, young man," Nox murmured. He stuck his hands in his pockets and set off for the Butterfly.

CHAPTER FIVE

CADE'S DRESSER was named Killian, a whiz with a needle and thread, capable of turning any suit or tux into a slightly sluttier version. He loved working for Cade—at least that's what he told him all the time—because his body was made perfectly for the current trend of menswear.

Lightweight material, body conscious, and all tucks and corners to accentuate the male form. Between Cade's broad shoulders and slender waist, his alterations were mostly just to better show off his assets—and Killian's ability to take in a pair of pants to accentuate Cade's ass was legendary.

According to customer feedback.

Tonight's ensemble was Kyto, a Japanese designer who did a retro thing Cade quite liked. Notched lapels on the jacket, a slight sheen to the midnight-black material of the vest and pants—everything tightly fitted to show off Cade's muscular thighs and arms. The black-and-white polka-dotted tie and leather gloves were perfect finishing touches, as were the shiny black shoes.

He did a slow turn for the young tailor, earning a round of applause.

"Are you showing appreciation for my ass or your excellent work?" Cade asked, watching in the round mirror in the corner of Killian's room as he smoothed his carefully done spiked hair. Clear mascara accented his hazel blue eyes, and an understated gloss drew attention to his lush mouth. The Friday-night regulars were in for a treat.

"Both," Killian said with a wry twist of his mouth. In another life, Killian and Cade would probably be hanging at a tractor pull in South Carolina, bitching about the taste of the shit beer in the back row before disappearing behind a truck to swap blowjobs. Instead, they exchanged high-fives and Cade headed out the door to the casino floor to sell his body for a shitload of money.

Rachel met him at the model entrance, a narrow hallway lined with mirrors on both sides so they could make sure every visible inch of their bodies was ready for viewing. Cade watched himself move, checking out the way the suit curved around his body.

"You're late," Rachel called. She was wearing a tiny silver dress; more sequins than material, with a matching collar around her neck. Her hair, gathered, curled, and draped over her left shoulder, fell past her hem.

She gave him a peck on the cheek when he reached her; the five-inch fuck-me heels finally brought her to the height of his shoulder.

"You owe me five minutes at least," he said, dry and bemused as he fiddled with his cuff links. "As your favorite and all."

"It doesn't matter. McClannaugh's plane was delayed by weather. You have a free evening."

Cade sighed. "If I had known, I would have slept longer."

"I'm not running a spa, my love. You're here to make money. Go out there and tease some wallets so I can book you up for the rest of the weekend."

After a well-placed slap on the ass, the door opened and Cade stepped into the bright chaos of the Iron Butterfly's main floor.

The posh luxury of the Iron Butterfly was miles away from the standard casino fare: no sirens or flashing lights, no machines spitting coins. Every game on the floor had a human behind it, every table designed for comfort. From the lavender-silk-draped ceilings and walls to the massive round light fixtures that looked like starbursts, the low lights and luxurious carpet, the curved seats—everything had been engineered to make you want to sit and gamble for hours.

Waitpersons in various states of barely dressed—each with a chain of butterflies tattooed around their neck for ready identification—circulated the floor, whispering offers of assistance. There were no menus at the Butterfly—ask and ye shall receive.

Cade walked down the center of the floor. The circle patterns were everywhere—subtly textured into the textiles, the rugs—including the way everything was laid out. Six bars were stationed within the room, ten gaming tables situated like spokes in a wheel around them.

He skirted the outermost tables; those were reserved for the lowest-tier guests. A deposit of ten thousand dollars didn't leave much room for him to make money.

The top-tier tables—those were his destination.

He caught some nods from regulars, smiles from waitstaff, and a wink from the second quadrant bartender, who was an insatiable flirt and hot enough to expect a promotion as soon as someone washed out.

At the far end, fanned out against the front of the building's floor-to-ceiling windows, the top tier waited. Here sounds were muted, the staff-to-client ratio was one-to-one, and Cade could seed a week's worth of business by bending over to pick up a dropped napkin.

Over at blackjack table one, Alec held court, a sultan's sister giggling against his shoulder. She wore jewelry worth enough to feed a small country, sparkling against the black sheen of Alec's suit. They made a striking couple.

Cade shifted over to the roulette wheel, where a small crowd had gathered to watch Mr. White perform his usual Friday-night routine. Cade caught the older man's eye, then flashed a subtle thumbs-up, which gained him a gloriously bright smile from his favorite client. They exchanged a nod. Then Mr. White turned his attention back to his other favorite thing at the Iron Butterfly—gambling.

Twenty-five thousand dollars, as long as it would take him to lose, only at the wheel. Only bet red. Several whiskey rocks, a lobster dinner, and a reminder to Cade he would see him next Thursday. For their date.

The crowd—thankfully—gathered for the former, not the latter.

Cade lingered for a few minutes. Mr. White, looking like an extra from a James Bond film, cut a serious figure with his signature gray pompadour and a tuxedo that was at least thirty years old—the man rolled old school and classy from top to bottom.

Someone bumped against his arm, and Cade turned to bestow a charming smile on the person's direction. Models never frowned. Models were always wrong and the customer was always entitled to whatever the hell they wanted.

"Sorry," he said, focusing on the man standing next to him.

"No problem" came the smooth response.

Cade struggled to place the man—the neatly styled sable-brown hair and trimmed beard, the vintage tux that shone under the subdued lights of the casino floor. Put-together and drop-dead gorgeous, with technicolor blue eyes and lush eyelashes and the jaw of a matinee idol, just hanging around in the high rollers' area.

This was Cade's favorite type of customer.

He extended his hand, working the sleepy bedroom eyes like the pro he was. "Cade."

"Patrick Mullens," the man said, his voice husky and charming. He slipped his hand into Cade's.

Firm, confident. Callused.

Cade blinked but never lost his game face. A working man's rough palms hadn't graced his presence very often; it was stranger yet to find them in the top-tier area.

"So, Mr. Mullens, what brings you to the Iron Butterfly tonight?" Cade angled his body towards him, brushing their arms together. "In the mood to win?"

"Always" was the response. Mr. Mullens did the full body scan—from the tips of Cade's shiny black loafers all the way up to his face, where a big smile awaited. "Are you a good luck charm?"

"I'm a sure thing," Cade deadpanned with a wink.

Mr. Mullens laughed, deep and rich. "So let's go find ourselves a drink."

He put a warm hand at the dip in Cade's spine; Cade couldn't help but hiss a little. That asshole from earlier bruised him, and….

Mr. Mullens moved his hand away—up instead of down.

"So, I haven't seen you around here before," Cade said as they reached the bar. "Is this your first time?"

"Oh no—but it's been a while. I don't get down here much," Mr. Mullens said smoothly.

"I can't imagine forgetting you, no matter how long you were gone." Cade continued walking, feeling the subtle directing the man was doing against his back. Far end of the bar, in the corner, where it was darker than most spots and uninhabited at the moment.

"Flattering." Mr. Mullens leaned in as he chuckled, breathing against Cade's ear, warm and intimate. "I've seen you around."

"Oh?"

"Your face a couple of stories high, every time I walk down the main drag. You seem to be doing well for yourself."

"I do all right." Cade did a once-over of his own, letting Mr. Mullens be very much aware of his interest. He licked his lips, making sure the other man was watching as he did.

They reached the corner of the bar; Mr. Mullens pushed Cade closest to the wall, limiting his avenues of escape.

Mr. Mullens seated himself on one of the high-backed leather stools, gesturing for Cade to take the other—but Cade knew how to play this game perfectly. He leaned against Mr. Mullens's arm, resting his other hand on the bar top.

Close enough to touch. Close enough for Mr. Mullens to enjoy Cade's body heat and scent.

He fluttered his eyelashes, and his companion signaled the bartender.

"So what's your pleasure, Mr. Mullens?" Cade purred as the man pulled out a diamond money clip practically choking with hundred-dollar bills.

"Scotch, blackjack." He did another full assessment of Cade's body. "Pretty boys."

Cade blinked. "Well, you've come to the right place," he said automatically, even as his brain stumbled over the man's choice of words. "Maybe I can keep you company for a while."

Mr. Mullens's mouth curved into a smirk. "Why do I think you're going to cost more than a bad streak at the table?"

"Because you're a very smart man." Cade leaned over as the bartender waited for their order. He pressed his hip against Mr. Mullens's leg, lingering as he said, "Two scotches."

The bartender knew to bring the most expensive thing they had. And Cade knew if he turned his hips just so, Mr. Mullens would get a clear accounting of just what he was hiding under this suit.

A hand brushed down Cade's back—Mr. Mullens clearly wasn't going to take his time with this transaction. He avoided the bruised area, then curved around to press his big, warm palm against the swell of Cade's ass.

The bartender returned with two square tumblers of amber liquid. He didn't linger, didn't ask for payment. Just disappeared quietly back to the other side of the bar.

Cade handed one to Mr. Mullens—who didn't remove his hand from Cade's ass—and took the other for himself.

They clinked glasses.

Cade took a quick sip—he liked to stay sober on the floor—and shifted his hips just enough to give Mr. Mullens another reminder about the length of his cock.

The man didn't even twitch. He did dip his fingers a bit, sliding down to press between Cade's legs from behind.

"Spread your legs a bit," Mr. Mullens murmured suddenly, taking Cade entirely by surprise. He thought they were playing subtle.

Sex acts on the floor were prohibited, but no one said anything about getting felt up, so Cade opened his stance, leaning forward to press against Mr. Mullens's leg.

Escalation, thy name is a full night's pay.

But instead of cupping Cade's dick, Mr. Mullens slid his hand down the interior of each thigh, one then the other.

Not sexual but… a frisking.

Cade twisted in an attempt to move, but the man was having none of that. He tightened his grip on Cade's thigh, keeping him still.

"Mmmm, stay right there," Mr. Mullens said quietly, leaning forward to whisper in Cade's ear. Warm breath tickled Cade's ear as the man began to move his hand again.

"You're going to get me in trouble with my manager," Cade whispered, rubbing small circles against Mullens's tight thigh. "Maybe we can take this somewhere else?"

"Shh" was the only response he got—but Mr. Mullens's fingers were making the case for something else. One finger stroked between Cade's legs, working the length of his perineum with increasing pressure.

Cade's breath whooshed out—he rocked gently against the thigh still tight against his dick. He usually had to work a little bit… harder… for this sort of attention; most of the men he slept with wanted to be wooed and seduced and made to feel like they were the only person in the world. They wanted Cade all to themselves, to make their fantasies come true—and then, if he was lucky, he might get to come.

Mr. Patrick Mullens seemed to have another agenda entirely.

The little circle of their bodies kept moving, electricity and movement begetting more electricity and movement until Cade was seriously uncomfortable—aroused and rocking his dick against the zipper of his fly.

Mr. Mullens moved his fingers back to Cade's ass, pressing his palm hard against the center. Then nothing until a smack in the same spot that nearly pitched Cade onto the floor.

Cade's wits were rapidly leaving him, but he was a professional if nothing else, and a guy with good hands who wanted to play Daddy Dominate would have to pay for the privilege.

"You don't like rules, do you?" Cade whispered, only partially manufacturing the hitch in his voice as Mr. Mullens teased the back seam of his pants with a finger. He fixed his gaze on the other man's face, taking in those fabulous blue eyes and rock-solid jaw. "Wouldn't you rather do this somewhere more private?"

For a second Cade wondered if he was pushing the sales pitch too far—Mr. Mullens's face went unreadable, from smug amusement to blankness in a second. But the switch flipped a second later as that lush mouth curved into a grin.

"How much for two hours?" he asked, flicking his tongue against the corner of his mouth. "And how much more to tie you up?"

Cade didn't bother to wait until his hard-on went down—they were all adults here, and frankly, letting all the patrons see him in all his flushed and horny glory, leading Mr. Mullens by the hand across the floor, was some damn good advertisement.

"Two hours, with props," he said to Damian as their paths crossed near the elevator bank.

Damian smiled serenely—the only time Cade ever saw the man look anything but pissed the hell off was when he was charging a customer. He took Mr. Mullens's card and waved it against the sensor sewn into his pocket; a second later, Damian got confirmation in his earpiece.

"Mr. Mullens, I hope you have a wonderful time." Damian stepped aside to let them pass.

"Oh, I'm sure I will," Mr. Mullens purred, as Cade led him to the shiny brushed metal doors.

"Twenty-ninth floor," Cade told the elevator. Mr. Mullens lounged against the purple velvet wall, arms crossed over his chest. Cade mirrored him from the other side.

Cade felt a little more in control now. This was where he turned two hours into four and a one-time treat into a regular customer. Slowly, he untangled his arms, then reached up with his right hand to unknot his tie. The other hand—that was the one Mr. Mullens's gaze immediately locked into. With that hand, Cade began to toy with his belt buckle, sliding his legs shoulder width apart as he did.

"You wanted to fuck me right there at the bar, didn't you?" Cade said softly, thoroughly enjoying the moment.

Mr. Mullens seemed lost momentarily, but he came back to attention as soon as Cade spoke.

"That would have cost me extra, I'm guessing" was the retort, something that Cade couldn't quite identify lurking beneath the surface.

Cade paused, then eased his tie open.

"You were breaking the rules," Cade said, trying to get Mr. Mullens's attention back on the matter at hand. "Might have gotten reprimanded."

Mr. Mullens tipped his head to one side. "What are we talking about? Demerits? Scrubbing the toilet?" He heaved off the wall and started walking toward Cade. "A spanking?"

There was definitely something there—mocking, maybe? Cade just threw him a smile, sliding his hands into his jacket pockets as the elevator dinged.

"This is our floor," Cade said, ducking around Mr. Mullens's broad shoulders as the doors opened.

CHAPTER SIX

SOMEWHERE ALONG the way, Nox lost the thread of what he was doing.

All he wanted to do was find the kid, get him to reveal the source of the letter to Sam, and be gone. He was good at this—extracting information and disappearing before anyone got too attached. Before he made an impression.

This dumb model, though—sexy and charming, seducing Nox like the pro he was, all big eyes and a quiet voice, asking to be taken somewhere with his softly spoken words and his perfectly sculpted body, asking for money in exchange for his services.

That ass he could bounce a quarter off of.

Nox adjusted himself as he walked behind Cade, who was swinging his hips like he wanted Nox to drop dead behind him.

No—like he wanted Mr. Mullens to come to the suite and fuck him.

Not going that far, he thought to himself, even as his dick throbbed and his mouth went dry with want.

Stupid. Stupid professional seduction bullshit. That kid in the dark alley that was all spit and fire, taking swings at Nox's head and refusing to back down, now dolled up and playing a role, just like he was. His head swam with the fade between what was real and what was not, for both of them.

Cade turned around at the double doors at the end of the hall. He leaned against them, waiting for Nox to catch up.

This kid.

The suit hugged every inch of his long, lean body like it had been sewn onto him. He blended "boy next door" and "sexy"—freckles and pale eyes, high cheekbones and a full mouth. The husky voice completed the package.

Oh right. And the package.

Nox tried to remember why he was there. Concern about who sent Sam a letter. Right. *Focus.*

Nox morphed back into Mr. Mullens.

"I forgot to ask, handcuffs or rope?" Cade asked, a smirk on his lips.

Nox closed the distance between them—and Cade reached out to grab his lapels. He pushed his hips out as Nox banged into him, and they crashed back against the door.

Not kissing him, Nox thought, frantically trying to keep his traitorous body in check.

"No kissing?" Cade murmured, turning his head to one side as if Nox had spoken out loud. "That's okay with me." He ducked his head to Nox's shoulder, their slight height difference making their legs slot together perfectly. He inhaled deeply….

Then stiffened up against Nox's body, suddenly tense.

"Let's get inside," Nox whispered, rocking his hips forward. "I have a flight to catch in a few hours."

Cade relaxed, nodding as he reached behind him, fumbling for the door handle.

"Got it." He slid his hand over Cade's, turned the handle. When the door opened, Nox pushed Cade inside.

The Monarch Suite was lush and dramatic, shades of white layered with silver. Floor-to-ceiling windows showed an expanse of the city filtered by sheer white curtains. A white leather sofa curved in the center of a thick silver rug, a huge bed, low and modern, draped in patterned velvet fabric in the room beyond. Glass tables and a long bar finished off the space, clearly designed for sensual comfort.

Cade pulled out of Nox's hands, still a bit distant. His gaze kept darting over Nox's shoulder. "Something from the bar?" he asked, stripping off his tie and then dropping it on the floor. His jacket followed, revealing a trim waist and killer shoulders as he turned around.

"No."

Nox's hands trembled for a second as he reached for his bow tie, watching Cade shed clothing as he walked to the corner.

Vest.

Belt.

Shoes.

Shirt.

Every move revealed another piece of the puzzle, another stunning curve of muscle or smattering of freckles across his skin.

Nox untied his tie, unbuttoned the top button of his shirt.

Cade poured himself something clear from a cut crystal decanter.

"Music. Seven," he said, and a soft jazzy number began to play.

The perfect staged seduction.

Cade said, "Lights. Four," and they reduced to a dim haze, the room now illuminated by the brightness from outside.

The kid was trying to distract him.

"Handcuffs," Nox said, sauntering across the floor. "To answer your question."

With a wave of his glass, Cade indicated the bedroom beyond.

Nox walked into the room, breathing deeply to center himself. He shrugged out of the tux jacket and left it draped over a white accent chair near the end of the bed.

A sound behind him and Nox turned slowly. In the doorway, Cade leaned, elbow against the frame, hips cocked to one side, dressed only in an unbuttoned pair of pants and those leather gloves.

Nox pretended the way he dragged his tongue over his bottom lip was Patrick Mullens, and playing a role.

"Get on the bed," he said, dropping an octave as actual need began to overpower his reason for being here.

The kid said nothing. He walked slowly to the side of the bed closest to Nox, then sat down. Before he could lie back, Nox held up his hand.

"Facedown."

Something flickered behind Cade's eyes. A challenge. Some fear. Their gazes locked for long minutes—too long, as Nox began to sweat, catching beads of perspiration on his tongue.

Still no words. Cade turned, then crawled and settled in the middle of the bed, arms over his head and crossed at the wrists, legs spread. This was not his first rodeo, clearly.

Nox pressed the heel of his hand against his dick as desire rolled through him.

He went to the side of the bed—nightstand, a white basket filled with the proper accoutrements for seduction. Lube, condoms, a pair of shiny silver handcuffs, a length of white rope, a pale pink vibrator.

If only he had the time....

The silver handcuffs in hand, Nox climbed onto the bed. He tamped down the urge to slap that perfect round ass or run his tongue down the grooves of his spine. No, the only thing he let himself do was run his hand from the lowest curve of Cade's back—careful not to touch the bruise he'd put there earlier—then up to brush against the spiky softness of his hair and farther up, to his slender wrists.

He snapped one cuff on, then hooked them through the handily provided white leather loops attached to the headboard before snapping the other on.

At the very least, after tonight Nox would have enough jerk-off material to last a year.

Nox felt the interrogative words on the tip of his tongue when he caught the subdued notes of music from the other room. Voice commands would be a safeguard if something went wrong with a customer—the other possibility being someone watching on closed-circuit television.

Two things Nox didn't want to find out the hard way.

He sucked in a deep breath, then swung one leg over until he straddled the small of Cade's back.

Nox flattened his palms against the padded headboard in an attempt not to come; he could feel the front of his pants dampening, thighs shaking as he stalled his hips from rubbing himself to an orgasm.

Cade trembled underneath him.

He leaned down, their bodies aligned—and he was insane, truly out of his mind, because God, this felt amazing—and pressed his mouth against Cade's ear.

Before he could speak, an alarm shrieked through the room.

CHAPTER SEVEN

CADE STRUGGLED against the handcuffs, pulling frantically at the restraints. The minute the fire alarm went off, his client jumped up and flew out of the room like a wanted man.

Leaving him there.

Leaving him handcuffed to the fucking bed, hard and confused and *Jesus*.

Voice commands weren't working. The alarm screamed relentlessly until Cade started to feel nauseous.

Something about that guy—something was off. For a few panicked minutes, Cade thought he was the hooded guy from the street—but no. The height was off. This one was taller. Sounded different.

Smelled….

Different but familiar?

Cade cursed as he twisted his body, trying to get his knees under him so he could get some leverage.

He heard a door open in the other room. He turned his head and shouted, "Hey, in here!"

"Got it, got it." Rachel. She came into view as the alarm continued to wail. From the side table, she grabbed the small key for the handcuffs. "What the hell happened?"

"Customer freaked when the alarm went off," Cade panted. "Is there a fire?"

"Bomb threat," Rachel said, her voice tight as she unlocked the handcuffs.

Cade hissed as his abraded wrists came free. "Goddammit," he spit out. Rachel helped him sit up, tugging him off the bed as soon as he was upright.

"We have to evacuate," she said tightly. "Zed's furious."

"So am I," Cade muttered, pulling off his gloves, then rubbing his wrists as he headed out the door.

THE POLICE swarmed the entrance of the Iron Butterfly. In the middle of the chaos of emergency personnel and the crowd of people flooding the street, Cade shivered under the blanket Rachel had hastily thrown on him as they hurried down the back steps. It was starting to snow, little pellets smacking down and making a crunching sound as Cade walked gingerly in wet socks down the block.

"Midfuck, eh?" Alec said, startling Cade.

"Chained to the fucking bed. Didn't get farther than that." Cade's teeth chattered.

"Come here." Alec pulled Cade farther down the street, out of the immediate crush of frantic guests and the employees attending to them. On the next block sat a small restaurant catering to those looking for some quiet and coffee. They were closed, but Alec rapped on the window until a server came over.

"What happened?" the girl asked as she opened the door.

"Faulty alarm—can we sit for a spell?" Alec asked, full-wattage charm and flirty lilt to his voice. "Do you mind?"

The girl was young—too young to see through Alec's blarney. "Oh, you poor things—come in!"

While she went to beg her manager's good grace, Alec tucked a chattering Cade into a chair, then stripped off his socks. "Come on, feet in lap and let me give them a rub."

"Stop trying to fuck me," Cade grumbled—then put his feet in Alec's lap.

"You look like a sad drowned rat—not interested. Also I'm a bit pissed at whoever decided to fuck with us tonight. My client is quite the big tipper," he sighed, rubbing his hands together before applying them to Cade's skin. "What about you?"

"What about me? Asshole got me facedown on the bed, handcuffed, and then split when the alarm went off." Cade trembled under the wet blanket. His whole body ached. *My God, what a day.*

Alec offered one arched eyebrow in disdain. "The stud you left with? Shame. I was going to ask you his name—I haven't seen him around."

"He said he didn't come to the Butterfly very often."

More police cars and armored vehicles sped by. Fucking false alarms and fake bomb threats—they usually turned out to be some dick who couldn't cover his bets and needed a way to sneak out.

"Name?"

"Patrick Mullens."

Alec seemed to thumb through a mental Rolodex, then shook his head. "No, not anyone I recall." He'd begun to massage Cade's feet, digging his fingers deep into the arches.

Cade stifled a moan, biting his lip to get his focus back. "He was acting strange—I don't know." Cade shrugged.

"You think he called in the threat?" Alec's hands stopped moving.

"No—he was with me the whole time."

"Could have had somebody on the outside do it," Alec offered.

Cade shook his head. "That doesn't make any sense. Does he really think he can skip out on a bill? They're gonna charge his account anyway." He sat in silence for a few minutes while Alec worked his magic. "The whole thing is just…weird."

He knew he should just let it go, chalk it up to the nature of the business, but it gnawed at him all the same.

IT WAS almost two hours before they got back into the building. Rachel found them in the restaurant, sharing a plate of tiny Italian cheesecakes and a pot of espresso.

"Meeting, now," she snapped. They didn't get enough time to offer her a seat before all that was visible was the back of her head.

"I believe there's a meeting right now," Alec deadpanned.

Cade's socks were dry, after a bit of time spent in the oven of the restaurant, and he and Alec made a run through the accumulating snow back to the Iron Butterfly. In the lobby, Damian was directing the staff upstairs to their posts, offering complimentary drinks, meals, and accommodations to clientele for the rest of their stay—the words seemed to actually pain him. He spotted Cade and waved him over.

Limping from the cold, Cade crossed the lobby to Damian's side.

"Your client," he said, reaching into his pocket.

"That son of a bitch," Cade muttered. "Left me—"

Damian waved him off. "He paid double your fee and left you a 50 percent tip."

Cade blinked.

"And he left you this." Damian pulled out his tablet with the blinking message icon under Cade's name.

Holding the blanket closed with one hand, Cade took the tablet, then flicked the message icon.

> *Sorry.*
>
> *- Patrick*

CHAPTER EIGHT

THE ALARM echoed in Nox's head as he raced down the back stairs of the Iron Butterfly. He could hear doors opening as people began to panic and evacuate.

"Fire!" someone shouted.

"Bomb!" another screamed.

Nox moved quicker, his steps sure, his well-conditioned body moving with ease even as guilt wracked him. The warring began to slow his steps as his body screamed "go" and his conscience screamed "what about Cade?" He was two flights down when he turned around, fighting against the flow of people now hot on his heels.

He made his way through the river of frantic guests and staff trying to escape the building. They broke his momentum, pushing him backward until he struggled to the side and pulled himself onto the railing.

Deftly, he climbed, hauling himself up like a kid on the monkey bars, swinging up and over until he reached the floor he'd come from.

He wasn't going to leave that kid alone and handcuffed to the bed.

His fight-or-flight response had kicked in wildly at the first sound of the alarm. It sounded like the evacuation, like the klaxon at his mother's sanitarium that terrible night. His heart pounded violently—he needed to get out, wanted to, but no.

You don't leave people behind.

Nox got back to the floor and pushed the door open. In the hallway, red lights flashed and flared; Nox focused on running back the way he came, to get back to the kid, to—

He saw her at the other end of the hall.

A tiny dress, long legs, a drape of red hair. She couldn't have looked more different than the last time he saw her, standing on the deck of the ferry with a murderous look in her eyes.

He froze.

She was running down the hallway, knocking on doors and shouting "Evacuate!"—the irony made him dizzy.

When she spotted him, his heart clenched, but she showed no recognition, no reaction beyond her purpose for being here. "Sir? You have to get out of here. I'm sure it's just a false alarm, but—"

"In the Monarch Suite. Someone is still in there," he managed to grind out. He gestured down the hall.

"Oh, okay—thank you." She smiled, then pointed toward the stairwell door. "Please head downstairs to the lobby."

Nox stepped back as if she were coming after him, when, really, she just turned and went in Cade's direction.

Nox turned and ran.

SHE WAS alive.

He made it to the street, momentarily confused by the lights and crowds and policemen and emergency units. Snow fell, but it wasn't the pretty kind that dusted the street and cabs. An icy mix and a wind kicking in from the north. A storm, possibly a bad one.

Nox didn't bother to hail a cab. He took off down the main drag toward the south exit of the District. If someone was following him, he didn't want to lead them back home.

He slipped in his dress shoes, the lifts he used to appear taller screwing with his balance, the icy deluge picking up as he walked as quickly as he could manage. The crowds thinned as the weather worsened—he could see the wall ahead, lights dimming as fewer businesses and advertisements populated this area.

If she recognized him, there would be guards following. Or cops alerted to pick him up. If she knew who he was, she'd send someone to the house....

Oh God.

He got off the main drag quickly, ducking onto a small side street. It looked more residential—newly built apartment buildings with wide front windows and tiny balconies—no one out and about, no activity for the entire length of the block. Worker housing, he thought.

A parking garage sign caught his eye; he went purposefully into a side door.

He needed transportation.

The tiny electric car was his first choice. It wasn't hard to break into—this model had a nasty habit of shorting out, and Nox knew what the hell he was doing with wires. Four and a half minutes—a record, considering his hands were shaking and he couldn't stop looking over his shoulder.

She was alive.

She looked right through him, but that meant nothing. He was already on the Iron Butterfly cameras. That man had scanned his card.

If she recognized his picture even though the name was different.... Seventeen years had done a lot to change his appearance, but Nox had recognized her right away. Was he burned into her mind the way she was in his?

Swallowing down the panic, Nox quickly started the car. He could barely maneuver inside the curved interior, but comfort wasn't his priority. He needed to get home.

Nox used a second pass, one he had tucked in his sock, to exit the parking garage. The streets were nearly deserted as he eased onto the main road; a few cops crawled down the strip, making sure the tourists got to their destinations safely as the rest of the force seemed to be streaming in the other direction toward the Iron Butterfly. Plows and salt trucks were already lined up at the south entrance, ready to make sure this part of town was accessible at all times.

He went north.

The snow hit the windshield; the tires ground in protest at the slick road. He drove onto the Freck Memorial Highway, going past the District line until the paved road ran out and the uneven broken concrete of the old highway began.

He took the car as far as he could, abusing the undercarriage until it whined and shimmied with each bump and crater it hit. When a tire blew on an especially hard hit to a buckled piece of pavement, he stopped.

A few wires snipped and touched together—the smoke started a second later as he exited the car. Nox cracked the window, then slammed the door, white tendrils creeping out as if to follow.

He walked through the growing piles of snow, hands in his pockets for warmth, head down as he walked toward home.

The tux and silly shoes provided no actual protection or warmth against the building storm that obscured the moon and his vision. Instinct was the only reason he knew where he was. Each step seemed to pull him closer into the memory of that night, and every moment, his worry intensified.

If Jenny wasn't dead, that meant someone knew he was alive.

And if she was the one sending Sam the messages.... Nox stumbled over some debris in the center of the sidewalk. No one lived in these abandoned brownstones; they'd long been ransacked and left for ruin. The power grid didn't extend here, and the people a block over ran off squatters. You got what you worked for, that was the motto—if you wanted to siphon off electricity, go fuck with those bastards in the District, not here.

The cold seeped through his tux and undergarments, into his skin until his teeth chattered uncontrollably. He thought about Sam and Jenny—and then his scattershot attention went back to the young man he left handcuffed to the bed.

Did Jenny get him out?

Was there real danger—a bomb, a fire?

What was his role in this whole deepening mess?

The burning attraction he'd felt, the clouding of his mind thanks to a nice ass and practiced bedroom eyes.... Nox felt a wrench of shame twist his solar plexus. If he'd let his dick lead him into trouble....

Nox would never forgive himself if everything he'd worked and battled for was undone by his base desires.

He struggled all the way back to the house, relief coursing through him as he came up on his block. He went through the back entrance, keying in his password with blue fingertips. Inside the townhouse, it was utterly silent save for the ever-present tick-tick-tick of the grandfather clock. Sam slept quietly upstairs, the neighborhood tucked in for now. The snow would chase the dealers and junkies inside for at least a few hours, which meant Nox could thaw out.

And figure out what to do next.

He sent a message to the Iron Butterfly through one of his many accounts, overpaying for his time with Cade (guilt, shame, desire, which set the whole cycle off again), and setting up another appointment to cover his tracks. Not that he was going back there, of course.

Apologizing to Cade was a difficult decision, but need twigged in his gut.

For seventeen years, his job had been to protect Sam. Whatever needed to be done—blood on his hands, marks on his soul—it didn't matter. His son was everything to him, and he'd die before he let his flesh and blood be harmed.

In this kitchen, Nox had made decisions and deals that cemented his life and future. He would stay here on this godforsaken island, he would raise a child as his own, and he would be a shadow for the privilege of being left alone. Every night he walked the Old City to keep the violence out. Every day he climbed to the top of a building and ran wires in the unfinished walls.

Nox Boyet died on Evacuation Day, on an overcrowded ferry in the middle of storm-swept waters. That simple fact—his name on that stone memorial—kept his son safe.

Jenny's name a few lines down had reinforced that belief. But not anymore.

The warmth of the house began to permeate Nox's sopping-wet clothes. He stripped off the tux and threw it onto the floor of the pantry. The kettle on, Nox went to the downstairs bedroom where he kept some of his clothes.

All the while, Nox's brain switched between two things: the woman in the hallway and the woman on the deck of that ferry. Now in the safety and warmth of his home, he could find a more rational space to think. Could he be imagining it? Could it just be a wild coincidence?

Everything about that night was imprinted on his brain—the fear, the hopelessness, the moment he decided he would do anything to survive. The gun in Jenny's hand, the bodies on the floor of his parents' bedroom, the impact of her words on his future. No detail escaped him. He couldn't forget that night if he tried.

Interlude
Before

NOX MAKES it up to the hospital, soaked to the bone and terrified. He's walked most of the way, except for the ride to the northernmost tip of Manhattan with a guy in a pickup truck. He gives the driver a hundred dollars and winds up at the gates to Morningside Sanitarium.

Ambulances and BMWs speed past him, kicking up the standing water accumulated on the driveway. The grounds resemble a lake, each crack of lightning illuminating another group of puddles joining together to form something rushing and dangerous.

He runs to the front steps and then into the building, boots squelching on the linoleum.

It's chaos.

People wander the halls in their pajamas, screaming and babbling, a few nurses here and there, frantically running from patient to patient. An alarm sounds down a distant hallway, a klaxon of warning.

Get out. Get out now.

Nox doesn't stop to ask directions. He knows where his mother is; he knows she's down the center hall, up one flight, and down six doors. This is the nice floor, where people pay extra for private suites and personal attention.

The ward is empty.

Or almost empty—he hears someone crying out in pain.

He runs until he's out of breath, reaching her door and pushing it open in a frantic effort. The scene in front of him doesn't register for a moment—the woman in the bed, straining and screaming, blood spreading out under her on the sheet.

She's giving birth.

His mother is giving birth.

Nox drops his bag. He rushes to her side out of pure instinct: take her hand, reassure her.

Scream for help.

"Mom, Mom, it's me. Just… just calm down, okay? Just breathe."

She doesn't know who he is. He doesn't know how to deliver a baby, but he's had health class and seen movies, so he knows to push up her nightgown, and oh God, so much blood. She's screaming and screaming and suddenly there's a head and he lets go of her hands to help pull this tiny person into the world.

Even after the baby—a little boy—slips free, his mother keeps screaming. He panics inwardly—there's so much blood, and all the health class videos in the world cannot capture how awful this moment is. But outwardly… somehow he remembers his mother cannot help him and everything in this moment is dependent on him. His actions.

He lays the baby on the bed then runs into the hallway. He knows from previous visits there's a nurses' station – and it's there he finds a first-aid kit.

Back in the room, hands shaking, Nox ignores the fact that his mother has stopped screaming. He pretends she's resting—eyes closed, chest barely moving—as he uses scissors to cut through the umbilical cord. It takes so long—his fingers cramp, his shoulders shake, but then finally the baby is free of his mother. Their mother, whose chest isn't moving anymore.

Nox rubs the infant clean with his mother's dressing gown, wrapping him up afterward. He doesn't cry until the baby opens his mouth and lets out a tiny mewl.

CHAPTER NINE

RACHEL HELD her emergency meeting on the abandoned casino floor.

Chairs were knocked over, poker chips and spilt drinks littering the carpet.

Chaos.

Zed was a force of nature, stomping around the room in a rage, cursing whoever did this to a violent death. His black-inked arms bulged out of his short-sleeved shirt, his bearded face contorted into an expression of pure ugliness.

"If it's any one of you...." He stopped, glittering black eyes taking in the semicircle of cold, damp, and terrified employees. "You will wish yourself dead when I find out." He let the words sink in, then stalked to the bar, leaving Damian and Rachel to take the floor.

Seemingly distracted, Rachel indicated Damian should speak.

"This interruption in service has cost us a great deal of money. For the next seventy-two hours, clients will not be charged for services. Which means...." He didn't even have to finish. No one dared mutter or moan their displeasure, not with Zed standing right there.

Everyone knew what the bottom line was.

No one was getting paid for services rendered.

"Regardless, we need you to step up and make sure the clients leave here with the intent to return—we can't afford to lose business over this." The warning note in Damian's voice was clear. New casinos were under construction even as they stood in this room—larger, more lavish, more to offer clients. The Iron Butterfly's reputation beat all of that, but once it was gone, they wouldn't get it back.

"Any questions?" Rachel asked, stepping into the center of the group. She cast her gaze on each of them in turn, lingering in the back, where Alec and Cade stood. Her look was a challenge.

Alec—with the balls of a giant—raised his hand.

"Oh Christ, you're going to get murdered," Cade whispered, but Alec ignored him.

"I'm not in the mood, Alec," she started, the edge in her tone absolutely brittle.

"It's relevant, I think," he said. "Do the police have any suspects yet?"

Zed took this one. He strode back into the group, arms crossed over his chest. "No."

"Call can't be traced?"

Damian stepped between Zed and Alec as if to deflect the explosion. "Not that I'm aware of," Damian offered.

A quiet murmur went through the group. Cade watched as Rachel's face hardened.

"How odd," Alec said, leaning back against the roulette table.

The room went dead silent.

Cade imagined everyone's thought bubbles were exactly the same—with all the security and promises made by the city police, why were they having no luck tracking down this person who kept calling in bomb threats to the local casinos?

"Get out of here," Zed snapped. "Clean yourselves up, then start checking in with the clients. Crawl room to fucking room if you have to, but make sure they're satisfied."

Everyone dispersed—everyone but Alec, who was beckoned over to Rachel with a crook of her finger.

"Don't wait up for me, darling," Alec cooed as Cade fled with the rest of the models.

THE WEATHER was too bad to go home, so Cade let himself into the suite he and Alec used for days they needed to stay at the Butterfly. Given his "trauma" and the fact that his customer was long gone, Cade decided his cleanup was going to take all damn night. Everything in the Starling Suite was done in smoky greens and antique silver, a two-bedroom with a central living room and a well-stocked bar. He ordered a chicken sandwich from the kitchen as he stripped his clothes off; then he made himself a double whiskey from the crystal decanters.

In the bedroom, he slipped into a pair of white pajama pants and a heavy gray sweater, feeling the cold down to his bones. It had been a ridiculous and exhausting night, and Cade was done.

"Look up a customer," he said to the voice-activated computer. "Patrick Mullens."

A discreet wall screen lit up next to the bar.

Patrick Mullens, resident of Boston.

37. Lawyer. Clean bill of health.

Top-tier deposit.

Hot spot: blackjack table at 21.

Cade scrutinized the picture next to the stats. He got as close as he could, studying the man's body, the curve of his shoulders. He remembered the scent of the man in the alley, the man who'd seduced all sense out of him....

Pretty boy.

"I think you're hiding something," Cade murmured, touching his fingers to the picture on the bedroom wall. He traced the man's jaw and down his strong neck.

He tried Rachel a few times, but she didn't answer her pager or her phone. Same deal with Alec. The past twenty-four hours caught up with him, so he dragged himself into the bed, facedown like a starfish in the center.

Tomorrow he'd find out what the hell was going on.

RACHEL WASN'T anywhere to be found in the morning, nor was anyone else above a manager pay grade.

"Yet another emergency meeting," said Alec as they passed in the hallway. "Hush-hush and serious faces." He looked like he'd been attacked by a wolverine, his shirt split down the back and scratches on his neck.

"I hope you got a decent tip." Cade pressed the down arrow on the elevator.

"Decent tip, a gold watch, and an invitation to the palace this summer." Alec smirked. "You might lose me to a harem."

"Your dream come true—being put out to stud."

Alec walked backward down the hall, musing over this as he tried to rearrange the mess that was his hair. "I actually think that might be it." He checked his watch. "Where the hell are you going?"

The doors slid open and Cade put one foot into the car. "Emergency meeting."

"HOW CLOSE can you get me to Ninety-First Street?"

The cab driver snorted loudly. He was the lucky guy Cade chose of the line of cabs, anxiously waiting for business on a day when no one wanted to be outside in the escalating bad weather as yet another storm smacked into the island. "Are you kidding?"

Cade leaned forward. "How close?"

"Maybe Seventy-Ninth," he huffed in response, driving around a mammoth pile of broken concrete in the street. "You'll have to walk from there."

"Fine."

THE RIDE took forever. Cade stared out the window, once again on the outskirts, once again marveling that people lived like this. Even during the worst of times—summer droughts, dropping prices—the farm kept his family fed and sheltered. He and his brother, Lee, didn't want for much in their lives. Maybe they didn't have the newest or fanciest anything, but unless someone pointed it out, it escaped Cade's notice.

Until he came out of college with a degree in English literature and no prospects except being second banana to his brother in the family lineage of farm ownership. A farm suffering under the weight of a second mortgage and yet another drought, the huge plantation that had been in his family's possession for generations sold off to developers in small parcels. Now when you looked out the kitchen window, you saw condo complexes and McMansions built for the flood of Northerners who fled when the weather went deadly.

No, thank you. Some modeling turned into more modeling, which turned into an offer from the Iron Butterfly.

"ARE YOU a virgin?" the man in the nondescript black suit asks, and Cade laughs.

"Yeah—no."

"Do you enjoy casual hookups?"

Cade looks around the Wilmington, North Carolina hotel room, searching for secret cameras. "Is that an offer?"

"As you might have heard," he continues on without looking up from his tablet, "the state of New York has come to debate the issue of legalizing prostitution in the District."

He laughs again.

Twenty minutes later, as Cade snickers and thinks what a killer story this will be at the bar tonight, the man writes a number on a slip of paper, and Cade stops laughing.

"HERE. I can't go any further," the driver snapped, pulling Cade out of his daydream. They were close enough for Cade to spy the vague outline of the grocery store he'd passed the day before. "And don't take too long—we miss curfew and you're paying the ticket."

Cade stuck a wad of bills through the small opening. "Thanks."

"Oh. At least it's a safe neighborhood," he said suddenly, his tone changing as Cade opened the door.

"Why do you say that?" Cade paused for a moment.

The driver pointed at the red spray-painted words—*portus tutus*—on the wall of an abandoned apartment building. "That means they got protection. Keeping the dealers out. You'll be okay." He turned in the midst of counting his money. "You call me, I'll come pick you up."

"Oh—thanks. Give me, like, two hours." Cade's mind clicked and whirled; he thought about the hooded man keeping him from getting jumped by the street gang.

The driver jammed the money in his jacket pocket, dollar signs in his eyes. "You got it. But don't be late."

Cade was prepared for the weather this time—this wasn't his first winter, and even when the rest of the models were in hiding, he liked to get out and breathe real air once in a while. Heavy boots, layers of his warmest clothes, gloves, and a jacket he'd nicked from one of the designers. It wasn't usable inside the casino, but damn, it kept him warm.

No one was on the streets—most construction sites were closed due to the storm, and the lack of plowing kept everyone inside. He made his way to Ninety-First, down the side street, and over to the gate in front of the church house.

This all started when he delivered Mr. White's letter, so Cade figured it was the best place to start. With any luck, he'd run into the asshole (protector?) in the hood and ask him a few questions.

And see if his theory was correct.

The gate opened easily—the stairs were neatly cleared, with pocks in the leftover snow where someone had dropped deicer. He knocked and waited.

No answer.

The anger started to build again; he took it out on the front door, pounding until pain radiated up his arm.

Maybe they were at work.

Cade turned to see if there was anyone on the street he might be able to ask. Some hint folks in the other houses might be of help. No one at all was out and about—not on the street or peeking out from behind a curtain as far as he could see.

Annoyed with not thinking this through, Cade walked back down the stairs. He pulled his cell out to call the cab driver but caught nothing but static, a common problem in this sort of terrible weather.

The sun would be setting soon.

Which meant the kid would be back. Had to be, thanks to curfew.

Cade went back up the stairs and leaned against the door to wait.

An hour passed and then the second began. The sun was nearly gone, pushed down into the horizon by the oppressive gray clouds. He checked his watch again and again, tapping his feet against the concrete stairs.

He needed to get back to the District.

Chatter broke his concentration; he looked down the street to find two men dressed all in black sauntering down the street. He leaned forward to see if one of them was the kid.

Neither of them was.

The men looked rough and dangerous, with ripped leather jackets and caps pulled low over their eyes. They seemed to be taking great care looking at the remaining buildings on the street. Cade started to get a bad feeling.

He dropped down to a hunched position in front of the door, calculating his odds of outrunning them. Of hiding. If they hadn't spotted him yet....

"Hey," one of them called up.

Cade wrestled with what to do for a moment, then stood up slowly.

The older of the two men gave him that patented look over, from his shoes to his face in one filthy sweep. The little smile that appeared on his face made Cade ridiculously uncomfortable despite it being a staple of his business.

This guy didn't look like he cared about Cade's conversational skills or anything else.

"You lose your key?" the younger asked as they stopped in front of the gate.

"Just waiting for someone," Cade called down. "He should be here any moment." He pretended he could see someone in the distance.

The men didn't leave.

"You need to buy anything tonight?" the older man asked, pushing open the gate. "We can give you a little company while you wait."

Cade was trapped. "No," he said, losing the pleasantness from his tone. "My friend will be here in a minute."

The man didn't seem to register Cade's words or defensive stance. He took the first step, and a smile spread over his face. "I recognize you from the billboards." He cocked his head to one side. "You probably make some big money up there in that fancy casino."

Cade narrowed his eyes. He wished he'd brought something to fight with, a knife or spray, something to give him an advantage. He could hold his own—his father taught him and his brother to defend themselves when they were barely out of diapers—but two against one left even the strongest person at a disadvantage.

"Come on, baby," the younger one called, slinking up behind his compatriot with an entirely differently gleam in his eyes. "How about a party?"

The slow, fearful burn turned into a brutally hot fire.

"Asshole, if you think either of you is getting anything from me without a life-threatening wound, you are sadly mistaken," Cade spit out, his drawl sneaking back into his words.

The men didn't seem to be anything but amused by Cade's posturing—they continued up the steps, menacing in a way that made Cade remember that stupid could kill you just as quick as skillful.

When the older of the two paused a step down—his gaunt form and bad skin spoke of a serious Dead Bolt habit—he pushed back his jacket to reveal a large hunting knife tucked in his waistband.

"Gimme your money," he said, and Cade slipped his hands out of his pockets.

"No."

The guy lunged a second before Cade, who ducked and took the force of his attacker's body weight in a crouched position. Cade struggled to stay upright, but the guy knocked him against the door, pushing the wind out of his lungs. He went for the knife before the guy could get his bearings, but it clattered to the ground as they both struggled to reach it.

Pushed from behind, Cade smacked headfirst into the door, the reverberations of the metal door rattling him right down to his fillings.

He slumped a little, still reaching for the knife. It got kicked to the other side of the stoop, and Cade threw his full body out to try to grab it.

Someone in the distance screamed, the sound cutting through Cade's foggy brain.

His fingers had just touched the edges of the knife's handle when the weight of his attacker disappeared. Cade rolled over, his head protesting the movement, then looked up...

...to find a man in a black hooded jacket holding the drug dealer by the neck.

"If I ever see you here again, I'll kill you," he rasped at the man he held. With a flick of his wrist, he dumped the man down the stairs.

He rolled down and landed in a heap on top of his already unconscious friend.

Cade sat up, leaning back against the house as he tried to catch his breath. His knee hurt like a mother, his left hand abraded from the concrete stairs.

"Oh shit," he panted, looking up at his rescuer—fucking Patrick Mullens—right before he passed out.

CHAPTER TEN

CADE CAME to slowly, registering *cold* and *pain* almost at the same time. He was on his back, staring up at the jutting edge of a roof and the backdrop of a starless black night.

God, his head screamed, throbbing in tempo with his thundering heartbeat. The cold seeped through his clothes from the ground, even as the crinkle of some sort of blanket alerted him he was covered. A second later his teeth began chattering.

He had to get up. He had to move. Had to remember why he was here....

It took a while to convince his limbs to work. He got vertical, leaning heavily against the door, then rolled onto his knees. A painful hiss from that—he'd done a number on both of them. The blanket dropped to the ground. Gripping the doorknob, Cade struggled on weak and shaking legs to stand up straight.

By the time he was clutching the door for dear life, he remembered what happened.

Two guys had tried to rob him. The hooded guy saved him. And underneath that hood? Was Mr. Freaking Mullens.

He was right. The slick guy from the casino and the hooded douche bag were one and the same.

Anger fueled warmth and action. Cade made a fist with his undamaged hand and pounded on the door.

It felt like forever—Cade slammed against the heavy metal until the dizziness threatened to consume him again. How dare he—Cade had been mugged, groped, and now, what the hell, this guy was going to let him freeze to death under a piece of tinfoil?

Bastard.

In the midst of his banging, Cade heard something click on the other side. The door slid open to reveal the teenager, Sam, who looked like he'd just woken up. At the sight of Cade, his eyes got huge behind those black-rimmed glasses.

"What are you doing here?" he asked. "And Jesus, what happened?"

"Two guys…." Cade's voice was as raw and bruised as the rest of him felt. "Mullens—in the black hood."

Sam's face went slack with shock. He pushed past Cade to walk onto the stoop, seemingly unaware of the snow or cold. He turned back to Cade, who was clutching the doorjamb, just trying to stay upright.

"Where is he?" the kid demanded.

Cade shrugged. "Got knocked out. He kicked the fuckers down there." He gestured toward the bottom of the steps, where he'd last seen the thugs. Both he and Sam looked at the same time.

No one was there.

"What the hell?" Cade wheezed.

Sam turned and began to bustle Cade into the house. "He's going to kill me," he muttered.

Behind that fortified door and gray exterior, Cade, leaning heavily on Sam's arm, tripped into a whole different world. From the foyer—wood floors, a crystal chandelier—he could see a long hallway that flowed into a dining room straight ahead, a large staircase to the left and a living room that appeared to run the length of the home. The furniture was sparse but obviously expensive, and once upon a time, this home might have been considered a showplace.

It was also so fucking warm he could have cried.

"Holy shit," Cade murmured as Sam led him down the hallway. He trudged along, limping and leaning against the wiry teenager. A huge kitchen past the burgundy-walled dining room, two doors to his right just past the stairs—this place was a mansion.

At the second door, Sam stopped and gave him an apprehensive look over his shoulder. "He's gonna be pissed," the kid warned, and then he pushed open the door.

CHAPTER ELEVEN

NOX HAD spent his entire day in fearful rage.

When he returned to the brownstone in the middle of the night—cold, panicked—his brain had been crowded with memories provoked by the woman in the casino. His concern about the letter Sam received didn't touch the terror that she was behind it.

That she was alive.

For the rest of the night, Nox pored over the Internet, looking for information. He found her name on the ferry manifest from seventeen years ago.

She was dead.

Jenny Aglaya was dead. He'd watched her get on the ferry. He'd watched the ferry sink into the river.

No. He'd run back to the house, but everyone knew the ferry sunk in bad weather twenty minutes after pushing off.

He'd built his entire plan for keeping Sam safe and out of harm's way on that fact. The only person who knew Nox Boyet was alive—knew that Sam existed—had drowned along with thousands of others in the storm-swept Hudson River.

Sam found him in the morning, staring blankly at the screen.

Rachel Moon, the manager at the Iron Butterfly, native New Yorker, was at college in Boston when the Evacuation happened. Brighton Beach born, Russian immigrant parents, though never mentioned by name and long since deceased. Top-of-the-line manager, long coveted by other casinos. But she was completely loyal to the Butterfly.

He read the interviews.

She wasn't Jenny.

Couldn't be.

Nox conducted the rest of his day distracted and jumpy. He was short with Sam, late for work. He wanted to pack their bags and run away—*where to* was the $100,000 question—because if the two things were connected....

If she was Jenny. If she was sending the messages.

He could barely breathe.

The people who killed his father knowing about Sam, knowing about him.

His worst nightmare.

His forewoman, Addie, didn't keep them on the job for long. The storm and subsequent winds made it dangerous on the fifty-eighth floor of the massive tower they were building. The jobsite was a hazardous mess, and Addie's bosses weren't too interested in dead workers making the headline of tomorrow's news.

He got home hours before Sam—messengers were even more necessary on days like this, when no one wanted to go out—and restlessly prowled the brownstone.

He touched the hidden door of the safe room, brushing his palm over the oak trim. His mother had installed it after 9/11, convinced the end times were upon them—the terrorist attack was proof she'd been right all along. The world would descend in chaos and bloodshed and they had to be prepared.

When it was still not good but not bad enough for the hospital, Nox's father would hand over a credit card and let her buy until she felt a modicum of peace.

Their basement rivaled even the most paranoid of the survivalists'.

Over the years, those supplies had kept Nox and Sam alive. Hard times were never potentially deadly. They made it through.

Food, water, guns. Solar-powered radios and enough first-aid supplies to open a hospital. Blankets tested for the most extreme temperatures. Duplicates and triplicates tucked and neatly ordered on row after row of shelving, waiting for darkness to fall and the people in this house to have to fight for their lives.

Sometimes he thought she had been right all along.

NOX CHANGED into his black leathers and went out to walk the streets of his territory.

It started within the walls of his home, but it bled out onto his block. His terrible fear that someone would come into the house and take Sam propelled him into the darkness, around and around the block, until daylight.

Sam got older. The longer he could stay alone, the larger the circle Nox traveled.

Up here there was no industry, no outside investment, and therefore no cops. The nameless, faceless murderers who killed his father didn't return, but Nox went on his little missions so he could head off other threats to the peace of his household. Dead Bolt dealers and junkies drawn to the dark mess of the Old City, with no one to stop them from plying their deadly trade.

It made him crazy.

The guy is standing on the steps of Trinity, holding court like he's king. He's got a line of people waiting for his poison, out in the open, no shame.

Nox sees red.

He's eighteen years old, tired and hungry for something more than rice and beans and water. He rations everything out, not knowing when things will turn around. If they will. People who stuck it out through the storms and the Evacuation have packed up their belongings and left. Nox is alone in the neighborhood except for Sam.

This man, this criminal, smiles and laughs as he passes another clear baggie to another poor soul—and Nox feels a rage he's only experienced twice before.

He waits in the shadow until the man is alone, counting up money with a huge grin on his face.

He waits until the man walks down the stairs and steps into the shadows pooling on the sidewalk.

Then Nox strikes.

Everything crowded into Nox's head in a symphony of madness—past and present crashing into him like angry waves. He stared at the faded brick walls of his former school and tried to remember when this building was a joyful memory.

HE WENT home.

HALF A block away, Nox spotted people inside his gate, on his stairs. The Sig—because a blackjack was no longer enough to make him feel safe—was tucked in the back of his waistband, under his heavy black sweater, and his hand was on it before he consciously registered it.

None of the men were Sam, for which he was instantly grateful. The blond on the top step, he realized, was Mr. Creel—and as he moved closer, he processed that he might need to kill him if he'd brought danger to his house.

Then the other two men attacked, and Nox started running.

He pulled the first man down by the back of his jacket. Nox recognized him as local muscle for one of the larger dealers—that meant a green light for him to get four rib punches and a toss down the stairs. As he collapsed on the ground, Nox moved to the ongoing scuffle.

Nox plucked the second dealer by the back of his shirt. He was heavy, but that just gave gravity a hand in yanking him down the steps after Nox banged his head against the concrete railings and issued a threat.

At his feet, Cade sat up suddenly, looked up at him, and Nox felt a flash of fear as recognition dawned on the kid's face.

His hood had fallen back.

"Oh shit," the kid muttered before passing out again.

Nox's trouble just kept multiplying.

CREEL WAS down for the count, passed out and sprawled on Nox's front step. Adrenaline coursed through Nox's body like a fast-moving virus; he had to clean up this mess before Sam woke up or anyone noticed the commotion.

He carried an emergency blanket in his pack, and that became a cocoon for the kid lying unconscious at his feet. The kid's immediate safety taken care of, Nox dealt with the assholes at the bottom of the stairs.

Part of him wanted to shoot them both—bad enough they prowl his neighborhood, bringing death and destruction, but his house? He tried to keep his logical mind engaged before the animal shredded them both and left them to bleed out in the middle of the street.

One hand on each of their jacket collars, Nox hauled them down the block. The weight and effort taxed his body, pushing it to the limit as he gritted his teeth. Over tree roots and around broken sidewalks, all the way to the main drag. In the center sat an enormous pothole—that was the destination.

Arms screaming, he yanked them the last few yards. First the muscle, then the flunky, went facedown in the slush-filled hole.

If they woke up, they could crawl back to their tenements. If not? Well, that was the law of the jungle. Survival of the fittest.

He got two steps before a searing pain sent him down to one knee. Nox looked back to find the muscle had woken up—and pushed a small blade into the back of Nox's calf.

Nox kicked back with his good leg without hesitation. He caught the asshole in the face, just over the side of the hole where he'd crawled out. The crunch and whimper of pain gave him time to reach for the Sig and aim over the side.

He pulled the trigger once, the silencer muffling his deed in the quiet, cold night.

The blade was too deep for him to pull out, so he limped back home, only rage powering his movements. The dead man in the street meant nothing to him, meant nothing to the drug dealer who employed him. There were men to take his place, women to step up and do his job without anyone lamenting his passing. Nox knew the score— everything he did just slowed the tide, handicapped the inevitable.

But for the violence to be so close to home? He couldn't have that.

Jenny's face flashed in his mind, and he willed himself to move faster.

That pretty boy with the lush mouth was going to tell him everything: who sent the letter to Sam, about Jenny's doppelganger, and why he was drawing attention to Nox's front door. And he was going to do all that or end up in the middle of the street like the dead asshole who'd stuck a knife in his leg.

CHAPTER TWELVE

WHEN CADE finally found his bearings, he was lying on a bed in a quaint white-and-purple room that looked like something his twin female cousins would go out of their minds for. He tried to remember why his head and hands and stomach and everything hurt so fucking much. It took a second, but the full details came back in a rush.

"Dammit," he said out loud, shifting his weight to try to roll over. The resulting pain was a mixture of nausea and breath-stealing pressure on his side.

He remembered the guy in the black hood pulling him up and the blue eyes and considered whether Mr. Mullens might be triplets or clones. He remembered being told to stay awake, which seemed a terrible idea. Everything hurt, especially his head.

A nap would be wonderful.

Or it could kill you, another voice said. This one sounded sardonic and irritated and most like his brother, Lee.

This time I won't go the opposite way just to spite you, Cade thought as he pinched his palm in an attempt to stay conscious.

The door opened and one of the Mr. Mullens—the one in the black hoodie—stepped in, hood down and a full scowl on his dirty and bruised face.

He slammed the door behind him. The sound went through Cade's skull like a knife through hot butter—and that image called to mind made his stomach roil.

"Who are you working for?" the man asked, cold and fierce. He moved—no, limped—to stand over Cade, who rolled onto his back in a move of supplication.

"I just wanted to know…." Cade shook his head, trying to clear his mind. "I don't like not knowing…," he tried again, but Mr. Mullens's face kept contorting into something angrier and angrier.

"Why are you here?" he snapped.

Cade closed his eyes tightly, bringing his hands up to cover his ears. "Shut up," he moaned, fighting another wave of nausea.

"I'm going to dump your ass in the middle of the street in five seconds if you don't tell me who you're working for."

Thu-thump, thu-thump went Cade's temples. He pressed his hands harder against his ears as if to keep his brains from spilling out.

"Mr. White is a good customer," he whispered. "It was just a favor."

Then everything faded to black.

CHAPTER THIRTEEN

NOX LIMPED back into the hallway only to find Sam standing there, arms tight across his chest.

"Your leg...." Sam gestured, his face pale. Nox looked down and realized the reason for his son's expression.

There was a blood trail from the front door, down the hall, and crisscrossing between the doors as Nox stomped around.

"Fuck. Get the first-aid kit," Nox rumbled, leaning against the wall with a shaky exhale. As his anger simmered and the heat from the house permeated his bones, the pain and blood loss started to register with his body.

Haziness touched the edges of his vision.

Sam pushed him into the kitchen, then directly into a chair. The sudden drop made Nox's head spin. He gripped Sam's arm as he leaned over him. "We need to get that guy out of here."

"He's hurt and so are you," Sam said, kneeling at Nox's side. His hands were gentle as he ripped the material of Nox's pant leg. The small knife sticking out of the meaty part of Nox's calf didn't even make him blink.

He'd sewn up worse.

"I don't want him here," Nox started, but Sam put his hand up to stop the flow of words.

"Well, tough. It's after curfew." There was a serious, mature edge to Sam's voice, his face—Nox couldn't help but see the little boy, but it was clear times had changed. "And we need to make sure he's okay."

Sam had grown up.

They were both quiet after that. Nox braced himself as Sam removed the small knife. He bit his lip as Sam cleaned and sewed up the wound. It wasn't his first stabbing and it wouldn't be his last, and somewhere along the way, Sam had gotten good at playing nurse.

In another life Sam would have made a wonderful doctor.

Sam stood up, wiping his hands on his T-shirt. "I want to talk to him, see if he knows anything else about the person who wrote the letter," he said matter-of-factly.

"No."

Nox rubbed his face with both hands, shaken from the loss of blood and still on edge with Cade in his house. People weren't allowed in here, for very good reason.

He didn't want to sacrifice another life, but he would if it meant keeping Sam safe.

"Stop saying that." Sam sounded done. "Stop telling me what to do. I'm going to talk to him and make sure he's okay, and then you can kick him out, okay?" Sam's voice escalated into a shout. "Stop being so goddamned paranoid."

Not much could have driven Nox out of that chair, but Sam's anger—his determination to defy Nox—did the trick. He loomed over Sam, who lifted his chin defiantly. "I'm trying to keep you safe."

"You're keeping me prisoner! Out there—my parents could be looking for me! Did you ever think of that?" Despair crept into his voice. "You keep me in this house, you control where I go and who I talk to! And all this time, they could be—they could be freaking out, thinking I was dead when I'm not."

Nox's heart broke, but anger was the only emotion he could safely express. "I saved your goddamn life," he snapped. "Everything is about keeping you safe. Every piece of shit's blood on my hands—even that's about you."

A dark veil fell over Sam's face. "Maybe you should have just let me drown," he said slowly.

Nox regretted it as soon as he opened his mouth, but the words snapped out. "Yeah, maybe I should have."

Sam was gone before Nox could stop him, storming through the living room and then up the stairs. Nox tried to limp after him but gave up halfway—he hurt, he was angry, and he didn't think Sam would have any interest in speaking with him at this moment.

Nox felt shame at hurting Sam, because nothing could be further from the truth. He didn't regret saving his life, not for a single second.

He felt the burn in his leg from a wound that never should have happened. Distraction. The boy unconscious in the guest room.

His carefully ordered world was descending into chaos again, and he didn't spend seventeen years to watch it happen because he lost control.

He limped into the bedroom where Cade was sleeping, trembling under the thin blankets. Nox didn't question the logic of what followed—he stripped the wet clothes off Cade's dead weight, tossed each piece to the floor, ignored his concern at the bluish tinge to his skin.

This kid was a bridge to trouble Nox didn't need or want.

With trembling hands, he tucked the blankets around Cade's still limp body and watched him for a long, long time.

Who are you really? Are you going to be another stain of blood on my hands?

THERE WAS scotch in the bomb shelter, a nod to his father's tastes, Nox supposed. When his mother, Natalie, went into a paranoid state—when she was still able to function, before it escalated—she would spend hours on the Internet, reading survivalist blogs and doomsday warrior sites. His father would spend more time at the office when the deliveries began, sometimes five or six times a day.

Nox would find his own things to do—extra hours at the library, more time at the basketball court or running along the river. He'd use the back entrance to avoid her accosting him as soon as he got home to point out another article about government conspiracies and strange diseases in Africa.

She was so scared the end of the world would come, so worried they wouldn't have enough of everything to help them survive. For an hour or two after she'd unpacked the boxes and arranged the items on yet another shelf, there would be peace. Natalie would believe they'd have enough. That they'd be fine.

Then the panic would return.

Now Nox drank the bomb shelter scotch, his leg up on the ottoman as he sprawled in his father's desk chair. Of all the rooms they used, this one changed very little. Only the family pictures and his father's diplomas were gone, tucked away in the panic room, away from potentially prying eyes.

The Boyets were all dead and he was just Patrick Mullens, who—along with his son, Sam—lived here, in this abandoned house. That was the story to anyone who asked.

No one asked, of course. Nox kept everyone at arm's length: no friendships, no relationships, no one knowing the truth, not even Sam.

Especially not Sam.

The blood loss and liquor did very little to clear his tangled thoughts. He felt himself getting pulled farther down the rabbit hole until he disappeared into memories.

Interlude

IT IS the worst moment of Nox's life, and he thinks if he breaks down now, he might never stop crying.

And he can't cry because the baby in his arms is doing enough of that for both of them.

He stands in the hallway of the hospital, unsure what to do next. He needs to get home. He needs to get off this island. And now, instead of his mother, he has an infant to take with him.

"What are you doing here?" someone asks, forcing Nox out of his grief-induced fog.

A woman—a girl, really, maybe a few years older than himself—stands at the end of the empty hallway.

"I need help," he says, voice cracking.

Her name is Jenny. She says she came to get her grandmother, but she'd already been evacuated. Everything about the girl is calm and steady, and Nox is so grateful he can barely choke out his thanks.

Where did the baby come from? Where's its mother? Is the baby okay? Does he need a ride?

He explains everything in a shaky voice, as if reciting the plot of a horror movie he saw last week. "Yes," *Nox says to the ride, tucking the infant inside of his jacket. He feels woozy with fear and grief, his mother's blood still clinging to his hands and clothes despite his attempts to get it off.*

She has a large black Hummer parked right in front of the stairs, passenger door facing them. The rain has turned into some unrelenting force, and the water rises to the bottom step, lapping dangerously upward.

"Let's go. I'll take you home."

"I have money," Nox says, staring down at the sleeping baby against his chest. He can't believe this, doesn't understand why or how—how did his parents keep her pregnancy a secret? "For you, for helping."

The Hummer roars through the rising water of the highway. Visibility is next to nothing—he has no idea how the girl is keeping the truck on the road.

"I don't need your money," she says, tightly gripping the wheel.

She seems annoyed he's said anything, so he goes back to the baby, touching his tiny head, black fuzzy hair sticking up all over.

They pass stranded vehicles and National Guard trucks filled with people. A line of cars and trucks stretches in front of them—the bridge backed up for miles. Jenny swears under her breath, then takes a sharp right down a side street, water splashing up on either side.

"Get the phone out of my pocket," she says, using her elbow to point at her jacket.

Jenny has him dial a number—she needs two hands, and he can manage with one as the baby sleeps on.

"*Put it up against my ear,*" *she says, slowing the truck to a crawl as she tries to find the road ahead of them. The water rises a little higher, lapping against the doors.*

"*It's me. Yeah. Are you at the rendezvous point? I'm having trouble getting there—the water's too high.*"

A voice at the other end—a man, he can tell that much—answers, anger evident. Jenny's expression never changes.

"*Fine,*" *Jenny says coolly.*

She pulls her head away from the cell. "*Hang up. Then shut it off.*"

Nox does as he's told. Somewhere in the middle of his gratitude for being given this ride, he starts to panic.

He'd assumed a girl wouldn't hurt him. He'd assumed she has the best intentions.

"*Who are you?*" *Nox asks as the baby whimpers against his chest.*

Jenny laughs, tight and high. "*I thought you'd recognize my voice after all our little chats, Nox.*"

She sounds different all of a sudden, breathy and girly, and God. Oh God.

"*You worked for my dad.*"

"*Very good, Nox. Very good.*"

"*Why didn't you tell me?*"

Jenny didn't say anything. Nox's stomach pinched as his anxiety grew.

"*I need to talk to someone about my dad's will. It's just my brother and me now....*" *It hurts to say. His throat begins to clog with tears. The reality is he and the baby are on their own now. Their parents are dead and there's no one to call for help.* "*I don't know what to do, but you can help me, right?*"

Still not a word.

"*Jenny, can you please help me?*"

"*It's not that easy,*" *Jenny murmurs.*

They drive a little farther, Jenny pulling up and down roads to find the easiest to travel through. Finally he sees headlights through the windshield, a cluster of them up ahead. Jenny makes a sound—a sigh, maybe—so soft that he thinks he might have imagined it. Except for the cold chill that runs down his spine.

"Stay here," Jenny say as she eases the truck into a triangle formation with the other two vehicles. The baby stirs, so Nox's attention goes to him; he hears a compartment open and close and then the door.

It's a few minutes before he hears shots.

At first he thinks it's thunder, but then the Hummer door flings open and a soaked Jenny jumps into the seat.

"What—" he starts to ask, but the gun in her hand answers the unspoken question.

"Shut up," she snaps. She doesn't say another word as she drops the gun in her lap, then throws the Hummer into reverse and guns the motor.

The precision Jenny has displayed before was gone. She drives recklessly, pushing the truck through the flooding roads, following a route with flashing emergency signs every few hundred yards.

Road closed.

Do not enter.

Nox isn't someone who does a lot of praying, but right now he is. Head bent, the baby breathing tiny puffs of air against his cheek, Nox talks to whomever might be listening.

He prays for the baby and for himself, that whatever happens, it would be quick and painless. He prays for the souls of his mother and his father, and apologizes for not being able to save his brother from all this.

The Hummer comes to a sudden halt. Jenny's harsh breathing fills the interior, and Nox cringes.

"I have money," he says, trying one more time. "You can have it all...."

Jenny laughs as if he's told the funniest joke of all time. "Oh, honey, you don't have enough to buy me off."

They're in the middle of nowhere, maybe near one of the uptown parks. No lights, traffic.

Jenny turns in the seat to face him. Nox holds the baby a bit closer.

"I'll take care of him," she says, almost gentle, almost remorseful. "Don't worry about that."

"But you're going to…."

She shrugs, undoing the seat belt as she moves. She brings the gun up, points it at his head.

He closes his eyes, tears squeezing out the corners as he says another prayer. He is just sixteen and this is how he was going to die.

The shot doesn't come, but the jolt does. The Hummer begins to move—sideways—as it lifts from the road, sweeping down the street by a wave of water.

Nox is thrown against the door as Jenny swears violently. The gun falls to the floor as she grips frantically at the wheel—there is nothing she can do. They're floating away.

Nox grabs the door handle as the truck lurches to one side.

Inside his jacket, the baby whimpers in distress.

A moment ago he had been ready for death, but suddenly Nox is just pissed the hell off. This crazy girl wants to kill him? The weather wants him dead?

Fuck them both. They had their chances.

With Jenny's furious screaming echoing in his ears, Nox unhooks his seat belt. If the Hummer goes under, he'll need to swim to safety so the baby doesn't drown, and he wants to be ready.

They strike something—another car, a building, a light post, he can't tell what. All he knows is that the Hummer stopped moving. He glances out the window as Jenny tries to turn the engine on, slamming the steering wheel when it doesn't work. During a flash of lightning, he sees a huge building just beyond the front of the truck. A second flash and he can see turrets….

The courthouse in Harlem.

His art class had come here to sketch the Romanesque architecture last year, and Nox fights to remember exactly where they are.

121st Street.

He is thirty blocks from home.

A sideways glance. Jenny pounds on the steering wheel with one hand as she moves the key with the other. The calm, collected girl has been replaced by a wide-eyed fury, spit flying from her mouth as she stomps on the gas.

Nothing.

She doesn't have the gun.

Stay and be shot.

Jump out and at least have a chance.

Nox eases his hand on the handle, cradling the baby against his chest with the other.

Open the door, jump down, and run.

Open the door, jump down, and run.

Open the door….

Nox takes a breath, then shoves all his weight against the door as he pulls the handle. It takes him three hard pushes before the door opens. Water rushes into the Hummer as Nox fights against it. He floats for a split second before his feet hit the ground, water swirling around his legs, hips, and waist.

Behind him, Jenny screams his name. All he can do is force his legs to move against the swirling water and make his way to the other side of the building.

CHAPTER FOURTEEN

NOX LIMPED back to the kitchen, shaking and not having much luck regaining his fucking control. He could barely move, the pain radiating up his leg and aggravating old wounds he'd collected over the years. The scotch left him light-headed.

He was a mess.

In the fridge he found ice; he threw it into a dish towel and shuffled back down the hallway with his makeshift pack in hand. At the bottom of the stairs stood Sam, hands in his pockets, steely resolve on his face.

Nox sighed. "I'm sorry."

Sam shrugged, kicked his boot against the bottom step. "We end up saying that to each other a lot."

"I don't regret saving you," Nox said, leaning against the spindles of the staircase. He put the ice pack against the back of his neck in an attempt to get his frantic brain to chill out. Literally. "It was the best decision I ever made. Even if you have grown up to be stubborn and hotheaded."

A smirk. Sam ran his hand through his hair, clearly trying to stay mad at Nox. "Biology isn't to blame here—it's all your bad influence."

The press of the lie, and all the lies that followed, bore down on him. "Right."

"Maybe... maybe my parents *are* alive," Sam said softly. Suddenly. "Maybe they could help you too, Dad."

Oh God.

Nox grabbed the banister with one hand. Sam moved quickly to hold him up as his knees buckled. He couldn't do this right now.

"Come on, Dad, it's okay," he said, helping him up the stairs.

Interlude

NOX DIDN'T go into the church. He spots a minivan, stalled out and abandoned, up on the curb. The door is unlocked, so he hops into the front seat and drops immediately to the floor. Every ounce of fury that propelled him out into the storm still courses through his veins. He is going to save his brother and he is going to get off this fucking island if it's the last thing he does.

The baby is furiously unhappy to be wet and startled, squealing frantically against his chest. When Nox spots the tipped-over diaper bag on the middle seat, he almost cries in gratitude.

He lays the baby on the front seat, then reaches back carefully for the bag. There're some diapers, a baby bottle of water, a pacifier, and some baby clothes, all much bigger than his newborn brother. But everything is dry, and that's better than what they have now.

One ear out for Jenny, Nox jury-rigs the diaper to fit the tiny infant and swaddles him in layers of the clothes. After a few stressful moments, the baby drinks some of the water, his little mouth working around the nipple. Finally, the pacifier is a godsend as the baby sucks himself to sleep as soon as he's warm, dry, and hydrated.

Outside, the storm rages on. Nox hears the roar of a motor and headlights flash by.

The Hummer. Jenny has taken off.

Relief courses through him. They're safe for now.

IN HIS room, Nox sat at the edge of the bed, staring at the rug. He'd had the same carpeting since this was a nursery, a royal blue with thin stripes of gray. Sometimes the lines were lanes for his race cars. Sometimes they were a high wire he was balancing on precariously. He graduated to using them to measure how tall he was—if his feet were against the wall, how many of them had he grown since last time he checked?

Back then this house wasn't a prison.

"Dad, you should lie down," Sam said from the doorway. "I'll go get you some food, okay?"

Nox shook his head. "I need to talk to him again…."

"He's asleep."

"Sam…."

The teenager didn't answer; he turned and disappeared from view. Another bit of his control slipping away.

He did lie down finally, the gun next to him in the folds of the blanket. Nox eased a pillow under his knee to take some of the pressure off his lower leg, then stared at the ceiling until he drifted off.

Interlude

NOX WAKES with a start. Something woke him up, something….

Quiet.

The rain has stopped.

He leans up from his curled-up position on the floor—checks the baby, who is still asleep in his little nest of clothes and Nox's jacket on the seat—and looks out the window.

In the light of day, the devastation is obvious. Water everywhere, as if someone awkwardly placed a city in the middle of a lake. Several buildings are missing their roofs, and streams of water are cascading out of windows—up to the third and fourth floors. Cars float by, slamming into storefronts on the avenue.

Nox needs to get out of there.

He rewraps the baby, waking him, to his great annoyance, before sliding him into his shirt. The jacket goes back on, his backpack over his shoulders, with everything left in the diaper bag tucked away—he is ready to go.

The sound of a truck rattling past makes him drop down again. He peeks up and spies a National Guard transport slowly making its way through the flooded streets.

They are saved. Actually saved!

Nox throws open the door and shouts for help.

CHAPTER FIFTEEN

CADE WOKE up in his underwear, with a headache and five blissful seconds where he thought maybe it was because of a wild party with a client. Then he remembered.

"Shit."

The side table held a lamp spilling low light and a bottle of water, damp with condensation, so it had probably been sitting there for a while.

Cade drank the water down, then tested his legs and head with actual movement. He was still a mess of aches and pains and a terrible headache, but he could manage that. Now he just needed some damn clothes so he could get the fuck out of here.

The past twenty-four hours had not been good for his wardrobe.

"Never mind. Designer clothes won't really be necessary on the farm," he muttered bitterly as he stood up. Fuck, he was so fired.

A grandfather clock began to bong out the hour—ten o'clock, which meant he was a full hour late for his shift, without a call.

So fucking fired.

He should probably steal something to sell for all his troubles before he got the hell out of here—and then call the police to take this lunatic into custody, he thought, working his way towards the shuttered windows on the other side of the girly room.

"I guess you feel better," someone said. Cade whirled around in surprise.

The teenager—Sam—was standing there, looking exhausted.

"Yeah," Cade said slowly. "I need my clothes back."

The kid seemed to suddenly realize Cade was standing there in his underwear; he blushed a little and averted his eyes. "They're in the wash. I can get you something in the meantime."

"Awesome," Cade sassed. "You're a super helpful kidnapper."

"You weren't kidnapped. You got beat up on our doorstep." Sam tilted his head. "Why were you on our doorstep, by the way?"

Cade opened his mouth, then shut it, giving himself a moment to think. What if this skinny kid was in cahoots with Mullens? He just wanted to get out of here, and he wasn't about to trust anyone in this house.

"I wanted to see you, actually," Cade said carefully. "Try to figure out why me dropping off a note to you got me into so much shit."

"Oh." High spots of color appeared on Sam's face. "Sorry about that. I didn't—I mean, I don't know who this Mr. White is. I'm not even sure how he found me, to be honest."

Well, that didn't help.

And it kind of made things worse.

"Maybe we can talk a little and figure out what's going on?" Sam asked. "You're kinda stuck here for a while because of curfew—I'll get you some clothes and food, okay?"

Cade rubbed his face with both hands, nodding helplessly.

He was fucked. Might as well be warm and fed at the same time.

NOW DRESSED in a set of threadbare black sweats, Cade followed Sam through the dining room—no table, the burgundy walls stacked with books and boxes—and into the expansive kitchen. Everything gleamed and sparkled, from the out-of-date appliances to the vintage countertop.

"You have a damn nice house," Cade said, surprised that such luxury still existed in the city.

"Thanks. Dad has lived here since he was born—I mean, here in New York. We moved in here when I was a baby," Sam said quickly, opening the refrigerator and ducking inside.

"Is it just you two?" Cade trailed his fingers over the countertop, eyeing the various coffeemakers and old-fashioned appliances—dated, but still nicer than anything his mom had ever had. Let the interrogation begin.

"Yeah." Sam brought a package wrapped in white paper to the island. He tore the paper open, revealing a few pieces of chicken, small and thin—it had probably cost them a fortune.

"Divorce?"

"What? Oh God. No." The kid smiled nervously. "I mean—I call him Dad, but it's not biological or anything. That was why… uh—your friend, Mr. White. He said he could help me find my real parents."

"Oh. Wow." Cade didn't know what to do with that. Mr. White, eccentric old man, terrible gambler and white-glove fetishist, trying to help a kid in the Old City find his birth family? Did not compute.

"Yeah." Sam reached over to the pot rack and pulled down a frying pan. "I know it's a long shot and I know it's crazy, but—I want to know, if he can really do what he says. I want to know their names, at least."

Confused, Cade leaned against the cabinets, arms folded over his chest. "Don't you have a birth certificate or something?"

"Most of that stuff got destroyed in the floods, plus—I was born on Evacuation Day. So you know—zero chance there's paperwork to even have survived. My dad found me in an abandoned car while he was going to the dock to get on the ferry and, um, he pulled me out."

"Holy shit." The asshole in the hood who also liked to handcuff boys to beds had a heroic past.

"And because he stopped, he missed the ferry." Sam dropped his gaze, wrapping his fingers around the handle of the pan. "The one that sank."

Cade shook his head. "That's—he stopped to help you and ended up helping himself."

Sam looked up at that, a melancholy smile on his face. "We saved each other that day."

"But you still want to find out about your real parents?" Cade asked as Sam moved around the kitchen. Into the pantry for a bottle of olive oil, then back to the stove to prepare the chicken.

"I'm really grateful to him." The kid stopped, scrunched up his face as he made quick work of pouring the oil and placing the chicken in the heated pan. "I'm just... curious. What were their names? Where did they live? Why was I in that car alone?"

"You know you probably won't find out those things," Cade said frankly. "Some people just... well, you know. They never found them."

The chicken began to sizzle and pop in the pan. "Yeah, true. But if I can find a name, maybe there might be pictures online or something. I'd at least love to see what they looked like."

A name and some faces. That was all this kid wanted. Something about the sad slant of Sam's mouth and the longing in his expression touched Cade right in the center of his chest.

Cade knew the Creel family tree back to the 1600s. His mother's Natchez ancestors—he knew them too. There were bound books of lineage and history from both sides of the family in the library, with pictures and census information.

For all his mixed emotions when it came to his family, he could identify his great-great-great-grandmother from a black-and-white picture, and this kid didn't even have his mom's first name.

Fuck.

"Listen, I can get in touch with Mr. White and I'll let him know, okay? That you want his help."

The kid lit up like Christmas morning. "Thank you."

Cade leaned against the counter. "So maybe you can help me in return?"

Sam dialed back the glow a little. "How?"

CHAPTER SIXTEEN

NOX JOLTED awake. He breathed deeply to steady his panicking heart as he stared up at the ceiling fan. Dreaming of that night didn't help his muddled brain, and it made that skittering paranoia rise up like the tide, swamping over his rational thoughts. The fact that there had been no knock at the door was reassuring, at least—if Cade was their advance scout, he sucked mightily at it.

At some point Nox would have to confront the kid, find out what he knew, and make a decision about how he was leaving this house.

In the middle of this grim train of thought, the door rattled. A second later it swung open, revealing a delighted Sam, smiling brightly as he carried in the old breakfast tray.

"We made chicken and some rice," Sam said as Cade trailed in behind him. "And tea."

Nox glanced from his son to the man lounging in the doorway like he was posing for an ad, dressed in some old clothes of Nox's. Scrapes and bruises aside, he looked better than before—and very fucking smug to be out of that room.

"I'm going to have to send you guys a crate of vegetables," Cade said, arms crossed over his chest, his hip cocked. "That kitchen is a festival of carbs. By the way, I'm not your little prisoner anymore."

Sam helped Nox sit up carefully so as not to tip anything over—the tray was dressed up with the good china and silver, a cloth napkin draped over the side.

"You were never—" Nox started to say, but Cade held up his hand.

"Me, underwear; you, lock door. That shit is kidnapping." He gestured toward Sam, who was still fussing with the tray. "Fortunately you have a really awesome son and I'm considering not raining down the cops on your head."

Nox dropped his hand to the Sig tucked under the covers next to him. "You were the one trespassing on my property," Nox said slowly as Cade sauntered fully into the room.

"True. And you were the one who left me handcuffed facedown on the bed—also half-dressed—while you ran like a coward," Cade retorted.

Sam made a sound.

"Out," Nox barked at his son, who didn't need to hear that twice.

The door slammed.

Nox opened his mouth, but Cade held his hands up in surrender. "How about we call a truce?"

Nox fingered the Sig but nodded.

"I'm trying to figure out what's going on here, because right now I have about five different versions of you, and I'm not sure which one is real," Cade said, sitting down in the desk chair across from the bed. "Asshole in a hood doing some street justice. High-rolling Mr. Mullens with a domination kink...." He shrugged. "Douche-bag kidnapper. Coward in a crisis—but who saved a baby during a flood. How many of you are there?"

Laughter bubbled up in Nox's chest, but he tamped it down— Cade would probably add "psycho" to that list if he heard the sound that was trying to escape. "First things first—why did you come up here?"

Cade rolled his eyes. "Which time?"

"This truce isn't going to last very long if you're an asshole...."

"One of my regular customers asked me to deliver a letter to Sam. That's it. I said yes because I like big tippers who treat me nice." Cade regarded Nox for a second. "After that I got accosted—by you. Then I got felt up and cuffed to a bed—by you. When I came up to find out what the fuck was going on, I got mugged. Then you know the rest." He leaned back in the chair, looking ridiculously good in those old messy clothes.

Nox regarded him carefully. He'd become a very good judge of character over the years, a habit honed from being lied to over and over again until he could spot tells like it was a sixth sense. Young Cade was all sass and bravado for someone put into one ridiculous situation after another.

Ballsy.

Maybe he was telling the truth.

He hoped he was telling the truth.

"Who's the customer?"

"Jesus Christ," Cade muttered under his breath. "Mr. White."

No bells went off. Not in any sphere of his life, not over all these years. Which meant it could be an alias.

"What does he do for a living?"

"Gamble badly and not try to fuck me." Cade leaned back in the chair. "Your turn."

Nox considered his answer. "You already know my name...."

A scoff. "Patrick Mullens is a bullshit alias. You're not Spider-Man."

"Actually that's Peter Parker!" Sam yelled through the door.

Nox rubbed his forehead with the palm of his hand. Of course Sam hadn't gone far. "I'm Patrick—"

"You're not thirty-seven and you clearly don't live in Boston," Cade interrupted. "So I'm going to extrapolate you aren't Patrick Mullens either."

Nox didn't respond.

The door creaked open. Sam poked his head in, looking warily from one to the other. "Mullens *is* our last name," he said, casting a look at his father, part reprimand and part fear.

Cade side-eyed him.

"Nox," he said finally. "Nox Mullens. I use Patrick when I visit the District," he added, a simple lie—which earned another scoff from Cade.

"You can't use aliases. You have to use your government identification to get an account at the Iron Butterfly," he drawled. "So you're either Nox or Patrick. Or... neither."

CHAPTER SEVENTEEN

CADE WATCHED Nox's gaze flit around the room. The power dynamic shifted—he was enjoying that. Oh yeah. This guy tromped all over the place acting like he could do whatever he wanted, but he'd fucked with the wrong pretty face.

"Listen, I'm not going to turn you in. I'm going to forget all the shitty things you've done to me in the past twenty-four hours and appreciate things like that massive tip you left me and the fact that you saved my life. But." He held up his hand. "You need to let me know this isn't a scam and that money is going to show up in my account tomorrow."

"The money will be there, believe me." Something resembling a smile curved on Nox's mouth. "And my name is Nox."

"Mullens."

Not even a twitch. "Yes."

"And you have the credit to back your recent sexual transactions at the Iron Butterfly?"

"You have a one-track mind," Nox said as Sam made another uncomfortable noise in the background. "Yes. For the last time."

"So you're some kind of con man?"

Nox tipped his head to one side. Suddenly Patrick Mullens appeared on that bed, his smile absolutely devastating.

"Something like that," he said, all charm and sparkling eyes.

Well, shit.

Cade threw his hands in the air. "Fuck it, whatever. You're a con man, I still get paid, and it'll help when they fucking fire me." He looked over at Sam, who was trying to blend in with the wall as he edged inside. "Sorry."

Sam bit his bottom lip, pushed his glasses up from where they'd slid down his nose. "You're going to get fired?"

"I missed my shift, didn't call." Cade's amusement plummeted as reality set in. "Two cardinal rules broken and smashed to dust."

"Dad," the kid said in a pleading voice.

Nox toyed with the napkin for a moment, Patrick Mullens gone once again. "Get me the cell from the kitchen drawer."

CHAPTER EIGHTEEN

"RACHEL MOON, please," Nox said, all cheerful charm as he called the Iron Butterfly switchboard. His stomach was full of rocks, his heart thudding like a bomb about to go off.

"Speaking," the feminine voice on the other end of the line said.

"Ms. Moon, this is Patrick Mullens—I was there last evening during that unfortunate... alarm event." He let his tone drop into something disappointed.

"Yes, of course, Mr. Mullens. We are so sorry for the inconvenience. I apologize for any distress that terrible prank caused."

"It was quite upsetting." Nox went quiet for a moment to let her sweat. To listen for tells.

"I hope I can find a way to make it up to you," she offered quickly, and Nox made a sound of agreement.

"Well, I know there's a way you can help me," he said briskly. "I had Mr. Creel come to my hotel room for the afternoon—to make up for our interrupted time. He was quite apologetic about the whole thing—he's got a lovely begging voice." Nox laughed, low and dirty.

Cade glared at him from across the room.

"Oh. Well. Mr. Creel knows that all business should be conducted—"

Nox cut Rachel off. "He told me that, but quite frankly, Ms. Moon, I didn't trust your ability to keep me—safe—at the Iron Butterfly. I wanted my paid-for time, Cade did an admirable job in making it up to me, and I'm afraid I took a bit more than he had expected."

Rachel hummed in response.

"He's spending some time recuperating in my room. He'll be back in the morning." There was a finality to Nox's words—and it left Rachel in exactly the awkward position he wanted.

"Of course. Thank you for letting me know—I was getting worried when he didn't show up," Rachel answered smoothly. "Please let him know to check in with me when he arrives."

"Certainly. Good night."

Nox ended the call with a whoosh of air from his straining lungs. He glanced over at Cade, who looked mildly impressed.

"Not fired."

SAM DISAPPEARED after that, mumbling something about his own dinner—and most likely horrified by the implications of Nox's conversation. As for Nox, he settled into his now cold dinner.

"How about one more question?"

Nox shoved a forkful of meat in his mouth so he didn't have to answer.

"Why did you jet when the alarm went off? Dudes who rescue babies and kick street gang butt don't seem the type to run off at the first warning bell." Cade rolled his chair closer as Nox tried to ignore him.

"After everything that happened during the storms, you learn not to ignore warnings," Nox said simply. "Then I ran into someone I thought I knew in the hall, and…."

He caught himself before he said anything else.

"Who?"

Nox swallowed. "Your boss, Ms. Moon. I told her to go and unlock your cuffs."

"Oh." Cade settled back in the chair, looking at him curiously. "You thought Rachel was someone else?"

A beat.

"Yeah. Someone I knew when I was a kid."

"Well, Rachel's from the city. She was away at school during the Evacuation, though," Cade said easily, no detectable deception in his tone. "Her family's from—I think it was called Brighton?"

"Brighton Beach."

"Right, right."

Nox took a sip of his tea, eyes trained on his leg, which was throbbing in time with his growing headache.

"It's gone now," he said while Cade nodded, his expression sad.

"Yeah—she hates to talk about it." He laughed nervously. "She'd probably kill me for even telling you this."

A little jolt skittered across Nox's skin.

CHAPTER NINETEEN

CADE WATCHED Nox as he ate, feeling slightly creepy. There were more sides and personalities to this guy than he could figure out—at least the crazy asshole with the gun could be put in perspective after Sam's story.

"How old were you? If you don't mind me asking?" He rolled even closer to the side of the bed.

Nox gave him a side-eye. "When…."

"When you found him. Sam."

"He told you that?"

Cade squirmed a little under the intense glare. "Yeah. I think it's amazing, actually. Must've been fucking terrifying for you, finding a baby."

There was a long pause; Cade expected the anger to come, but instead, melancholy filled the room.

"It all worked out," Nox said carefully, his gaze locked on the empty plates in front of him.

"That's a pretty mild way to put it," Cade laughed. "I would have pissed myself."

"Adrenaline."

"You were alone—what? Seventeen, eighteen?"

A beat. "Sixteen."

Cade didn't hide his surprise. "Fuck. I'm even more impressed. My life at sixteen was hiding gay porn from my mother and trying to get out of feeding the goats."

Nox actually laughed. "That sounds better than my story," he said, almost wistful.

The moment stretched on, Nox staring blindly at the far wall, and Cade realized he wasn't getting much more than what he already had—and maybe he'd heard more than anyone else.

Nox seemed to come out of his little mental wander. He cast those brutally blue eyes in Cade's direction.

Their gazes locked for a moment. Then Nox looked away.

"You should probably head back to the guest room. It's pretty late."

"Uh, right, thanks." Cade pushed away from the bed, stood up, then put the chair back at the desk. "I'll talk to you tomorrow, I guess."

Nox didn't look up or say anything else. Cade let himself out of the room.

IN THE late morning Cade emerged from the guest room to find his clothes neatly cleaned and pressed on a chair and a cup of coffee on a small table nearby.

Weirdest not-kidnapping ever.

He was nervous about going back to the Iron Butterfly, fully aware that not being fired didn't mean Zed and Rachel would overlook his rule violation. He knew better.

Cade dressed slowly, feeling aches and pains all over his body. Well, at least when Rachel offered his ass to the more brutal customers, he would have a head start on hurting.

He exited the room, mug in hand, and walked a few feet. He heard a throat being cleared and looked up to discover a dressed Nox glowering from the top of the stairs.

"Oh, hi."

Nox gave him a nod. "Sam is going to walk you down to where a cab will meet you at the border."

Cade tried to rein in his surprise. "Great. Thank you."

Nox used the banister as support as he walked down. The baggy jeans and heavy wool sweater once again hid Patrick Mullens's suave flair.

"I realize we got off to a bad start. I just wanted to make sure that when you left here, you understood...." He glanced at the floor before lifting his eyes to Cade's. "I need to keep my business private, or else my son could suffer the consequences," he murmured.

"Right." Cade wasn't thrilled with helping a con man, but at the end of the day, who was he to judge what people did to make a living? He wasn't exactly living the purest lifestyle either. "Don't worry, okay? I'm not going to do anything to screw with your kid's life."

Nox looked relieved. "Thank you."

A creak on the floor turned Cade around.

Sam, dressed for the cold in a puffy jacket and woolen cap, stood there, smiling. "Ready?"

Cade checked his watch as he stood. "Yeah, I gotta go. You need anything else?"

"No. Thank you, though." Nox's face was guarded. "But I need to ask you...."

Cade held a hand up. "I can't for the life of me remember your address."

To beat the laugh, Cade got a smile that reached Nox's eyes.

SAM FELL into silence as they headed down the front steps, bundled against the cold. The sun was bright overhead, melting the snow into a manageable slush.

"So... you go to the school?" Cade asked, awkward as he considered the words. Did they have schools here? He hadn't seen anything on his treks up here that indicated schools or businesses beyond the one market. Hell, he hadn't seen many kids either.

"No. There aren't any in this neighborhood, and the only one up here in the Old City was too far to go every day," Sam answered. "So I did it online."

"Must suck to not hang out with your friends every day." High school was a fucking dream for Cade, playing football and writing for the paper. Out and proud, which meant he got about a 60/40 ratio of fawning to hate. The girls loved him, and there wasn't a better deterrent to asshole bullies than having a gaggle of cheerleader fag hags.

He'd learned to have a lack of shame very early on.

"Ha." Sam kicked through some slushy puddles. "I don't really—I mean, there's some guys at work who are nice, but that's about it."

Cade shook his head. "You're breaking my heart. How the hell do you find girls sitting at home, going to school on your computer?"

That cracked Sam up. "Well, I'm actually done with school now—I work full-time. And, uh, I don't really care about meeting girls." His voice cracked a little at the end.

Oh.

"That's cool. I didn't much care about girls either when I was your age." Cade skirted around a snow-covered root as they turned the corner. "Then we need to find you some nice boys."

Sam sputtered out an embarrassed laugh. "You know in these neighborhoods there aren't many teenagers, right? Like—there are some little kids a few blocks over, but people my age? No. They mostly got evacuated."

Or died. But neither of them said it.

Cade could see his cab idling in the distance. "You're saying this stuff and I feel like it's a challenge," he teased gently. Sam was a nice kid, cute as hell—Cade wanted to tuck him into a bag and ship him to the farm for home cooking and a few normal years of chasing boys and breaking hearts.

"I'd settle for you helping me find some information about my parents, to be honest. The rest of it…." Sam shrugged. "That doesn't really matter in the end."

"I disagree, and when we have more time, I'll give you a fabulous presentation on the joys of hot guys and having fun."

When they reached the edge of the pathway, Cade suddenly regretted his carefree song and dance. He'd be taking the cab back to his luxurious life—a safe life that had followed a comfortable and trauma-free upbringing. Rachel's words haunted him. How many people on the outside would kill for what he had?

This kid just wanted to know his name.

"Listen, you got a cell phone?"

Sam nodded, digging into his pocket. He produced an archaic model that further shamed Cade as he pulled out the latest bit of technology. One of his regulars owned the parent company in Japan and was generous with gifts.

They exchanged numbers, as the driver honked twice to let Cade know the meter was running.

"I gotta go—you okay to get home?"

"Yeah." Sam tucked his phone away, looking up at Cade with a bright smile. "Thanks for everything. I appreciate it."

"Sam, it has been my honest pleasure." He extended his hand for Sam, who shook it with enthusiasm. "You call me if you need anything."

"I will."

They parted ways, Cade watching the teenager retrace their footsteps back up the street.

Inside the cab, the driver gave him a strange look.

"A friend of mine," Cade said coolly. "Let's get going."

CHAPTER TWENTY

"I COULD go out for you," Sam said from the doorway.

Nox didn't bother to answer. He was using all his strength to stand up and pull his clothes on.

"You know you can't walk with your leg like that."

"Go to bed." Nox shook with the exertion as he pulled the black sweatshirt over his head, tightened the buckles along the shoulder, then attached the hood to the collar.

"Let me go with you."

"Sam."

"What are you going to do if you run into some dealers? Ask them to lie down so you can punch them? You can't walk, Dad."

"I'm fine."

"No, you're stubborn." Sam sighed dramatically. "I'm getting dressed. I'm getting the second Sig."

When had Nox lost control of this situation?

"Fine—you can come, but no gun."

SAM WAS six when he discovered what Nox did after hours. At that point Nox was still just walking the perimeter, keeping watch on their house lest someone sneak into the neighborhood. The paranoia was worse back then; Nox slept in tiny increments—a half hour here and there between taking care of Sam and going out on patrol.

Every time he closed his eyes, he saw Jenny and her gun. Every night he dreamed of her words.

Interlude

THE NATIONAL *Guardsman takes them to a makeshift hospital. They tend to the baby and give Nox a heavy blanket, two sandwiches, and water. There is chaos everywhere, injured people screaming and wailing, others frantically searching for lost loved ones among the beds. Nox stays in the corner on a cot, watching the nurse who has his baby brother on an examination table.*

"What's your name?" a man with a clipboard asks.

Nox starts to say his name—opens his mouth and makes a sound—but something in his gut tells him to lie. "Roy Grimes."

"How old are you?"

"Nineteen."

The guy gives him a look but marks down the number anyway. "And who's that baby belong to?"

A beat. "Me."

This time the guy doesn't write anything down and his look says "try another one, son."

"My girlfriend had him the other day at her house—we couldn't get to the hospital, and then we, uh, we got separated when we left our building on 118th Street." Nox gulps, tears coming to his eyes. He needs this man to believe him, needs it so desperately.

For the longest time, the guy says nothing. Then he scribbles down the information and walks away.

Nox pulls the blanket over his face and cries.

Later, they bring the baby back to him, warmly dressed in better-sized clothes and sound asleep, his little mouth pursed in a bow. "A little small" is all they say, assuring him he's fine. They tell him how to take care of the gross stump of his umbilical cord and give Nox a bag of formula and diapers and an extra blanket.

Nox falls asleep with the infant snug next to him. An hour later he is woken up by a flashlight in his face.

"They found your girlfriend!" A nurse smiles down at him, and Nox's heart stops.

THEY MOVED slowly, walking the blocks closest to the house. Sam, tucked into an extra hood and leathers, strode ahead while Nox stuck to the shadows, his leg screaming after forty minutes. The bad weather had chased the dealers and junkies back to their hovels, and no one was out.

After an hour Nox leaned against the side of an abandoned tenement and whistled.

Sam turned and jogged back.

"Let's call it a night," Nox said, but Sam shook his head.

"You go back. I'm going to walk over another few blocks."

"Sam...."

"Don't yell, because I'm going to run in the other direction now," Sam said with a smirk. "Go home!"

And his teenager took off in a sprint in the other direction while Nox cursed a blue streak under his breath.

Interlude

JENNY IS standing near the entrance of the makeshift hospital. She manufactures tears, cooing as she takes his brother in her arms.

"Oh, sweetheart," she whimpers, pressing herself into Nox's side. "Mommy's here." She curls her body against Nox, nuzzling her face into his neck. "Oh baby, I was so scared!"

He fights nausea at her convincing performance.

"You need to come with me quietly," she whispers in his ear as the adults watch the reunion with tender smiles. "Or something terrible is going to happen to these nice people."

He gathers up the baby things, his backpack, and the blankets, and follows Jenny out the door to a large covered jeep parked outside.

"You need not to run anymore," Jenny tells him as she drives down the wet empty roads to his neighborhood. "I can't help you if you run."

"You're just going to kill us," Nox says, cradling the baby in his arms. He knows he'll run again. He knows he'll kill her if he gets the chance.

"Maybe I won't," Jenny answers. "Maybe I won't."

CHAPTER TWENTY-ONE

SAM FELT like he'd been let out of a cage.

He would never be glad his dad got hurt—never. His love for his father was absolute. But oh God, it felt so good to be out on his own.

Work didn't count. The only reason Dad let him take the job was because he went everywhere with another messenger—someone his dad used to work with on a construction site—and never out on his own. He was just someone to open doors and carry heavy parcels, climb stairs when Steve didn't feel like it.

It seemed like he spent his life two ways: watched like a hawk or alone in his room.

He didn't understand it all. His dad was very specific about following rules and how the world beyond their front door was dangerous and how they kept to themselves because people couldn't be trusted in this city. And it all seemed logical because he'd never had anyone else but his father, never heard another opinion. Never saw anything from the few people he'd met except that same deep suspicion.

And he owed Nox his life, literally. Sam could have died in that car, but his father *saved* him. Was so absolutely brave that he saved a little orphaned baby and raised him all on his own. That was amazing— Sam didn't think he could be that selfless or responsible. With his own parents killed in the flooding, his father made their life here in the city on his own. Sam was in awe of his father.

Sam tried to be always grateful, always follow his father's orders to show his appreciation—he did. But sometimes he just wanted to be free.

And right now, walking along the dark streets of the Old City, when he should be feeling fear, Sam was euphoric.

He stuck to the shadows, following his father's route. He'd only been allowed to come along a few times, but he remembered every turn like it was habit.

A few blocks from the very edge of the Old City, where miles and miles of burned-out neighborhoods were interspersed with new construction sites, he spotted a white truck idling behind a building.

Sam stopped, ducking into the doorway of an abandoned high-rise.

Well, that was weird.

He considered turning around, but the thrill of being out on his own held him back. His father would make him go home. His father would lecture him about never calling attention to himself.

Sam crept out of the doorway.

He would only go see what they were watching—then he'd go home. They'd never know he was there.

He went the long way around, around the block to front of the building. There were no lights, no signs of activity, at least from the outside. So Sam took a deep breath, reminded himself that this was what he wanted—to make his own decisions, to be an adult—and walked around until he found an open door to the building.

THIS USED to be a hospital.

It had been stripped bare of everything, by looters, elements, and time. Sam's footsteps echoed as he walked down the hallway, the beam of his small flashlight helping him navigate. The musty smell of disuse and abandonment, the sound of his boots—nothing else seemed to be happening.

So why was anyone up here?

Sam did a circuit of the first floor. He reached the front entrance, sticking close to the wall so he could look outside through one cracked windowpane. The truck remained, but now a nondescript car idled behind it. Sam watched as a man jumped down from the cab, then walked to the driver's side of the car. After a moment of conversation, the man handed something to the driver, then quickly turned away.

The man got back in the truck and within minutes was gone in a cloud of exhaust as the truck took off downtown. A second later, the car came to life and followed in its wake.

Curious.

Sam waited a few minutes to make sure no one returned, then eased out the front door. His heart beat wildly in his chest. He had no idea what he'd seen, but it made him feel important.

Hands jammed in his pockets, Sam hurried home. He could barely contain his excitement—something he'd have to push down before he walked through the front door. His father could smell a secret, and Sam's poker face was crap.

A block away from home, Sam stopped. He tipped his head back to look up at the sky, making out a few stars through the cloud cover. Sometimes he imagined another life—getting off the island, going to college, living his life in a city where everything wasn't a struggle. He'd live in an apartment he furnished himself, he'd work a job he found on his own. He'd go to places where people drank coffee and talked over tiny tables.

He'd meet a boy who thought he was handsome and charming and they would…

Do things.

Sam bit his lip, trying to push away the suddenly intrusive thought of what his father and Cade might have been up to at the Iron Butterfly. To think of himself dating—well, that was amazing. To imagine his father?

No, thanks.

Dad had never dated, never brought anyone home. Sam didn't even know he was gay until a few years ago, when Sam was struggling with his own sexuality. He just thought—well, he just thought his father was too busy and too paranoid to date. Not to mention the lack of women in the general vicinity. Dad didn't have any friends—they only had each other.

Which was wonderful.

And not so wonderful.

Sam took a deep breath, let the cold air rattle around in his lungs. He didn't want this night to end. He wanted to feel this free, this alive, for just a little bit longer.

CHAPTER TWENTY-TWO

TWO HOURS later Sam came home. He was bright-eyed and panting from the cold, but the smile on his face told Nox he didn't even notice the weather.

His first solo patrol.

"Anyone give you a problem?" Nox said from his perch on the bottom step of their stairs.

"Nope." Sam stripped out of his leathers, clearly elated by his little adventure. "There was some stuff going on by the old hospital on 101st Street, though."

"What?" Dealers liked to hang out there in bad weather, and there were junkie squatters in the basement.

"A truck idling by the back loading dock for about twenty minutes. A car came up, and then everyone left." Sam put his boots on the mat near the door. "That was it."

Nox tucked it away for future reference. "Well, then—good job."

Sam glanced up at him in surprise. "Thanks. I was sure I was going to come home and get the full lecture."

"I'm tired—you can have the half lecture," Nox said, wobbling a little as he stood. "We have rules, Sam...."

"Right. I know. We have rules to keep us safe, because this city isn't," Sam sighed. "But, Dad—how long before you realize I'm an adult now? I can handle myself."

"You're right," Nox murmured. "You can handle yourself. I promise to remember that."

Sam brightened, his smile so warm it hurt. "No, you won't. But I'll keep reminding you."

Nox felt resignation and panic deep in his bones.

NOX SENT a text message to Addie before he crawled into bed. His leg hurt, his head thumped a steady rhythm, and there was no way he was going to work in a few hours. He didn't like to admit he was human and his body needed rest, but tonight—this morning, this moment—he was.

Not to mention the small part of him that didn't want to leave Sam alone at the house.

Just in case.

He pulled the covers over his head, moving gingerly until he found a comfortable spot for his various aches and pains. Of course there was no position that stopped his brain from racing.

Interlude

THEY ABANDON the jeep a few blocks away. The National Guard is herding people down the streets toward the Seventy-Ninth Street Boat Basin, and it's chaos. Nox thinks he can duck into the crowds of people and get away from Jenny, but she takes one look at him and makes a grab for the baby.

Now he knows he's not going anywhere.

They walk to his house. Ninety-First Street is less busy than the other streets, as most of the people have already left. Some National Guard jeeps rumble past.

He watches them go with a heavy heart.

Jenny stands behind him, cuddling the baby against her chest. She doesn't look like a murderer like this, doesn't seem like a person who would shoot a teenager in the head.

"Are we going to the ferry?" he whispers, fumbling with the key in the lock.

"Not yet," Jenny says.

Inside, Jenny gives the baby back to Nox, telling him to change and feed him.

She has a gun, so he does what she says.

In the kitchen, he takes care of his little brother, musing that he needs a name. Nothing comes to mind until he remembers his mother's favorite painter was Samuel Palmer, a British guy who did these pictures that looked like weird cartoons. Nox never saw the point, but his mother always lit up when she got to talk about his work.

"How about Samuel? You like that?" Nox asks the baby, who just lies there, his skinny arms and legs twitching. "Okay. I'm going to call you Sam."

The baby doesn't care. Nox changes his diaper, keenly aware of Jenny prowling around the house. She's in his father's study now, going through his desk.

Sam is clean and dry. Nox uses one of the formula bottles the people at the medical tent gave him—mostly he's avoiding moving from the kitchen. He sits at the counter, Sam in the curve of his arm, sucking down the thick liquid.

Jenny appears in the doorway.

There are papers in her hand and a smile on her face.

Nox's skin crawls.

"So let's you and me talk about what's going to happen," Jenny says as she sits down at one of the stools.

"Are you going to kill us?" he asks, blunt because he has nothing to lose at this point.

Jenny cocks her head to one side. She'd be pretty if her eyes weren't so hard and angry. "No. I'm not. I'm sorry for scaring you on the road back there, but...." She looks uncomfortable for the first time since he's met her. "Things got a little out of hand. But now? Now I'm in a better place to make some decisions for myself."

"I don't understand—" he starts to say, but Jenny cuts him off.

"Your father was murdered."

Nox takes a deep breath, looks down at Sam, who's fallen asleep with the bottle in his mouth. "I know."

"No, you don't. You think it was a mugging or a robbery, but it wasn't. He pissed off some people who then decided to kill him." Her

voice is relentless, all momentary softness disappearing from her face. "And they decided to get rid of you as well."

"What?" *Nox shakes his head. Crazy, stupid, sounds like a spy movie.* "That doesn't make any sense."

The sheaf of papers in Jenny's hand—she puts them on her lap, then knits her fingers together and rests her chin against them. "I worked for the same people your father did. He made some unfortunate mistakes with their money, and they punished him." *She doesn't look sorry Nox's father is dead.*

Nox looks at his sleeping brother.

"Did they tell you to get rid of me?"

"No, honey, I was at the hospital to take care of your mom. You weren't supposed to be there."

He swallows hard.

"Get her out of there, that's what I meant," *Jenny says, but something in her tone makes Nox shiver.* "And now you and me and that sweet little baby are going to get the hell off this island."

CHAPTER TWENTY-THREE

"I EXPECTED better from you" was all Rachel said to him as Cade stood in front of her ridiculous desk.

"Rachel—"

She held up one hand to silence him. "The only reason your ass isn't on the street is the ridiculously obscene tip Mr. Mullens deposited in your account—which is now, by the way, in my account," she said sharply. "Mr. White is waiting for you in Yellow Seven."

Cade shook his head. "It's not his regular day—"

"Seriously, Cade? Shut up and get over to the room now. If he tells you to crawl over and suck his dick, you better do it. If he tells you to lick his shoes? Guess what you're going to be doing? Go. Now."

The anger in her voice couldn't be charmed away, he knew that well enough. He'd seen more than one model thrown out—literally— weeping on the sidewalk while Rachel verbally eviscerated them.

She was practically being nice to him.

Without another word, Cade fled the office and immediately made his way down to one of the small rooms. Yellow Seven was nothing more than two chairs and basket of condoms—it was literally a fuck-and-suck space for the clients who were cheap and fast.

Cade checked his face and hair in the hall mirror before tentatively knocking. He looked like shit. His only hope was Mr. White thinking the client before him had a rough streak.

"Come in, dear boy," Mr. White called.

Inside, Mr. White was seated in one of the leather wingbacks. He smiled brightly when he saw Cade, patting the seat next to him.

Cade put on his best dimpled grin and perched on the edge of the chair. "This is a lovely surprise," he said softly as Mr. White touched his cheek.

"I couldn't wait until our regular meeting. Did you deliver my letter?" Mr. White asked, leaning forward in anticipation. His rheumy eyes were out of focus. He didn't seem to notice the rumpled state of Cade's clothes or his marked-up face.

"Yes, I did. Everything went fine," he said, smooth and charming as ever. Cade's mind went to Sam's sweet smile and his wistful words about finding his parents. Then he thought about the kid's father and, well, it was hard to drag his attention back to Mr. White.

"Marvelous," the man was saying, his hands wandering over Cade's knees and thighs. "Absolutely marvelous—can you take something else to him?"

"Of course," Cade purred, demure as he moved subtly away from Mr. White's wandering hands. "Anything you need me to do. I'm sure he's waiting to hear from you again."

Mr. White practically giggled with delight as he reached into his pocket.

It was another envelope, drawn out of the man's expensive Italian suit. Cade tucked it into his back pocket before being drawn into Mr. White's lap.

He steeled himself for more, but Mr. White just wanted to pet him like a beloved dog. "You don't understand how wonderful this is, my dear. How I've been waiting so long for this."

Curiosity lapped at Cade; he wanted to ask questions, to read the letter. Anything to help that kid. But he played it cool, the pretty messenger for Mr. White.

And maybe, just maybe, a hero for Sam.

CADE GOT home almost forty-eight hours after leaving. Serendipity Towers was the most ridiculous name, but the twenty-five-story high-rise was only a few blocks from the casino, which made his commute to work easy. Alec lived on the first floor, Cade on the tenth.

He dialed his friend's number as he flashed his ID at the front gate. It went right to voice mail.

"I'm home. Come up when you're done," he said before getting into the elevator.

The view was the best part. Cade could lie in bed and stare out at the East Side of the District, where fewer high-rises meant he could actually see the night sky. The bright lights of the casinos obliterated the stars, but it was enough, that little square of darkness.

Two rooms were all he needed—an enormous front room with a kitchenette, a leather couch, and a chest that doubled as a table; and his bedroom with the adjoining bath. No television, no music, no electronics. His phone was his alarm clock. Here, he wanted silence and peace.

Cade took a hot shower, trying to ease his aches and bruised back. He stayed long enough for the water to go cold, and let his mind wander.

It kept wandering back to the enigmatic Nox Mullens.

He'd known a lot of men in his twenty-five years—literally and figuratively. He'd fucked them for work and pleasure, punched them in bar fights, and fled South Carolina to get away from one's quiet disapproval of his life.

Nox was a beast unto himself.

Chilled from his shower, Cade stepped out and grabbed a towel from the rack. There was something intriguing about someone who couldn't be figured out in five minutes. And seduced in ten.

Naked, Cade slipped under the covers of his bed, pulling the blankets over his head until only his eyes peeked out. He angled himself so he could see his little patch of sky, a sliver of gray blue over the gleaming tower of 21.

Maybe it would take an hour to figure out Mr. Mullens.

And half as long to seduce him.

CHAPTER TWENTY-FOUR

NOX WALKED down to the hospital two nights later, his leg healed enough for him to manage. Sam made noises about going with him, but Nox found an alternative to that—he sent Sam to the boat basin for some "recon."

To visit the weeds, but Sam didn't need to know that.

101st Street was not a residential zone. The city couldn't decide what to do with it, so it festered as an eyesore and drug den that wouldn't be dealt with until some casino needed a better view.

He skirted through the shadows until he reached the block over, then climbed the fire escape of an old apartment building. The roof provided an excellent view of old Mount Sinai's loading dock.

And the white panel truck currently idling in front of it.

Nox settled in. There were binoculars in his pack, and a thermos of coffee. The Sig sat in his waistband, a knife in his boot. For now, he'd watch.

DEAD BOLT.

He'd recognize those small white boxes anywhere. Two years before, Nox had interrupted a larger sale near the old Central Park Zoo. Dozens of slender white boxes filled with pool-blue powder.

This was at least a hundred times that big a potential bust.

Nox chewed his lower lip as he dropped the binoculars. Eight men total, no one he recognized from the neighborhood. They each brought out at least twenty boxes in the hour he watched. The idea that the old hospital held that much poison turned his stomach sour. So close to the neighborhoods. There was a tiny school just opened up, only four blocks to the south.

He wanted them out.

One of the men got into the driver's seat and put the truck into reverse.

Nox gathered his things. Time to follow.

THE WHITE panel truck wound its way through the Old City—bless the shitty streets so Nox could keep up, even with his bad leg. It pulled into a small abandoned parking garage on the East Side, near the border of the District.

Nox hid behind a pile of concrete.

The man jumped out and went inside, leaving the truck unattended.

Perfect.

Nox waited, creeping closer as he watched the door the man disappeared into. After ten minutes, he ran to the truck and stepped into the cab.

Keys—how thoughtful.

He started it up, slammed it into reverse, and drove away with a squeal of tires.

The Dead Bolt floated on the surface of the Hudson for a few moments before sinking under the rays of the sunrise. Behind him, the panel truck burned.

All in all, it was a good night.

Until he got home and realized Sam wasn't there.

CHAPTER TWENTY-FIVE

THERE WAS nothing at the old boat basin, nothing but weeds and silence and clumps of dirty snow that hadn't melted yet, obscured by the copse of trees. Sam trudged around in circles, not even running across a deal to break up.

Boring.

He knew his father had sent him here for the express purpose of doing nothing—yet another attempt to keep him sheltered like a child.

A motor caught his attention. Sam tucked himself into the trees and watched as a white panel van just like the one he'd seen the other night wound its way through the rough streets, heading up toward the construction zone above the Old City.

Sam had a second to make his decision: Call his dad? Let him know? Or just follow the van to see where it was going?

He was jogging up the road, the red taillights his guide, before he finished his last thought.

SAM HEADED for the zone above the Old City, where casinos and high-rises were slowly being built. He wondered what would happen to their neighborhood when the city planners decided the real estate could be sold. Would they lose their house? Where would they go?

The truck was parked in front of a high-rise, the future home of gamblers who didn't want to leave the bright lights of the island for their more mundane lives on the mainland. Sam crept closer, trying to see how many men were in the vehicle.

He didn't realize there was someone else standing there, cloaked in the shadows, until he was right up on him. Sam stumbled back as the figure turned around. He didn't have enough time to run; Sam could do nothing but fall to the ground as the tall man leaned down and grabbed him by the collar.

"Oh, you're in some trouble now," he said, pulling Sam up off the pavement.

BATHED IN the headlights of the white truck, Sam sat on a concrete barrier, handcuffed and shaking with fear. The man had a shield and a gun, and he kept asking Sam about the explosives he might have been carrying. No amount of pleading and apologizing and confusion over "bombs" made any difference. He'd left Sam there to go make a phone call several minutes ago—Sam contemplated running off, but that big gun at the cop's waist kept him riveted to the spot.

"Yeah," the cop said into his phone. He paced back to stare at Sam. "No, I don't think so." He paused, smirked. "Good idea."

Another car drove up—a police cruiser—and the cop looked annoyed. "Gotta go."

Sam dug his heels into the ground; his arms were starting to hurt, pulled behind his back like this, and just thinking about what his father was going to do made him want to throw up. His father always told him not to trust cops, and this—this reminded him his father was usually right.

A uniformed officer got out of the car. He swung a flashlight in Sam's direction, then moved closer. "Detective Francis?"

"Yeah." The cop walked toward the flare of light. "What's your name?"

"Uh, Mason Todd. I'm a patrolman—dispatch said you wanted me to pick someone up?" The newly arrived policeman sounded young and uncertain. Sam suddenly had hope he might have a sympathetic person to reason with.

Patrolman Todd stepped into the light, meeting Detective Francis halfway. He was tall and slim, and when he looked over at Sam, he looked concerned.

Oh thank God.

"He was trespassing on the site," Officer Francis said. "I think he's our bomber."

"Did he have anything on him?" the patrolman asked.

Detective Francis walked past him to the truck's door without answering. "Take him back to the precinct and have him held on suspicion for the bombings," he said, opening the truck's door.

"Is there some evidence—" Todd tried again.

"I'll be down there to sign everything in two hours. Three at the most." Francis climbed into the truck.

"Sir? Excuse me, sir?" The young cop ran over to where Francis was now sitting. "Is this truck evidence or—"

"Patrolman, take the suspect to the precinct and do what I fucking told you," Francis said. Sam winced at his cold tone.

"With all due respect, sir, I don't feel comfortable with this."

The truck's engine turned over, and Francis backed the truck up. Sam's heart beat ridiculously. Could he persuade the young cop to let him go?

Todd had to step back as Francis swung the truck in his direction, narrowly missing him. When the truck was out of view, he walked back over to Sam.

"What's your name, son?" he asked, and Sam tried not to huff. Up close, he could see Mason Todd had a baby face—they couldn't be more than a few years apart in age.

"Sam Mullens."

"What are you doing here?"

"I was just walking around. I know it's past curfew, but I was bored," Sam said, using his canned response. It was what his father told him to say if he ever got picked up on patrol.

"How old are you?"

"Seventeen.

"Do your parents know where you are?"

"No, my dad's asleep," Sam said automatically. "He's going to be so mad at me...." The pleading note in his voice was not acting. "I don't know what that guy is talking about with bombs or whatever. I mean, I haven't even heard anything about that."

Mason Todd frowned at Sam. For a moment Sam thought he might be let go, that this guy could see he was innocent, but that crashed down when the young cop sighed and reached for Sam's arm. "Let's get you down to the police station."

CHAPTER TWENTY-SIX

CADE SAT in the employee lounge, listening to Alec's voice mail yet again. He frowned, ending the call instead of leaving a message. Five, ignored. And Alec "busy with clients," according to Rachel. Feeling a little put out, he put his socked feet up on the tufted ottoman as he waited for his shift to begin.

Killian's choice tonight was a tight white tux shirt tucked into a ridiculous pair of leather pants. The boots that went along with the outfit weighed about twenty pounds, so he was saving those for last. Black eyeliner and spiked hair—Cade was made up to look even more fuckable than usual.

His phone vibrated in his lap, and assuming it was Alec, he answered without looking at the screen.

"I need your help," said the man.

Cade literally felt his desperation through the line. "Who—"

"Nox. It's—they arrested Sam last night. He's at the main District precinct."

"Oh shit." Cade got up off the couch and headed for a private corner. A few models were scattered about, and nosiness was a hobby everyone shared.

"What do you need me to do?" Cade asked, lowering his voice as he tucked himself on the far side of the room.

"My ID isn't going to work at the police station," he answered finally.

Oh shit, again.

"My shift doesn't start for a while—let me... fuck, okay. I'm going to head down there and see what I can do."

"Thank you," Nox said and disconnected the call.

RACHEL WAS not pleased when Cade told her he had a private appointment with Mr. Mullens—despite the man's overtipping habits.

"I'll be back by my shift," he insisted, having changed into a more sensible suit—something Rachel eyed as he twitched, trying to get out of there. "You can keep the tip again, okay?"

One perfectly manicured eyebrow raised. "Your tip and your fee. If you're late, you're fired."

Cade ran out of her office.

The District police station was an incredibly uncomfortable place.

It sat in the old Port Authority building, massive, hulking, and ugly in the middle of all that pretty bling. Huge concrete barriers prevented attacks or any vehicles getting close. Cade flashed his District ID at least ten times before he reached the front desk inside.

"Sam Mullens," he said yet again, spelling it out for the annoyed woman behind the desk. A man and a woman in flak jackets, carrying semiautomatics, walked behind her.

"See Detective Francis on six." She slapped a visitor badge on the desk.

He didn't dare ask any questions.

More people in flak jackets, more guns and hard stares. Cade put on his best pretty smile, tucked his hands in his pockets, and pulled his shoulders back like he was going to church.

The elevator left him at six, where scads of plainclothes police officers swarmed around.

"Detective Francis?" Cade asked at least five people before being directed to a tall man with curly hair and a smirk. He was leaning against a desk in a cheap suit.

Cade disliked him on sight.

Which meant he turned the star wattage up to an eleven.

"I'm Cade Creel." He extended his hand and gave the "you might know me" pause.

Detective Francis shook his hand, the smirk getting uglier. "Right, right. You're a model." He said the word like it was "terrorist" or something. "I've seen your face on the side of a building."

Well, that wasn't going to work.

"Then I don't have to explain who my rich and powerful friends are," Cade said archly, looking around the room with interest. "I'm looking for a young man who was brought in today."

The detective folded his arms across his chest. "Name?"

"Sam Mullens," he said casually. "I think there might have been a mix-up."

"Oh no, no mix-up." The policeman laughed, nasty and nasal. "Someone's been setting off bombs at jobsites uptown. We caught him sneaking around after curfew." He paused, then pursed his lips. "How do you know him?"

"He's our messenger, actually." Cade was proud of the way he kept steady as he pulled his cell phone out of his pocket. "Let me give my boss a call, get the bail process going."

"No bail."

Cade let his eyes get big. "No bail? For a kid out after curfew? That seems a little harsh."

"I told you, the bombs—"

"Did you catch him setting them off?"

The policeman chuckled. "No."

"Was he carrying anything?"

"Just a house key."

"Well, then," Cade said, matching the officer's rude smirk. "I believe there's a fine for being out after curfew, which I'm prepared to pay."

"I said there was no bail." The policeman's tone took a sharp turn.

Cade pressed a few buttons on his phone, then put it up to his ear. "I'm sorry, you're not a judge and I know a few so, let me just…."

Alec's voice mail picked up again.

"Judge Perez? It's Cade," he said, layering some serious flirtiness to his voice. "Yes, well, this isn't exactly a pleasure call. I need some assistance from you."

Alec did an amazing Judge Perez, an impersonation that had gotten them out of some scrapes in their early days in the city, when they didn't quite realize the lack of humor and love of bribes when it came to the police force. A frequent customer, Perez had a tendency to be overserved most of the time, and he rarely remembered his day—it was embarrassingly easy to convince him he'd made calls bailing out friends of Alec's or smoothing over issued fines.

His voice carried past Francis to several officers standing nearby. They looked up from their tablets, first at Cade, then at Francis.

Francis threw his head back and laughed. "Fuck you, son." He stood up, flicking his middle finger before walking away.

"Sam Mullens. I need to have him released." Cade kept talking to Alec's voice mail as one of the policeman turned to murmur something to the woman next to him. "Do you need the arresting officer's badge number?" He gestured toward the people watching him. "Do you know it?" he asked them.

The woman smiled slowly, then wrote down the numbers on a piece of paper.

Cade kept up his pretense of a phone call, perched on the edge of Francis's desk. He talked loudly and drew attention from more people—a few even asked for his autograph.

It was fucking performance art.

After twenty minutes—and two more pretend phone calls to Alec's voice mail—Officer Francis appeared with a disheveled Sam in tow.

Try as he might, Cade could not contain his smug grin. He was happy to forgive Alec for not getting back to him in the past few days—clearly he'd gotten the messages and done his Judge Perez for the folks here at the police station.

"Thank you so much for your help," Cade murmured, pulling Sam to his side. "About that fine…."

All Officer Francis's shit-eating grins were gone, as was the attitude. He gave them both a nasty look. "Get the fuck out of here."

"Thank you so much." Cade wrapped his arm around Sam. They were going to get the fuck out of there as quickly as possible.

"Oh my God, my dad must be freaking," Sam murmured as they power walked past the front desk attendant and the concrete barriers. Across the street, standing on the street corner in an impressive suit and cashmere overcoat, was Nox.

Quietly freaking out, no doubt.

"Good guess." Cade laughed nervously as they crossed the lines of cabs and limos. Nox was rubbing his hands through his hair like he was about to pull it right out.

"How the hell did you manage this?" Nox said as they reached his side. Sam pressed against his father, ducking his head like he expected a scolding. He got a hug instead.

Cade rocked back on his heels. "Me and Alec—one of the other models—we have this system. I call him, he pretends to be Judge Perez. Or he calls me and I pretend to be the health department." He waved his hand. "Sometimes you need an exit strategy."

Nox smiled—and this time it wasn't the charming grin of Mr. Patrick Mullens. This one was real. "Thank you. I didn't know who else to call."

"Wow, how flattering." Cade winked at both of them. "Go home, okay? I have to get back to the Butterfly before even a phone call from the debonair Mr. Mullens won't help me keep my job."

The tourists pushed past, oblivious to the conversation—Cade gave them a salute, then turned to walk away.

"Thank you!" Nox called after him.

Cade raised his hand and headed off.

CHAPTER TWENTY-SEVEN

"WHAT HAPPENED?" Nox directed Sam down the street; he had stolen a car from the parking lot at 21 and left it around the corner. "You weren't supposed to be up there." He tried to keep his tone even, even as he wanted to scream out worry, to try to get his son to understand what could have gone wrong.

"I went down by the docks and there was another one of those white panel vans. I followed it up to the work site," Sam murmured, head down. "The cop who arrested me, he was just hanging out there. Like he was waiting."

"What's his name?"

"Francis. He called another cop to actually arrest me." Sam's voice hitched. "That second guy—he tried to tell Francis he didn't have cause, but it didn't work. The other guy kept apologizing for having to follow his orders."

An asshole cop on the take—what a shock.

"Who was the other cop?"

"Um—Mason. Mason Todd." Something in Sam's voice made Nox look at him a bit more closely.

"Was there something else?"

"Nope." Sam sped up. "That's it. I'm sorry, okay? I really am. I know I keep screwing up."

Nox directed Sam around the corner; the small sedan sat in front of a coffee shop.

"These aren't mistakes, Sam. This is you disobeying me, and it stops now." Nox unlocked the passenger-side door. "I called the messenger service, and you've been relieved of your duties."

"Dad!"

"Get in the car, now."

They drove out of the District and abandoned the car near the Circle. Not another word was spoken.

CHAPTER TWENTY-EIGHT

AT SERENDIPITY Towers, Cade knocked on Alec's door, frantic. One of the bartenders had admitted to him that no one had seen Alec for seven days. His assumption that Alec had been listening to his Judge Perez messages was clearly wrong. Rachel's "client" bullshit was a lie—a fact he couldn't confront her with, since she'd taken to staying in her office even during shift.

Damian took over her duties on the floor.

Cade was fucking terrified.

Every day the atmosphere at the Iron Butterfly got a little more strained. Damian insisted it was due to the upcoming Anniversary Weekend, but even he didn't seem to believe that line of crap. Zed was always "in meetings," and the high rollers' table stayed packed with unfamiliar players.

Mr. White sent Cade a huge spray of lilies with an apology—he would miss their weekly meeting but promised to make it up to him—and a reminder to give Sam the letter.

Shit. He'd completely forgotten the second letter with all the drama of getting Sam out of the police station.

After twenty minutes, Cade gave up. He tried to use his pass on the door, but it didn't work. He tried the phone and got a "voice mail full" message.

Cade went upstairs and got into some warm clothes. He was headed up to deliver Sam's letter.

THE DAYLIGHT made the trek a little easier. Cade didn't worry as much about baby gangbangers and drug dealers. Of course he also didn't linger, walking as fast as he could up to Ninety-First. The denizens of the neighborhood gave him the same treatment, though—out-and-out staring as he hurried to Nox and Sam's home.

Nox answered the door in full scowl.

Then blinked when he saw Cade.

"Hey."

"Hi." Cade tried false brightness, but it collapsed under the weight of his burdens. "I have another note for Sam, and, uh—I need your help."

"I think I owe you at least one favor," Nox said, opening the door a little bit wider.

They settled in the kitchen, Cade leaning against the counter as Nox poured them coffee. He spilled the story about Alec, worry permeating each word.

"Do you feel like Rachel might have something to do with it?" Nox asked, handing him the mug.

Cade frowned. "Rachel? Um—she's a hard-ass at work, but I don't think she's capable of hurting someone."

Nox's expression flashed something dark. "How well do you know her?"

"Why are we talking about Rachel? Alec's the one missing." Cade tamped down his annoyance as he sipped his coffee. And tried not to react to the bitter taste.

"And she's the one lying."

The fierceness took Cade aback—he ducked around Nox and walked to look out the back window.

"Who did you think she was? When you saw her?" Cade asked.

Nox didn't answer.

"I'll get Sam so you can give him the letter."

SAM OPENED the envelope with Nox standing over his shoulder. Sam didn't crack a smile or get excited like he had before—he barely gave Cade a second look as he stood there in his sweatshirt and jeans, hair a mess and glasses smudged.

He blinked down at the note and gasped.

"My mom's name is Jennifer and, uh, my father's name is Roy Grimes," he whispered. Nox made a sound next to him—anger, maybe—and Sam's face fell. "I mean…."

"Wow, that's great, right. You have names," Cade said, trying to navigate this heavy moment and feeling painfully out of his depth.

"Dad, can I… can I use the tablet for a little while?" he asked in a small voice, but Nox shook his head.

"You're grounded. Go upstairs," Nox said shortly.

"Dad."

"Now."

Sam gave Cade a sad look and disappeared up the stairs.

Nox started pacing as soon as the kid's door slammed. "No fucking way," he muttered. Then he stopped and glared at Cade. "No more notes."

"Hey, don't shoot the messenger. I get this is stressful for you, but think about your kid, okay? He just wants to find out what happened to his folks."

"His parents are dead," Nox snapped. "Your friend Mr. White is fucking with him and… and…." He stopped, visibly reining himself in. "No more. Those names are a fucking lie and a trick. Do you understand me?"

Cade nodded. He'd seen this guy kick a drug dealer down the stairs, but that was nothing compared to the barely contained anger he was simmering with now. "Okay. No more notes."

Nox exhaled. "You need to stay away from Rachel."

"She's my boss!"

"She's not what she seems."

"Great. I'll take your word for it, Mr. Con Man," Cade snapped. "I came up here because I thought you might want to help me find someone's who's missing—that's your thing, right? Playing hero?"

"Not for the people making a buck off my city by turning tricks," Nox spit out.

Cade's gaze narrowed. "Fuck you."

He got two steps away when Nox grabbed his arm. "Sorry—just stop. I don't want you to leave."

CHAPTER TWENTY-NINE

NOX FELT like he was about to explode in a million pieces.

Mount Sinai's building yielded almost three hundred boxes of Dead Bolt. He'd set the first floor ablaze the night before, just after another truck took off for the downtown location.

He set that on fire too.

It felt like every little dealer he'd kicked in the head over the past few years had joined together to make all his efforts worth exactly nothing.

Sam stayed in his room, furious and hurt by Nox's actions, pulled away from his job—his only freedom—and denied access to the tablets or phones. Locked in his room like a child when Nox went out.

Cut off.

"It's for your own good" fell on deaf ears.

How could he explain after all these years? He hadn't needed an excuse for so many years—he'd filled the role of mother and father to Sam, raised him, and then one day the question came up.

Sam was seven. In a lesson from his online school, they were discussing family trees and Sam asked.

Who was his mother?

He could have answered then. He could have explained Sam was his brother. Explained their mother and father were dead, but then— Nox thought—he would have to say more.

Natalie and Carson Boyet were dead. So was their son Nox. The family was gone as far as everyone thought, and Nox—well, he had convinced himself it was the only way to stay safe.

So he spun a story for little Sam, a story that divorced him from the sad facts of his life. It seemed so much smarter—a way to stop the questions and tie it all up in a neat and loving bow.

Nox had found Sam and saved him and protected him. That part wasn't a lie.

And now? It wasn't Nox's paranoia anymore. Like his mother had been right about the city falling into ruin, Nox's fear of the outside world was becoming justified.

Jennifer and Roy Grimes.

Jesus.

Only one person knew about him. Only one person could have written that name for Sam to see. Mr. White was a front, and Rachel Moon was a lie.

Because Jenny was alive.

And now, this ballsy boy with the beautiful face and fierce determination wasn't going to listen to his warnings either.

He held on to Cade's arm, feeling it flex under his grip.

"I'm sorry for saying that. And I'll see what I can find out about your friend," he said slowly.

Cade relaxed slowly. Their bodies were curved close, like they had been at the Iron Butterfly that night.... Nox felt his body respond even as he fought to stay on track.

"Thank you." Cade seemed to drift closer, then shook his head. "I should go."

"Why don't you stay a little while longer?"

Nox didn't want to be alone.

CHAPTER THIRTY

THEY DRANK tea in the kitchen, sitting on stools at the island, thighs touching. Cade kept meaning to pull away—this inexplicable attraction was mixed up in so many layers of lies; every conversation was a game because they didn't trust one another—but he never did. He felt drunk with the desire, even knowing this was a client.

Although he was never actually a client, after all, was he?

"I need to go," Cade said again, even as Nox ran his warm palm down his back.

"You have time."

Cade leaned forward, lifting his ass slightly off the stool.

An offering Nox took as he slid his hand lower, pushing and pressing until Cade was bent over the counter, legs spread, Nox's fingers notched between his thighs.

He felt stupidly easy, which was hilarious considering his line of work.

So hard it was starting to hurt, Cade tried to move—up, away, *something*—but Nox moved quicker, pushing the chair aside to crowd behind him. He leaned forward, lining up their bodies perfectly, rocking his hips forward.

"You're gonna fuck me on your counter?" Cade asked, swallowing down a moan. "With your kid upstairs?"

"Or I could just push you down to the floor and stick my cock in your mouth until you shut up," Nox whispered back, molding his hands down Cade's chest in long, luxurious strokes until he reached his hips. He turned him around in the cage of his body so they were still perfectly aligned.

So they were doing this with masks firmly in place. It was probably safer that way, because Cade had gone about fifty steps past his rules into unchartered territory.

Cade licked his lips. Then he did it again when Nox's expression darkened into something that gave him weak knees. "Yeah?"

"Yeah." Nox traced his finger around Cade's lips.

Cade opened his mouth, catching Nox's fingertip as he went around once again.

Nox smiled, another of those genuine ones Cade found so fucking fascinating—then slipped his finger farther into Cade's mouth, watching his lips with those too-blue eyes.

Cade was good at this, he knew, puckering his lips around Nox's finger with a tight seal and sucking him in. His eyes fluttered shut as he concentrated on the motion of his tongue, the drawing in and movement of the flesh in his mouth.

"Show-off," Nox murmured.

Cade didn't answer. He felt Nox's dick against his, growing with every grind and pump of his hips. His eyes flickered open for a second as he opened wider, and he took two more of Nox's fingers into his mouth. He rubbed his tongue over the undersides, tasting the tang of Nox's skin.

Nox didn't have to tell him he was good at this or that it was getting to him—the proof was in his ragged breaths, the way he was gripping Cade's ass with his other hand like it was trying to get away.

Cade sucked harder.

Maybe he was an attention whore. He liked hearing Nox's throaty growls, liked the vibrations of want fluttering through his body and filtering through to Cade's chest.

He ran his tongue over the groove of each finger, twisting his head to take him deeper.

Cade let his mouth pop off with a dirty wet sound, looking up at Nox with heavy-lidded eyes.

Chapter Thirty-One

Maybe If I let it happen this once, I'll stop wanting it so badly, Nox thought, knowing full well that was a bullshit lie he was feeding himself.

He reached down with his free hand, flipped the button of his jeans, and dragged the zipper down, sighing with relief as the pressure eased and his dick sprang free. "Cade," he said hoarsely, licking his lips. Nox tucked his free hand at the back of Cade's neck, caressing his Adam's apple with his thumb.

Nox didn't push—didn't have to. Cade dropped to his knees without hesitation, breathing soft puffs of air on Nox's dick.

"God, yes," Nox murmured, cock jerking just from the way Cade slid between his legs. He thanked whatever deity listening that he had some kind of control. For the moment, anyway.

Cade didn't go the seductive or the coy route; he opened his mouth and slid his slick tongue down the underside of Nox's dick, dipping his mouth down as far as he could into Nox's pants, then jerking back up and sucking the head between pursed lips.

The moan that Nox let out was dirty and too loud, but God, he'd never felt something so perfectly intimate in his life. A few times at the casinos, to keep up appearances. Furtive touches as a young teenager with Patrick all those years ago, when he was optimistic and still thought he might eventually fall in love.

Nothing compared to Cade sliding down to take him all the way, bumping the back of his throat, and oh—Nox grabbed the countertop with both hands as Cade kept swallowing, massaging his length in the wet heat of his mouth.

"Good... fuck, so good," he gasped, fighting himself over whether he should keep his eyes open and take the risk of watching Cade destroy him as he bobbed and sucked his cock.

He'd wanted this since that first night at the Butterfly, and he was done fantasizing—done jerking off in the shower imagining that he had Cade on his knees in front of him and feeling like a dirty bastard for turning him into wank material.

Cade fluttered his eyelashes, hollowed his cheeks, and moaned deep in his throat, leaving Nox light-headed as he grabbed the back of Cade's head.

The eyelash flutter alone just about made Nox go insane, rocking his hips forward, unable to keep still a second longer.

Nox held out as long as he could, pushing himself and Cade to the point where he was trembling and desperate, fingers getting tighter and tighter in Cade's hair, if only to disguise just how much his hand was shaking. He gave no real warning, just a hard tug to Cade's hair and a loud yell, head snapping back and hips snapping up as he came down his throat.

Cade carried the perfect whore routine down to the swallow, the held-back choke, the sensuous cleaning of Nox's dick with his tongue. Nox loosened his grip on Cade's hair, and he sighed as Cade slowly slid off his dick.

"Sure shut me up," Cade muttered, dropping his hand to his own erection even as he looked up at Nox, lips shiny and damp. "Now come down here and get me off."

CHAPTER THIRTY-TWO

CADE GOT back twenty minutes before his shift started with an aching throat and a fever—he felt like he was going to walk into a goddamned wall.

His entire body throbbed, and Killian kept asking him if he was all right as he stripped down so he could get dressed.

He was fine.

No, really.

So what if the insides of his thighs were reddened from Nox's beard, or his dick ached from a hand job that made him come so hard he bit his tongue. So what if there was a bite mark on his hip that he had to be careful not to touch or he'd probably come again.

Killian mentioned none of this, just stuffed him into a disturbingly tight pair of navy blue slacks and white button-down, open to display his chest. His dick lay half-hard, curved down his leg, manipulated and placed for maximum notice—Cade was shaking by the time Killian finished with him.

"Enjoy your night," he said, pushing Cade out the door.

He was very popular on the packed floor.

Three high rollers with no luck at the tables happened upon him at the bar. They didn't try much wooing, just ordered him a drink and asked how much for all of them at the same time.

He barely got a number out when Rachel's voice cut through the babble.

"Sorry, gentlemen," she said, resting her hand on Cade's back. "He has a previous appointment."

"The Monarch," Rachel whispered as he walked away, staying behind to soothe the hurt feelings of the trio.

Cade tried not to run, hoping desperately he was right and Nox was waiting.

The elevator couldn't move fast enough, and Cade's legs didn't move as quickly as he wanted them to. He made it to the door of the Monarch Suite and pushed inside…

To find it empty.

Cade checked the bedroom, the bathroom. No one was there.

He came back to the living room to find Rachel sitting on the couch. "I thought you said—"

Rachel indicated the seat across from her by pointing the toe of her shoe in that direction. "Sit down, Cade. We need to have a chat."

Interlude

JENNY LOOKS at the teenager across from her, holding that sweet little baby so protectively, and tries to remember what her job was in the first place.

Oh right. Get rid of the wife, take care of the kid, rendezvous with the papers from the safe at Carson Boyet's house. Make a shit ton of money and get the fuck out of town.

Nothing has gone as planned, not a damn thing.

She tries to figure out where it shifted, where the big score stopped being her main goal and she changed the script.

Maybe it was when she realized Natalie was pregnant.

Maybe it was when they told her to kill a teenager and an infant because things had gotten "complicated."

No shit.

So here is the new plan: She has the papers they want. She's going to take the kids off the island, drop them off somewhere far, far away, then blackmail the shit out of these assholes until she gets her money.

Ballsy? Sure. But fuck them. Fuck all of them.

"We're gonna pack up, go down to the ferry, and go somewhere...."

Nox makes a face. He doesn't believe her.

"Somewhere safe, okay? I'm not going to hurt you."

"You pulled a gun on me," Nox snaps. "While I was holding a baby."

Jenny rolls her eyes. "I'm sorry."

"You're sorry? Oh my God." Nox clamps his mouth shut as if he realizes he shouldn't argue with the lady with the gun. "Whatever. When do we leave?"

"When it gets dark."

She gets him to give her his school identification, tucks it into her pocket.

ALARMS SOUND outside. Emergency vehicles race down the street. The rain starts again in earnest. Jenny sits in a chair by the front window, watching and waiting.

Nox is on the couch, talking to the baby he's now calling Sam. Jenny ignores the chatter because it's annoying and she doesn't want to care.

The lights go out.

Nox has battery-powered lanterns, which he gets from the kitchen.

"My mom was right" is all he says.

They sit in the dark. Jenny has the gun in her lap—and she grabs it when the front door rattles.

"Hide," she murmurs, and Nox takes off up the stairs. Jenny raises the gun as the door opens.

CHAPTER THIRTY-THREE

THERE WAS a police cruiser on the outskirts of the Old City.

Nox sat on the roof of the Museum of Natural History, now a disco catering to the young and hip who wanted to dance the night away instead of throw money down the toilet at cards. For Nox, it gave him a good vantage point to watch who was entering his part of town.

The police didn't come to the Old City without good reason, and crime wasn't a good enough one, hadn't been for a long time. They were looking for something. Someone.

Music leaked out of the doors; drunk revelers tripped down the stairs, shouting and shrieking their way to the street. Gypsy cabs slowed, looking for fares in a place no self-respecting driver would be. Nox watched for a few minutes, saw the young girls tottering on too-high heels, so liquored up they didn't feel the cold even in their skimpy dresses. He saw the men waiting in the shadows.

For a moment he considered leaving, but something pulled him back.

Nox walked to the edge of the roof and jumped to the church next door. He slid down the side, then walked boldly around to where the men were standing. Whispering.

He caught enough words to understand the plan. He waited until the girls turned away before striking.

The blackjack took out the first man before the second could react. With three quick blows, they were out, piled at his feet like garbage. He left them in the shadows for the junkies who lingered near the barrier and the baby gangbangers with something to prove.

Unaware of their potential fate, the girls got into a cab.

Nox watched them go, then continued on his way.

AT SERENDIPITY Towers, Nox became Patrick Mullens, a man in a nice suit holding an all-access key card. He tried to forget Cade's apartment was here, sticking to his mission.

Break into Alec's apartment. See if he could find anything.

So far none of his contacts at the other casinos had panned out. They knew of Alec, knew where he worked, but no one had seen him for at least a week. So with a pass from Brownigan, Nox walked right through the front door of the towers and then up to Alec's door.

No one was in the hallway, which made this easier; he slid the card into the reader and waited. And waited. When the green light flashed, Nox got into the apartment as quickly as possible.

He took a small flashlight from his pocket, shone it around the room.

Empty.

Not just empty of an inhabitant but empty of personal belongings. Aside from a few pieces of basic furniture—most likely included in the rent—the place had been picked clean.

The smell of bleach, the lack of rugs. Nox sighed as he surveyed the space.

Cade's friend wasn't missing, he was long gone. Whether he was alive or dead, Nox couldn't say.

CHAPTER THIRTY-FOUR

CADE SAT down across from Rachel. He watched her expression, his own nerves subsiding as he realized she was unsettled.

He'd never seen that before.

"Cade, I've always liked you," she started, tapping her heels on the floor. "You have a good head on your shoulders."

She stopped—and he waited.

"A very long time ago, I made some mistakes. I was young and I listened to the wrong people, let them manipulate me into doing things I didn't want to." She shuddered. "What I told you about where I come from and where I was during the Evacuation—that wasn't true."

Cade's breath caught in his throat.

Nox was right.

"My parents died when I was very young, and I was taken in by some family friends." Rachel's expression turned dark, as bad as he'd ever seen her when someone fucked up. "Their business was—let's just say it makes what we do now look like church camp."

Cade nodded, pressed his palms against the sofa.

Nox—Jesus Christ. He had to let him know.

"I went to work for them because I didn't have a choice." She stopped again, her eyes flashing with anger. "You understand that. I didn't have a choice."

"I understand, Rachel," he answered because he knew she needed to hear it.

"And I did things I regret, but—at the time, they seemed to be my only chance to survive." She looked away, staring at the door. "I reached a point, though, where I couldn't—I wouldn't do the last job required of me. I could have walked away with a lot of money, Cade. More money than I could have imagined when I was that young, but I couldn't do it." She stressed each syllable. "I let that person I was be erased and I… I remade myself."

Rachel turned again, and he saw tears in her eyes. "I became Rachel Moon, and I became successful on my own terms. That girl I was before—she's dead. It's not a lie, it's not a cover-up, it's the truth. Jenny is dead."

Cade nodded, leaning forward even as he wanted to bolt out the door. "I get it, Rachel. I do," he said gently.

"Tell him Jenny is dead," she repeated as she stood up. "That's the truth."

CHAPTER THIRTY-FIVE

NOX LEANED against Cade's door, checking his watch a few times as he waited. He could go inside—he had a pass—but something held him back. Cade's shift should be over by now. He was about to leave, feeling ridiculous for standing there for so long, but God, since this morning, this afternoon—he could still taste Cade in his mouth, and the need... the want. It was in his head so deeply he couldn't leave without seeing him.

Down the hall, the elevator dinged, and like he could sense it, Nox turned to see Cade stepping off.

Their gazes met, and the grateful smile on Cade's face was everything he wanted to see.

They didn't talk. Cade opened the door and Nox followed. A single light flipped on.

And this was what Nox was thinking about all damn day. He groaned into Cade's mouth, sliding his hands down to the small of his back, tugging him in even closer.

He kept a tight hold on him and edged him back toward the bedroom, struggling to get Cade's shirt off without breaking the kiss.

Cade moved in complete cooperation with Nox's aggressive hands—shirt off, walk backward, navigate hallways and furniture. By the time Nox got them to the bedroom, both their shirts were gone and Nox had unbuttoned Cade's pants. "Everything off," he said, his voice a low growl.

Cade took a tiny step back and reached for his waistband as he toed his shoes off. Everything was fast and slow at once—Cade watching Nox watching him, drawing out each second of anticipation, and then he was naked, completely stripped in Nox's space.

"Cade," Nox murmured, and so help him, he actually licked his lips like Cade was a steak dinner and he hadn't eaten in a week.

"Come here." Cade tugged him closer. "My turn."

Cade lowered his eyes and went to work, quickly and effectively stripping Nox out of his clothes. No more touching than necessary—just the occasional brush of fingers against Nox's skin until he was naked.

Nox gave in for a few long moments, letting them both look their fill, then reached around Cade and pulled him in, nice and snug against his body, hands low on his hips. "Suck me now. Then I'll fuck you," Nox murmured, leaning in closer, lips brushing his neck.

Cade's smile was smug and dirty. He opened his mouth, teasing and drawing out the anticipation before he whispered, "That sounds like a good plan." He stroked his hands down Nox's back, then around his hips. "On my knees or...."

"Mmmm, yeah," Nox sighed and Cade laughed.

"You really like to play boss, don't you?"

"You're so distracting," he said, tightening his grip on Cade's hips. "If I had time, I'd chain you to that bed and fuck you until you couldn't walk."

"Big talker." Cade slapped Nox's ass hard, and the sting propelled Nox to start moving again.

"I need—" Nox started to say, but Cade bit his lower lip, sucking slowly before pulling off.

"I'm a professional, son—nightstand, top drawer."

Professional. Right. This was sexual relief. This was an understanding between two adults.

The detour was blessedly short thanks to the compactness of the room. He caught Cade around his waist, kept him close as he leaned over to retrieve what they needed.

And then, after he'd tossed the condom and lube bottle onto the bed, Nox took Cade down and pinned him to the mattress, kissing him hard and growling into his mouth as he did so. "Where were we?"

Cade moved underneath him, an echo of that moment against the wall on the first day they met. But this was so much better—skin to skin, the full expanse of Cade's gorgeous body for Nox to use and take.

"I can't suck you like this," Cade said, kicking at Nox to get off him. "Come on, put that cock in my mouth." The words were breathless and practiced, but there was nothing fake about the hard-on pushing against Nox's thigh.

He scrambled up, knee-walking over to Cade's muscular chest until Nox straddled his shoulders. Something dark flitted across Cade's pale eyes, and Nox moaned as he grabbed his cock to stroke.

"Mmm, that's mine," Cade moaned, opening his mouth. He laid his tongue against his bottom lip, begging with his eyes and the urgent tugs of his hands against Nox's hips.

Nox fed his cock into Cade's mouth, teasing against his tongue then pushing in deeper.

It was slow and torturous. Cade sucked on the head, flicking his tongue against the vein just under the cap. His wet mouth was heaven as Nox slid his cock deeper.

He couldn't keep upright.

Nox dropped his hands to the bed and watched, felt, as Cade seemed to cease breathing or moving anything but his mouth and tongue and back of his throat.

Cade dug his nails into the muscled flesh of Nox's thighs, slowing his thrusts enough for Cade to slide his mouth even lower at his own practiced pace, until he swallowed around the cock in his throat.

"Oh, oh," Nox panted, stilling his hips as Cade did all the work even with limited movement. Nox gripped the sheets with both hands, sweating and aching from every suck. Nox groaned, yanking at Cade's hair to pull him off slowly.

"Fuck," Nox whispered as he slid down Cade's body. "Your mouth…."

Cade looked supremely pleased as Nox rubbed his wet-with-saliva cock down Cade's chest and stomach. "You gonna fuck me now?" he murmured, reaching down to stroke himself as Nox moved off for a second to grab the condoms and lube.

He moved them closer, then dropped back down on Cade's body.

"Spread your legs," he mumbled against Cade's lips. He knew Cade was well aware of what to do to make the experience the most sensual, but then he also knew Nox got off on telling him what to do.

Cade opened his legs, cradling Nox with his body, relaxing in his tight embrace.

Maybe there would be another time for this. Maybe next time he'd be patient and slow and unselfish, let Cade have his pleasure before taking his own. But right now, there was no space for thoughts like that. He pushed a condom into Cade's hand without needing to explain, swearing under his breath until he managed the lube, until he got two fingers rubbing right over Cade's hole.

"I like you like this," Nox whispered, nuzzling at Cade's throat, finally easing his fingers inside his body, and God, how was it even possible that anything could feel this good? "Fuck, you're the most gorgeous thing I've ever laid my eyes on."

He watched Cade's face, shifting his fingers inside him, waiting to feel him relax just that little bit more. The lube on his fingers began to burn, and it took a second to realize that this wasn't just slick to make fucking easier. This stuff had a kick.

"Uhhhh," Cade stuttered under his breath, as the heat of the lube began to hit him. "God, that stuff is… fuck…." He arched up, straining against Nox's body. "Oh fuck it hurts," he moaned, but it was clear from the blissful expression on his face that he welcomed the pain.

Nox's dick pulsed against Cade's stomach.

Cade laughed/moaned. "That's enough. Just fuck me," he breathed out, pulling his own hair.

The burning on his fingers started to physically hurt, so Nox began pulling out, blindingly slow and with an extra twist at the end. He manhandled Cade onto his stomach, then up onto his knees. "Move your legs apart a little more," he said as he shoved Cade into position.

"If I had my way, I'd bring you home with me, leave you chained to the bed so I could fuck you every night," he choked out, waiting a beat and then pushing into Cade with three hard strokes. He was once again lost in his desire for Cade. The words were his fantasies and this beautiful man was like a gift he never conceived of having.

That fantasy was caught in Nox's mind now, the intense heat of Cade's body sending him into orbit when meshed with that need he'd had since the last time they were together.

"Chain you to my bed, blindfold you, keep you and use you...." He grunted and moaned, every thrust deeper and more violent.

"Yes," Cade bit out, the words muffled by the sheets.

There was more in his head, more visions of things he'd do if time and circumstance permitted, but the tight heat of Cade's body had done in his power of speech beyond the muttered *fuck yes*. He dug his fingers into the flesh under his hands. His thrusts rocked them lower onto the bed.

"Please," Cade begged in a rough voice, his cheek dragging over the covers with each thrust. The tight grip he had on the bed didn't stop that from happening. "God... please, fuckin' touch me."

"No."

Nox fucked him harder, pushed Cade flat on the bed so he could get more friction that way, so he could take it all, completely.

"Yeah, yeah. Take it, whatever you want," Cade gasped.

"Say that again," Nox ordered, voice sandpaper rough. "Tell me again."

Cade moaned. "What... whatever you want. T-t-take it," he whispered, eyes tightly closed as he pushed back against Nox.

Nox growled. He tugged Cade's hands above his head and pinned them there, biting his shoulder while he held him down.

"Oh my God," Cade said faintly.

Nox's vision went a little gray as his orgasm rocked him with a sudden viciousness. He pushed down once more, hard, and then pulled out, still pulsing in the condom. "Turn over," he said roughly, fully in control of what he wanted right now.

Cade reached out to grip the covers and turn himself over. Quickly he was on his back, looking up at Nox through hooded eyes. He was gorgeous, bottom lip bitten red and his body glistening with sweat.

Their gazes locked, Nox leaned down, flicking his tongue over the swollen head of his lover's cock, teasing for a long, cruel moment. He made sure Cade's eyes were begging as he swallowed him deeply.

"Oh, fuck," Cade breathed, eyes fluttering shut and head flopping heavily back to the bed as Nox took him in.

Nox swallowed until he tasted Cade at the back of his throat. He slipped his fingers back into his lover without announcement or prep, fucking him again.

Cade parted his legs greedily, giving Nox all the room in the world. Pulling off Cade's cock with the most obscene slurp outside of a porn movie, Nox locked his gaze on his lover's face. He continued to thrust his fingers, his smile wicked.

"You're driving me crazy," he murmured, twisting a third finger inside Cade's body.

Cade moaned, planting his feet on the bed and raising his hips to fuck himself on Nox's fingers. "You're one to talk. Oh Christ, right there."

Nox was about to make a smart remark about Cade still being able to form coherent sentences when his lover's body stiffened and the pump of his hips, the tension in his body, told Nox he was close. He managed to be smug and swallow at the same time, deep-throating Cade to catch the last few pulses of his orgasm.

Cade choked out Nox's name, shivering when the pressure on his sensitive dick became too much.

Nox loved that moment, that shift when pleasure transitioned from amazing to overwhelming. So he pushed just that little bit more before he licked his way up and off to rest his cheek against Cade's thigh. "Good?" he murmured.

"Understatement," Cade whispered, unclenching his fingers long enough to touch Nox's shoulder. Nox smiled up at him, biting sort of gently at his hip.

Cade shivered in response.

CHAPTER THIRTY-SIX

CADE LAY in boneless bliss under Nox's ever-wandering hands. He knew they were going to go again, but first he needed to tell Nox what Rachel said.

"Come here, I need to tell you something," he said gently, drawing Nox into his arms. There was an awkward moment of fumbling—first time with a lover, first time in a long time for Cade just experiencing the pleasure of curling up in someone's arms. "Rachel told me something tonight…."

He repeated her words verbatim, feeling Nox tense up throughout and vibrate with anger at the end.

"Jenny's dead," he finished, clutching at Nox's warm skin to keep him close. "She doesn't want to hurt you. Or Sam."

Nox shook his head, all the warmth of their holding each other gone. "I can't know that for sure."

"I believe her."

Nox got out of the bed as quickly as he had fallen into it.

Cade listened as Nox fumbled into his clothes and lay there as he stormed out the door. He lay there and smelled the spunk and sweat on his sheets, from sex that was just for him and not for money, sex with someone he wanted for just that. He rolled himself tightly in the blankets, pretended they were arms pinning him to the bed as he watched his little piece of sky through the window.

He slept and dreamed of the farm, and his mother stroking his hair and telling him to stop trying to be someone else and just come home.

WHEN HE arrived at the Iron Butterfly late in the afternoon, his ID didn't work as he tried to enter the building.

Billy the security guard ambled over—strangely out of place from his usual post at the back door—took the key card out of his hand and examined it, then slid it into his pocket.

"I'm sorry to inform you you've been terminated, Mr. Creel," he said. "You need to leave the premises immediately."

"What?" Cade stepped back, shock coursing through his body. "What the hell are you talking about?"

"You've been terminated. Please leave the premises or I'll be forced to remove you myself." Billy sounded like he would enjoy that.

"You're crazy. Get me Rachel on the phone." He looked around wildly; the front desk staff was pretending they couldn't see him or hear him. "Get me Rachel on the phone!"

"Get out of here," Billy repeated, stepping around the desk to loom over Cade. "Now."

Cade turned and walked back to the street, his entire body shaking. He pulled his phone out and hit the icon for Rachel's cell as he began to walk mindlessly.

Voice mail.

"Rachel, what the hell are you doing? How could you do this to me?" he shouted, drawing looks from the early evening crowds. His recording time ended and he hit the icon again; he was headed for the cab line before he could think about it.

He flung himself in the first available cab. "Ninety-First Street."

The guy turned around, looking at him like he was crazy.

"I know, I know—as close as you can get, and hurry up. It's almost curfew."

CHAPTER THIRTY-SEVEN

NOX WOKE up facedown on damp concrete.

"Oh good, you're awake," someone said. A boot connected with Nox's side, rolling him over onto his back.

He remembered leaving Cade's apartment. He remembered making it all the way up to the Old City. He was maybe ten blocks away from home when...

Someone jumped him.

No, several someones jumped him, forcing him to the ground and stabbing something into his arm. For a second, there on the cold, wet floor, Nox panicked. What if it was Dead Bolt? What if....

"Just a sedative," the voice said. Deep. Masculine. Amused. Reading his mind. "You'll be fine. I just needed you a bit more amenable to a conversation—and less inclined to try and kill me."

Footsteps echoed around him. Nox closed his eyes as his vision swirled.

"What are we going to do with you? So insistent on sticking your nose where it doesn't belong." The footsteps stopped for a moment. Nox felt a shoe prod against his shoulder. "I would appreciate it if you would stop destroying my product before it even gets to the streets."

Nox's anger rolled through him. *Son of a bitch.* "Fuck off. Keep your poison out of my neighborhoods," he spat back, kicking out. "I'm not stopping 'til you're gone for good."

The man sighed dramatically. "Well, that's not going to happen."

The prodding became a kick, half-assed but still painful as Nox twitched in response. "You and I have had a perfectly good relationship up until now. I've left you alone because quite frankly you were doing me a service. You catch one of my employees slacking off, you break their hand—I know whose employment I have to... terminate. And I appreciate it, I really do." The footsteps came closer as Nox twisted his head, trying to clear his vision enough to see. "You do a service for me, young man. You keep the streets safe and you keep my product in the hands of the right people."

Nox bit his lip until he tasted blood.

"But now? Now you're expanding your little mission, and it's pissing me off." Nox felt the tip of a shoe against the side of his face, pressing his head into the cold floor. "Those trucks are just transports. They're moving a desired product. Supply and demand—how else can I meet the needs of my clientele?"

"I don't care," Nox spat. "I want you out of my neighborhood."

"I'm afraid that isn't going to happen."

The shoe disappeared, but a second later it connected with Nox's side, near his kidney—hard. He swallowed a moan as the pain radiated across his back.

"Since I'm not going anywhere, let's make a deal, all right? You stop destroying my trucks, and I won't let the police arrest your son in two hours for those nasty bombings."

Nox's heart stopped. "Leave him alone. He hasn't done anything wrong."

"I don't give a damn about him." The voice laughed. "But the police? Oh, the police like him for the bombings. It would close the case for them, another feather in their cap as far as crime in the District goes. They have evidence, you know, about him being the Vigilante stalking the streets of the Old City, killing drug dealers and junkies. He's crazy, you know—terrible thing." A sound, a movement, and the man was closer. Nox felt knees digging against his side. Softly, the man murmured, "Crazy like his mother."

Nox moved—or tried to. The room spun and dipped, his vision going black as he made it to his knees, then tipped back to the ground. This drug dealer—the man behind the trucks, the man behind Dead Bolt, the one whose name no one would tell him—knew who Sam's mother was.

Which meant he knew who Nox was.

The man had stood up. His voice trailed away, back to being all business. "So one more time. You promise to stop destroying my trucks, I give the police a different suspect to lock up. Do we have a deal?"

"Leave my son alone. I'm the one you have a problem with," he gasped, trying to get up again. He couldn't let this man hurt Sam. "Take it out on me. Leave—"

A heavy boot connected with his stomach hard enough to knock the breath out of him for a second. Another to the back—there were at least two of them raining kicks upon him.

"Pay attention," the man said, his voice growing fainter. "I'm not saying it again. Stop destroying my trucks or the police get the boy."

The footsteps echoed in the distance. A heavy door slammed. The blows finally stopped after a particularly vicious one to the left shoulder. As the sounds receded until he knew he was alone, Nox panted and shook on the cold wet floor. Then he passed out.

CHAPTER THIRTY-EIGHT

CADE WAS running up the pathway to Ninety-First Street when his phone rang.

Rachel.

"Jesus, what the hell?" he yelled, not slowing down as the sun began to sink in the distance. "Why did you fire me?"

"You're better off out of there," Rachel said, clipped and brusque. "Stay away from the Iron Butterfly, Cade, believe me."

Cade jogged to the corner. He could see the street, he could see— a police cruiser parked at the other end of the block.

Oh God.

"What's going on, Rachel?" He panted, ducking behind the grocery store, now closed up for the night.

"The less you know, the safer you'll be. And don't go back to your apartment for a few hours. I'm texting you an address—it's better if you wait there for my call." Rachel disconnected, and Cade smacked his hand against the brick wall.

A second later an unknown number came up on his phone. He didn't recognize the address—which meant it wasn't in The District.

What the ever-loving hell was going on?

CADE, IN the midst of his mental gymnastics, remembered the back entrance to the house.

He walked up to Ninety-Second, then cut through the deserted lot behind the townhouse. He could see the door as the sirens went off and curfew went into effect.

Hiding behind the small wall separating the property lines, Cade pressed the icon for Sam, praying he was home. Two rings. Three.

"Hello?"

"Sam, I'm at the back door, let me in," he whispered, staying alert in case a cop was walking by. Or another pack of drug dealers.

"Okay, okay."

He heard fumbling and movement through the line; Cade jumped to the top of the wall, then over the short, spiked fence, and kept low until he came to the door. A light went on in the kitchen and the door opened.

Sam pulled him inside and shut the door behind him.

"There's a cop car—"

"My dad isn't here," Sam blurted. "He's been gone all day and I can't find him."

"Shit." Cade stripped off his coat and walked to the front of the house. The flashing lights from the cruiser illuminated the entire block. "We need to stay inside and hope he makes it back here."

He turned around to find Sam on the verge of tears behind him, twisting his hands.

"This is my fault," Sam whispered. "That man and me wanting to know who my parents are."

Cade shook his head as he took Sam's hand. "Stop it. You didn't ask for this—it's just people meddling and playing games. You didn't ask for this," he repeated, but the boy just bowed his head, breaking down into tears.

"My dad...."

"Stop, okay? Just stop. He's going to be fine. He can take care of himself," Cade said gently, pulling Sam into his arms. "Deep breath."

The back door opened just as someone pounded on the front door. Cade reacted on instinct.

He pushed Sam toward the stairs. "Up, right now. Stay in your room and lock the door."

"Police!" The pounding began again.

Cade took every ounce of his remaining courage and opened the door.

A uniformed rookie stood on the front step, shining a flashlight in Cade's face.

"Can I help you?" he asked, calm and sweet as he could muster, like he was addressing a Girl Scout offering up some cookies.

"I'm looking for Sam Mullens," the man said. Man? Boy playing dress-up. He looked like he was maybe twenty, with shorn blond hair and a baby face. Not an ounce of menace in him.

"He's asleep," Cade said. "Anything else?"

"Sir, I really need to speak with him."

There was a desperation there, an urgency in his tone that didn't say *cop*. It said *personal*. Cade paused before he closed the door in the kid's face. "Maybe I can get him a message."

The cop sighed, looking worriedly over his shoulder. "Tell him Mason came by. Tell him he needs to be careful."

"Mason? You helped Sam when he got picked up."

Cade almost hit the floor in relief when he heard Nox's voice behind him. A hand touched his back, and Cade leaned into it. *Thank God.*

"Yeah, that's me." Mason flicked his flashlight over Cade's shoulder.

"I'm his father. Is everything all right?" Calm and cool. Only Cade felt the tremor in his touch.

"Just please—tell him to be careful." Mason looked down the street again, fear clearly written in his expression. "Tell him Mason said to be careful."

And with that the rookie turned, jogged down the steps, and disappeared through the gate.

Cade slammed the door, resting his forehead against it as Nox engaged all the locks over his shoulder.

"What the hell is going on?" Cade asked, turning into Nox's embrace.

THEY SAT in Sam's room, on the bed, sharing what had happened. Sam cried again when Nox described what had happened to him in the past few hours. Someone was threatening to frame Sam for the bombings. Nox had been dropped on the corner of their block by these guys, which meant they knew exactly where they lived. Cade shook as he soothed the teenager, rubbing his back in circles. It was something his mom would do when the world seemed entirely too much for Cade to handle. When his gaze met Nox's and he saw the fear, the worry, Cade felt something unlock in his chest.

I'll kill anyone who tries to hurt you, he thought, surprising himself. Cade refused to fight the realization. At this moment, he was being included in this little family and determined to pull his weight in fixing the mess. Cade slid his hand across the bed to rub the back of Nox's hand.

"He needs to get out of here," Nox said, all quiet anger. "We have to find somewhere the cops can't find him."

"My apartment—" Cade started to say, but then he remembered Rachel's warning. "I don't think that's a good idea. Too many nosy models," he said, covering quickly. "But I—I might know a place. Somewhere, uh—it's just somewhere that was recommended to me. Someplace safe." He knew mentioning Rachel's name would throw a wrench in this little plan, so he kept that part to himself.

For now.

They packed a bag for Sam, then snuck out the back door, hiking through the shadows and down to the Circle the back way. Cade gave Nox the address, cheeks burning with fear—thankfully unnoticed as they tramped through the dark.

Please let me be doing the right thing, he thought to himself. *Please let trusting Rachel be the right move.* Because she was trying to keep him safe. If she didn't know Sam and Nox were with him....

It would be fine. It had to be.

Interlude

IN THE panic room with Sam, trying to shush the infant's cries, he can hear people outside, walking around his mother's bedroom. They've been here for over an hour, looking for something. Looking for him? He doesn't know, and he's scared out of his wits.

Finally there's a knock on the wall.

Jenny calls to him though the hidden opening. "It's okay. You can come out now."

He thinks he shouldn't believe her. He thinks he should stay here, but he can't stay in this little room forever.

With the crying baby against his chest, Nox opens the door.

There's a smear of blood on Jenny's face, a smoking gun in her hand, and two bodies lying on the floor behind her.

"They worked for the people who killed your father and you were next," Jenny says.

He takes her at her word.

Chapter Thirty-nine

Sam felt sick to his stomach.

He sat on the floor of an abandoned printing company, watching as his father stalked around, checking windows and doors and closets. Cade trailed behind him from room to room.

No one looked at Sam, and he was glad for that, because he didn't want to see their disappointment. Dust and God-only-knew-what kicked around; he covered the lower half of his face with his jacket, breathing in the harsh scent of detergent. His eyes watered, allergies and irritation and his own stupidity fueling his tears.

Mason had come by to warn him. Something fluttered in his chest, amazing and painful at once. He couldn't tell his father, not now. He couldn't say, *Mason and I have been talking. There's a disposable cell you don't know about. We have feelings for each other....*

It was more fuel to the fire, more proof that Sam was a screwup.

"Everything seems okay," Nox said, coming back into the small office where Sam had been parked. "Are you hungry? I'm going to head out, pick up some more supplies."

The gruffness of his father's tone made Sam feel worse. If only he hadn't followed the truck that night. If only he hadn't been picked up by the police.

He'd even trade meeting Mason if it meant this wasn't happening.

"I'm fine," he whispered, wringing his hands in his lap. "I think I'm just going to go to sleep. If that's okay."

Leaning in the doorway, a newly arrived Cade gave him a grim smile from across the room. "It's been a rough couple of hours. That sounds like a great idea. You got something you can sleep on?"

"My sleeping bag." Sam gestured past Cade to the cubicle area where a secretary once sat.

"There's this storage room like two doors down," Cade said, looking at Nox. "Seemed a little less disgusting than the rest of this place. No moldy carpeting."

"Yeah, good idea. You should sleep in there." Nox didn't look at Sam, busying himself with checking his gun, then tucking it back into his waistband. "Cade'll show you where it is."

"Thanks," Sam whispered. He got up and walked past his father. He paused, hoping for a hug, a touch. Something—anything—just so he knew Nox forgave him for screwing up so badly.

"I'll see you in the morning," Nox murmured. When he reached out to squeeze Sam's arm, Sam almost started to cry.

AFTER CHANGING into a pair of heavy flannel pajamas and socks, then brushing his teeth via a bottle of water and a bucket in the "bathroom," Sam went to the storage room where Cade was cleaning up. A camping lantern sat on a pile of broken shelves, bathing the small space in a gentle glow.

"I can do that," he said softly, but Cade ignored his comment. He went on sweeping the clutter into the corner until there was a space for Sam to lay his sleeping bag.

"It's not the Butterfly, but it'll have to do," Cade mused, hands on his hips as he surveyed his handiwork. "I'm gonna see if I can go to my friend's apartment and pick up some bedding. There's a draft...."

Probably a hole in the roof, but Sam didn't mention that. Cade wasn't used to living like this, but Sam remembered winters where the only thing keeping them from freezing was the fireplace and the dining room furniture they fed to it every night.

Sam spread out his sleeping bag—designed to withstand blizzard conditions—and laid his backpack down to use as a pillow.

"This is not me tucking you in," Cade said dryly. "Just... supervising."

Sam smiled wanly. He crawled into the insulated bag, pulling the fabric up to his neck. The room was dusty and it smelled of mildew; beneath him the ground was hard. He didn't say anything.

He missed his bed.

"Get some sleep," Cade said softly, lightly kicking at his feet. "We'll figure it out in the morning."

Sam nodded because he didn't want to cry in front of Cade.

"Night."

Cade turned and left, taking the light with him. Sam had one of his own, but he didn't bother. At this point he just wanted to sleep and try to have a few moments where he didn't feel so absolutely terrible.

In the next room, he heard murmurs of conversation, and then someone's phone rang. Fear gripped Sam. He sat up, trying to listen in.

A minute later the light reappeared, along with Cade.

"Sam?"

"Yeah."

"Sorry. We're going to head out for a little bit, pick up some supplies."

"Oh. Okay." Sam smiled faintly. He didn't want to be left alone. "Not too long, right?"

"An hour, tops." Cade's voice softened. "Are you going to be all right?"

"Yeah." He refused to cause more trouble. "I'll be fine."

Cade ducked back out, closing the door behind him. Sam waited for his dad to come in, but he never did. He fell asleep with tears on his face and a heavy fist in his heart.

A FEW hours later, Sam awoke to rough hands pulling him out of the sleeping bag and dragging him out the door.

CHAPTER FORTY

"I DON'T like leaving him," Nox muttered as they walked down the street toward Cade's apartment on the other side of the District. The cold weather kept most people inside, but Nox and Cade stuck to side streets and moved quickly just in case.

"He'll be fine. No one knows he's there but you and me," Cade said, chattering in the chilly night air.

Nox grunted in response, worry fluttering in his chest. He wanted to get to Cade's apartment, pack up his things, and make some phone calls. Figure something out. Because right now some asshole knew far too much and Nox knew nothing.

He didn't like that feeling.

"You don't know who that man was? The one in the warehouse?" Cade asked softly.

Nox didn't want to answer, but Cade was putting an awful lot on the line for him and Sam. "I've never been able to get much information about him. The dealers have never met him—he keeps himself pretty well hidden."

"But he takes the time to talk to you?"

Nox side-eyed his lover. "I couldn't see his face."

"Right. But he talked to you. He didn't send someone to do it." Cade frowned as they turned down another side street, and pulled his coat collar up around his ears. "Maybe you know him."

He shook his head. "I don't know many people. They're either dead or they...."

"Don't know who you really are—like that guy," Cade finished.

They walked the rest of the way in silence.

When they reached the entrance of Serendipity Towers, it was late enough to avoid the doorman. Nox used one of his spare IDs at the guest entry, and when the green light flashed, Cade pushed open the door.

Nox pulled his cap low over his eyes and Cade kept his collar up. They looked away from the mounted cameras in the lobby, hurrying to the stairs.

AT THE apartment, Cade quickly showered while Nox made some calls on the disposable cell. Except he couldn't seem to reach anyone—not his forewoman, Addie, or his forger, Brownigan. He didn't dare leave messages. Instead he paced and stalked the apartment until finally he just threw the cell into the garbage in frustration.

Hide Sam. Give up his patrols, his attempts to stem the tide of drugs in his neighborhood? He didn't know what to do, didn't have a plan, and that was terrifying. For so long he'd hidden away in that house, clung to shadows and lies to keep them safe. And now everything was spinning out of control.

A hand touched his shoulder. Cade, clad only in a towel, stood beside him, his eyes warm and pleading.

"Can you just tell me? I need to know what's going on here."

Interlude

NOX BARELY keeps himself from throwing up as he walks past Jenny into his mother's bedroom. There are dead men on the floor, two of them, bullet holes in their foreheads.

One of them is Roy Grimes, his neighbor's nephew.

"Oh my God, Roy was...."

"Watching you and showed up to kill you," Jenny supplies. She pushes him out of the room, past the bodies, and into the hallway. "Go pack your bag. Get what you need for the baby. We're getting out of here."

He does what he's told, laying the finally calmed Sam in the center of his bed. He rushes around, packing and freaking out and trying to find a way out of this. How can he trust anyone, let alone Jenny and her supposed change of heart?

He hears thumps and crashes.

Jenny is pulling the bodies out of the house.

THEY LEAVE *the house in the dead of night. Jenny carries Nox's bag. The papers are tucked in her jacket, the gun in her waistband. Nox follows with Sam, a step behind.*

They're getting on the ferry; they're being evacuated. They're going to New Jersey, to a shelter, Jenny tells him. From there they'll move to Philadelphia, where she has some friends.

With every step, his stomach clenches.

"Where are the people you worked for? Are they here? Are they...."

Jenny shakes her head. "The people pulling the strings are in Colombia, Nox. They're as far away from this shithole as they can be. I'm the last employee here on the island."

"How can you know that? Those men...."

Jenny turns to face him, so utterly calm he imagines she's an android with no discernible feelings. "Because I called my employers and told them what they wanted to hear. You're dead, Nox Boyet, dropped in the East River and everything. Got your identification to prove it and some lovely shots of you on the floor of your mother's bedroom with your face blown off.

He stumbles over his own feet.

Nox digests this information.

"So they think I'm dead. And they don't know about Sam."

Jenny's lips go into a tight line; she shakes her head, looking heavenward in apparent exasperation. "No, they don't. Just you and me know about that."

He slows his walk until he's two paces behind. Three.

They approach the Seventy-Ninth Street Boat Basin, where a huge crowd of people waits. It's mostly orderly; people clutch their loved ones and bags. Some are crying.

Nox follows Jenny.

She goes up to a National Guardsman wrapped in a yellow slicker and holding a clipboard. She talks to him, and Nox thinks.

Calculates.

The people who tried to kill him are out there, far away, not here. They think he's dead. They don't know about Sam. Jenny is one of them. He can't be sure she won't change her mind.

He can't be sure she isn't taking him to these people.

If he leaves the island, he's entirely at her mercy.

He's not leaving with her—he knows that.

Sam twitches against his chest, inside Nox's jacket. His little brother is the only person he has left in the world, and he's going to do everything he can to save him.

They start loading people onto the ferry as the rain begins to fall in earnest.

CADE HELD his hands as he talked—the whole story, every piece of it. Something he'd never done before, he realized as his voice got hoarse from the spew of memories.

"Holy shit," Cade whispered, eyes wide and skin pale. "Holy...." He tightened his grip on Nox's fingers. "You're pretty fucking badass, can I just say that?"

Nox choked out a laugh because he didn't want to cry. He let Cade pull him into a tight embrace.

"So we've established you're, like, a freaking superhero or something, but listen—I'm going to help you any way I can," Cade said softly, laying his head on Nox's shoulder. "We're gonna go back and get Sam, and we'll just—we'll figure it out, okay? I'm going to help you."

Nox let himself breathe and sink into Cade's arms. Maybe he didn't have to do this alone anymore.

They sat there quietly for a moment, enjoying a false peace. Out there, things were fucking insane, but here?

Here was just a big bed and moonlight through the window and a few minutes of pretending everything was okay. Nox knew it couldn't last. He could feel it like a premonition, the clock running out on this quiet moment. He felt the warmth of Cade's body aligned with him, he felt their breathing sync, and he knew it was coming.

His cell phone vibrated in his pocket a second later. Nox had a moment of refusing to acknowledge it. *Just five more minutes,* he thought. *Five more minutes.*

"You should get that," Cade murmured against his shoulder.

Nox slipped his hand in his pocket. It vibrated again. A text.

Your brother isn't safe.

I can help.

But you must come here, alone.

A second text from the unknown number popped up a moment later. It was the address of a place that still haunted his nightmares: Morningside Sanitarium.

Nox went cold, bones and blood and vital organs freezing in one instant.

He didn't say anything. He felt Cade tense, one hand gripping Nox's hip as if to anchor him to the bed. "What's wrong? What is it?"

"I have to go." Nox finally found his voice. He didn't look at Cade, just put the phone back in his pocket and stood up.

"Where? We have to get back to Sam."

Oh God. "Stay with him until I get back." He reached for the gun, ever present, tucked into the back of his pants, then extended his hand to Cade. "You know how to use this?"

Cade's eyes widened. He nodded, taking it from Nox without question. "Where are you going?"

Nox shook his head, finally facing his lover. "Stay with Sam and wait for me. Please."

Cade opened his mouth to argue.

"Please. I know I'm asking a lot…."

"I told you I would help." Cade stood, a strange picture in his towel and holding Nox's gun—the ballsy kid who had no reason to be doing this. Nox felt something twist in his heart.

Now? This was the moment when he felt something for someone? How fucking ironic.

"Thank you," Nox said softly. He took a step, leaned in, and then laid a gentle kiss on Cade's mouth. "Thank you."

CHAPTER FORTY-ONE

HE MOVED up his familiar trails to the sanitarium, hooded and cloaked as the Vigilante, following in the footsteps of a teenager in frantic search of his mother.

That boy didn't know what his life would become.

He braved all that rain and destruction, battled his fear, and walked into a truth he hadn't imagined in his wildest dreams.

And now Nox stood at the steps of the Morningside Sanitarium, prepared to face down the unknown once again.

This time, though? He was armed.

LIKE THE factory, the sanitarium had fallen victim to age and neglect. Its tableau of abandoned wheelchairs and gurneys spoke of the tumultuous night when people were running for their lives and the addlebrained weren't a priority.

Every man for himself.

Nox walked up the stairs to the double doors, neatly repaired but not painted, as if to give the illusion that nothing had changed in seventeen years. But a closer look revealed reinforced windows on the top floors, security cameras hidden behind ivy on the curved façade.

The fresh tire tracks to the underground garage.

When the door opened without an alarm or more than a push, Nox knew they were expecting him.

Nox followed his instincts, winding around the debris to the second floor—his mother's floor—and made his way to the door of her suite.

Pale pink walls filthy with dirt and mold, the bed removed by looters, perhaps. Nothing remained of that night but the echoes of his mother's cries.

"Thank you for coming," a voice murmured behind him. Nox turned slowly. A man in an impeccable gray suit stood in the hall, smiling. No shadows here.

"Mr. White," the man supplied helpfully.

Nox nodded. "You could have called the police, told them where we are. But you didn't."

"Hmm, yes. A well-placed call to the chief of police and they were throwing all their manpower to tracing you at the construction site you were working at in Harlem." He dusted off his sleeve. "I believe you and your coconspirators are bunked down on the uppermost floor after having disabled the elevators."

"That was very clever of us," Nox said, turning fully. He felt the blackjack against the small of his back and met the man's smile.

"Indeed. You're quite the master criminal." Mr. White tipped his head to one side. "Tea?"

Nox followed Mr. White down the hallway. They turned left and entered a side office. And stepped into another world. The walls were clean and painted a dove gray, the furniture—office and living space both—all classic and expensive-looking. In the corner, a young woman in a maid's uniform was preparing tea.

The bad guy's lair, Nox thought, and he almost laughed.

"Have a seat." Mr. White gestured to a small green settee, taking his own seat in a leather club chair to its left. "Millicent will bring you a cup."

Nox settled on the edge, planting his feet, casually glancing around, assessing the space. No other doors in sight, no place for any guards to hide.

"Why did you send those letters to my son?"

Mr. White smiled. Smirked, actually, smoothing out nonexistent wrinkles in his pants' legs. "I wanted to get to know him a bit better. He must be curious about his origins."

Nox bit the inside of his mouth. "I'm his father. That's all he needs to know."

"No, you're his brother," Mr. White said.

A high-pitched whistling noise from inside his head almost knocked Nox to the floor. "I'm his father."

"Poor Natalie," the old man murmured. "So much suffering. And her boys—so much hiding and lying. She'd be sad to see what's become of you."

Nox stiffened in his seat. The girl came over with a tray set for tea, a wildly misplaced moment of civility.

"My mother didn't know where she was half the time," Nox said harshly. "Someone should have been taking better care of her."

"I tried," Mr. White said with a sigh. "Oh how I tried. But your father dropped her here without a word, left her here to rot."

Ill, Nox rubbed his hand over his face. He didn't want to hear this or know about the neglect his mother suffered at his father's hand. He didn't want to talk about people long dead—he just wanted to know why this man had a fascination with his brother.

His son.

"You need to leave Sam alone," he broke in as Mr. White murmured to himself. "I don't want him to know how our parents died, okay? You have no right to upset him."

Mr. White shook his head. "I have every right."

Sweat trickled down Nox's back. *Crazy motherfucker.* "Stay away from Sam. All I want to know right now is how you knew about Roy Grimes."

Clearly perplexed by this, Mr. White took a sip of his tea. "Roy Grimes?"

"In the letter," Nox snapped, "you said his parents were Jennifer and Roy Grimes. That's a lie. How did you know those names?"

Mr. White nodded. "Oh yes. She told me to use those names."

Oh God, he was right. It was Jenny—Rachel. She was behind this.

"She?" Nox choked out.

"Natalie. She sends me messages," the old man whispered, leaning forward as if to not let anyone hear. "She told me what to write on the notes. She saw it was time for Sam to know."

Nox got up then. He walked around the couch until he came to the door, fists knotted at his sides. He wanted to scream and trash this room, this entire horrible building, and for one second, he was glad he gave the gun to Cade, because had *he* had it, Mr. White would be dead already.

So Rachel—Jenny—was sending the information to Mr. White, a crazy old man.

Of means?

"Does my mother send you money too?" Nox asked, turning around slowly.

Mr. White squinted. "Yes. How did you know that? Does she send you messages as well?"

Nox ignored him. "That's how you knew where we lived, those names. The way you pay for your time at the casino."

"Yes, yes." The old man took another sip of tea. "Do you know Cade? He's such a lovely boy. Natalie told me to send him on the errands."

Nox's stomach turned. "He doesn't know her... my mother? Does he?" *Please, please let Cade be innocent in all this*, he prayed.

Mr. White set his cup down, looking over at the nurse then back to Nox. "Natalie said to use him because he had more freedom to move around. Because he's her favorite." He made a face at that.

"Her? My mom?" The conversation was giving Nox a sick headache. As much as he wanted confirmation he was right, it felt like daggers being slipped into his heart.

"No, Rachel's." Mr. White's displeasure showed on his face. "Horrible woman."

Wait.

Nox moved slowly back to the couch. "You don't like Rachel."

"She's rude to me. She tried to have me banned, but Zed knows...." That lost expression settled back on his face and his eyes went out of focus.

"Knows...?"

Mr. White cocked his head to one side. "Knows what's good for him and his casino."

The nurse was skittering in the background, moving toward the window, then back to the corner.

Nox narrowed his eyes. "What's her problem? Are you expecting someone?"

"We're the only ones here. This is my home," Mr. White said. "No one comes here but her. And you. It's so beautiful here—I don't know why everyone stays away."

Nox wanted to slap him. "Maybe it's the blood on the walls."

Mr. White sighed, crossing his legs carefully. "I wasn't there. It wasn't my fault."

"You should have done something." Nox's anger rolled and receded. "They all died." His mother hadn't stood a chance, but everyone else, the people he passed that night, out of their minds and unable to escape—they all drowned.

God, if he could only snap this bastard's neck.

Mr. White shook his head. "They were suffering, each and every one of them. It was the... merciful thing to do."

Nox's throat froze for a moment, his brain misfiring information. "You—you left them here to fend for themselves on purpose," he said, slowly. Carefully.

"No. We locked the doors and opened the valves so the flood waters would move quickly throughout the lower floors," he responded so matter-of-factly that Nox had to shake his head to clear the buzzing sound.

Not incompetence. Murder.

"Why would you do that? Why not just let the National Guard get those people out?" asked Nox slowly.

"The owner sent word to take care of them," Mr. White said, as if he was giving directions to a garden party. "And I agreed. We locked the doors and let the water take them. Since my beautiful Natalie was dead, what use was this place anyway?" he added, a sad droop to his mouth.

Nox's stomach dropped. "Your Natalie."

The old man looked away, staring into the distance as if lost in a memory. "He didn't love her like I did."

Nausea crawled up his throat; he swallowed again and again to keep from vomiting on his shoes.

"She wasn't well—she didn't... she could barely understand what was going on around her when she was here," Nox choked out. "The drugs. She was *sick*."

"Such a beautiful girl. So docile and giving," Mr. White rambled on as if Nox had said nothing. "She would lie there so sweetly, without protest.... When I found out we were expecting, I was so delighted. We could be a family...."

Nox threw himself across the room, lunging for the man's neck. The white-hot rage blocked all rational thought as he knocked Mr. White to the floor. The teacup flew in one direction, the chair in another. Nox straddled his chest and wrapped his fingers around the papery-skinned neck of this... rapist.

Mr. White didn't fight him, didn't even try to knock away his hands. He closed his eyes, a smile blooming as Nox choked the life out of him.

This man was his brother's biological father. This rapist, this monster. This piece of garbage.

He squeezed until Mr. White stilled under him, and a death rattle escaped as he pulled his hands away.

When Nox sat back, he stared down at the elderly man, so harmless-looking. So peaceful.

Sam's father.

He closed his eyes and tried to stem the flow of his tears.

When he opened his eyes, it was to Millicent stepping over her charge's body, pointing out the keys to Mr. White's Hummer.

Chapter Forty-two

Cade packed his bags after Nox left, lost in his thoughts. He chose only the important things to fit in his duffel and backpack—clothes, shoes, a few pictures and mementos, sheets, towels, what food he had in the cupboard—because life as he'd known it for the past few years was over. It was looking more and more like his future was in the past.

Back home on the farm in South Carolina.

With one last look around—his bed, his view, his fancy clothes—Cade stepped out of the apartment. The gun Nox gave him sat in the inside pocket of his overcoat, a heavy reminder that he was in danger, in the middle of a fucking mess he had no idea how to get out of.

He took the stairs down to the lobby, pausing briefly at the door to the first floor. Alec was still missing. He didn't ask Nox about it because, well, things being what they were, it wasn't the top of his priority list.

I hope you're safe, wherever you are, Cade thought morosely as he exited the building through the heavy door into the parking garage.

He stuck to the back alleys again, stopping briefly at two separate cafés to grab a large coffee and then a few sandwiches. Somewhere in all of this, they'd have to remember to eat.

At the printing place, Cade went through the back entrance. It was dark and hauntingly quiet. He assumed Sam was still asleep as he made his way to the office where they'd set up camp.

The camp light provided enough illumination for Cade to unpack a few things. A heavy cable-knit sweater to put on when he took his overcoat off and a second pair of socks when he kicked his boots aside. There was no furniture, so he made use of the duffel as a seat as he drank his coffee.

Fuck, he was tired.

And scared.

And confused.

Because somewhere along the way, he'd lost the thread. A simple favor had woven him into the fabric of a weird little family, a world of violence, a place where no one told the truth about who they were.

Cade had always maintained a persona to keep himself emotionally safe, and now? Now it was shattered by this compulsive need to be around Nox, to help him, to make sure he knew he wasn't alone. And it made no sense at all, because Cade was smarter than that. Way smarter—and if he was hearing this story from a friend, he would haul off and slap them for being so stupid.

He's going to get you killed, his brother's voice bitched.

Cade didn't disagree, but he also didn't leave.

THE NIGHTMARE was ugly as nightmares went. Cade ran through the streets of the Old City, a screaming mob on his heels. He could hear their violent threats and feel the fire of their torches, the whiz of bullets flying past his head. His lungs nearly burst from the struggle to escape, because he knew if he stopped, if they caught him, he'd be dead.

Up ahead he saw Nox, in his hooded sweatshirt, arms crossed over his chest.

"Oh thank God," Cade wept, using the last of his energy to push himself, arms and legs pumping as he desperately tried to reach Nox's side.

Because he'd protect him. He would stop the mob, because he had his gun out and he was angling it...

Against his head.

"No, no, stop! Don't do that!" Cade screamed, reaching out as if to swat the gun away. "Don't."

He was twenty feet away. Ten. Five.

"This way you'll be safe," Nox murmured, pulling the trigger just as Cade reached him.

CADE WOKE with a start, breathing harshly, as if he really had run from the mob.

As if he'd seen Nox kill himself.

When he heard a loud bang from the back door, then footsteps, the adrenaline rush still coursing through his veins prompted him to grab the gun with shaky hands. He clutched the weapon a bit tighter and left the safety of the office to investigate.

The shadows were easy to find cover in; he wove through and around and under, swallowing sneezes from the dust- and debris-heavy air. More heavy footsteps, this time closer.

Cade tightened his finger around the trigger of the gun. As much as he didn't relish the idea of shooting someone, he was damn sure he wasn't going down without a fight. He'd put himself between danger and Sam, and Cade wasn't about to let him down.

Panic coursed through Cade's body. Was it even Nox? Had the police found them?

A shadow moved in front of him so quickly he didn't have time to aim—which was a good thing, because it was Nox, a dark silhouette suddenly appearing in front of him.

Cade jumped back and nearly wound up on his ass. It was a reminder of the moment they met, which made him choke on a hysterical laugh. "I could have sh-shot you." Cade doubled over, swallowing a sudden flood of tears and giggles, his whole body shaking with the effort to breathe. The past few weeks, the past few moments— that fucking dream—it all caught up with him in a violent rush. When Nox rested a gentle hand on his back, he fought the urge to sob.

"Come on, you need to sleep. I got what we need for now," Nox said, his voice as soft as his touch. "Come on."

"I'm sorry," Cade murmured, trying to stand straight. His body felt like it weighed a thousand pounds and gravity was trying to bring him down flat.

There was a metaphor in there somewhere.

Nox didn't say anything. He wrapped an arm around Cade's shoulders, guiding him back to the office.

Cade leaned against the wall.

"Let me make you up a bed," Nox said. His expression was unreadable, and Cade couldn't bear to ask what was wrong. He knew what the problems were as each of them thudded through his head like a slide show of doom.

Tears started running down Cade's face then, and he couldn't have stopped them if he tried. He was so fucking tired and so scared, and what if the police found them? By the time Nox led him to the pallet on the floor, Cade had gone around the bend into someplace terrifying.

It was hopeless.

Nox slipped a coat over his arms, pushed the hood up over his head. He maneuvered him down onto a stack of mats covered with a blanket.

"You're fine. It's going to be okay," Nox said, and Cade realized he was talking out loud. As he rested his head back on something soft, Cade looked up at his lover.

Nox still didn't look him in the eye, his face drawn and hands shaking.

"You don't believe that," Cade whispered. He rolled to his side, precarious on the narrow makeshift bed, and closed his eyes.

IT WASN'T long—five minutes, maybe ten, if that. Cade tried to calm his breathing, tried to find a place where he could think again, where he could find the strength to keep going. The quiet shattered a second later as Nox's shouts echoed down the hall.

Cade sat up, fumbling with the covers and extra clothes to get up. He could hear Nox swearing and shouting, hear things being kicked and thrown down the hallway.

"What? What?" Cade yelled, running out the office door.

"Sam's gone," Nox said, running past Cade.

"He's—"

"He left, there's no note. His coat is gone," Nox said frantically, back in the office and digging through his bag. When he stood up and turned around, Cade wasn't surprised to see the Sig in his hand.

Cade swallowed hard. "Where are we going to look for him?"

He'd seen Nox's anger many times over the past week. He'd also seen his fear and his sadness, but nothing prepared him for the expression of pure loathing and fury playing over his features.

"We're going to see Rachel."

CHAPTER FORTY-THREE

THEY TOOK the back alleys from the printing place to the side entrance of the Iron Butterfly. It had the least amount of traffic—it was primarily for the cleaning and kitchen staff, and at this time of night, it wouldn't be used at all. Cade used his code with trembling fingers—it was a long shot, but it was all they had at the moment, since there was no way to waltz into the front door or, God forbid, try to get past Billy. Nox pressed up against his back with his gun out. He waited for the responding code, but instead, the door creaked open.

A kid, one of the lower-rung security grunts, opened the door with a panicked expression on his face.

"Rachel's expecting me," Cade said, putting his hand on the door and one foot inside, his smile as charming as he could manage under the circumstances. "She said to go right up."

"I—I need a pass," the kid managed, his voice shaking. He looked all of about nineteen and fresh off the ferry from someplace not so terrifying.

"You can call up to Ms. Moon's office," Cade bluffed.

The snick of Nox's gun put a halt to the conversation. It was pointed directly at the kid's forehead.

Cade pushed in, dragging the kid with him.

"Jesus, seriously," he huffed, pushing the quivering teenager to the floor. It didn't take much effort. "I was going to get us in."

"No time," Nox snapped, already stalking up the stairs.

"Gimme your pass," Cade told the security plebe—who handed it over without hesitation. "Thank you. Now do yourself a favor and get the hell out of here."

Cade pocketed the all-access pass, running after Nox.

You could practically hear the sonic boom as the kid ran out the back door.

The pass got them into the back stairwell.

Nox hadn't articulated his plan to Cade, but he was pretty sure it involved intimidation and violence.

"Rachel has a gun, in her desk drawer," Cade said, jogging to keep up with Nox's huge strides. "If you walk in there blazing away…."

"Call her. Tell her to meet us somewhere in the building. Somewhere private."

Cade swallowed as he pulled out his phone. He pressed the little icon for her name and waited for her to pick up.

"Goddammit, Cade," Rachel swore through the phone. "What the fuck is wrong with you? I told you to stay hidden."

"We—I did," Cade said, not looking at Nox as they reached the fifth floor landing. "Listen, I'm here at the Iron Butterfly. I need to see you."

Rachel let loose a string of profanities and spitting anger. "Why don't you listen to me? You can't be here," she implored. "I'm trying to save your life."

"I need to see you," he said again. "Please, Rachel."

"No. You turn around and leave right now."

"I can't," Cade said, stopping to lean against the wall. Nox continued up two steps, then stopped and turned around. "Rachel, Sam's missing. I was hiding him in the printing place and we were out and then—"

Nox's glare should have set Cade on fire. He could literally feel the flames on his face.

Staring at the gray-painted floor, Cade waited for Rachel to say something. Anything.

"Where are you?" she said finally, her voice low and cold.

"Fifth floor. The right stairwell."

"Don't move."

She disconnected. Cade looked up at Nox and shook his head.

"I'm sorry."

"She's the one who told you about the printing place," Nox said, his voice lethal.

"It was a place for me. No one cares about where I am. I thought it would be safe," Cade murmured, staring down at his feet.

The silence was broken by the door above them opening. They both looked up and Cade heard the click-clack of Rachel's shoes.

She came into view dressed in jeans and a sweater, her hair piled on top of her head. She looked anything but glamorous.

And she had a Beretta in her hand.

"He's here," she said, coming down the stairs slowly. Cade saw Nox tighten his hand on the gun, saw Rachel do the same. "They grabbed him, brought him here."

"Who?" Nox spit out.

Rachel shook her head. "I don't know them. They showed up about six hours ago and Zed's been freaking out. He told Damian to start erasing files in the office. He told me…." She looked at Cade, a tiny smirk on her lips. "He told me to pack my bags, as I've been fired. For my own good, apparently."

Cade climbed the stairs toward her, skirting around the ice sculpture that was Nox. "Where are they keeping him? Do you know?"

"No. Damian is the one who told me they had a teenager with them—tied up and scared shitless. I was hoping I was wrong." She glanced at Nox, who sneered in return.

"You're behind this…."

"Stop trying to pin every goddamn thing on me, Nox," Rachel snapped. "While I'm flattered you think I'm able to control a fucking drug empire, it doesn't work like that."

Nox stepped up closer to her, the gun unflinchingly pointed at her chest. "You sent those messages to Mr. White. The money."

"What the fuck are you talking about?" Rachel turned and ran up a few steps, Nox at her heels.

"You were behind the letters to Sam," Nox insisted.

Rachel grabbed for the door handle with her free hand. "You're as crazy as that old piece of shit. I'm not his boss, Nox. I'm nobody's boss."

The clang of a door opening many floors above them echoed through the stairwell. "Find Sam and get the fuck out of here—as far away as you can. They aren't waiting anymore."

Nox grabbed for her arm, but the sounds of voices descending from above reached them, and Rachel used the momentary distraction to open the door. She darted out before Nox could stop her.

He moved like he was going to chase her, but Cade took a handful of his shirt and tugged. "Leave her—we have to find Sam."

Cade's best guess as to where Sam was, was far away from where any of the guests or staff could trip over a tied-up teenager.

Zed's private suites were his first guess, a place that set his stomach churning. The security level there—even with the pass, it would be hard to get in.

"This is—it doesn't make sense," Cade whispered as Nox led the way up the stairs. "Why bring Sam here? The place is crawling with VIPs. They're at capacity for the Anniversary Weekend." They reached the staff floor; Cade hurried past Nox to use the pass. "Security is beefed up because of all the damn bomb threats."

He had just pushed open the door slightly when Nox grabbed the back of his jacket.

"What?" Cade turned around to find Nox had gone white, his face stark with terror. "What?"

"Get us here," he murmured. "Get us here on a weekend when the place is packed—everyone is here. The full staff, all the talent, the highest rollers... all those threats without any ransom demands."

It hit Cade between the eyes. "They're gonna blow the place. Holy Jesus."

CADE LED Nox through the talent locker room; everyone was on the floor at this late hour. Down the hall in Killian's workshop, a light was on.

"Wait, wait. I have to...." Cade left Nox's side, running toward his friend with a warning on his lips.

He ignored Nox's sharp whispers behind him—he wasn't going to let anyone die here if he could help it.

At the doorway, Cade heard faint music from the back room. "Killian?" he whispered loudly. "Are you in here?"

Killian popped his head out from behind a rack of suits. "Cade!" Surprise was written all over his face. "I thought you got fired."

"You need to get out of here, right now."

"What?" Killian halted his approach, his face reflecting wariness.

"I think something's going to happen tonight, and you need to get somewhere safe, please."

Killian stepped back and Cade could see him reaching for the silent alarm. "Cade, we're friends. And I know you mean well...."

"Just please—please get out," Cade begged.

Nox ran by in a blur of black leather, and he knew he had to follow. "Get out before it's too late."

"I HEARD static from walkie-talkies," Nox said when Cade caught up to him.

"Security doesn't use those here."

"That's what I thought."

Their conversation halted as they crept around the corner. Down the hallway, near the main elevators, two men stood in security uniforms, each with a walkie-talkie on his belt.

They were watching the descending numbers on the electronic crawl above. The doors dinged open and two more men walked out, each carrying a semiautomatic. They all took off down the far hall without exchanging a word.

Nox waited a second, then bolted down the corridor to follow.

The parade of fake security men ducked into the employee lounge. Voices reached Nox and Cade where they hid behind the last corner. The voices got louder until it was clear a fight had broken out. A second later, Zed stormed out in all his ferocious glory. Blood dripped from the corner of his mouth, his suit askew. He disappeared into the stairwell door and slammed the heavy metal behind him.

"Where is he going?" Nox whispered.

"Probably his private suites. If he takes those stairs up two flights, he comes out right by the entrance."

Nox nodded, then began to creep down the hall toward the employee lounge, one hand directing Cade to remain where he was.

Cade didn't like that, not at all. His heart pounded—he wanted to press the fire alarm, get people out of the building before the bomb went off. But he knew that would probably sacrifice Sam's life, and he couldn't do that. He just—

A hand slapped over his mouth and yanked him back with full force.

He went flying against the back wall, hit it with a thump, and sprawled onto the floor. His breath knocked out of him, he looked up to find Billy standing over him, both hands knotted into fists.

"You're not allowed to be here, Mr. Creel," he said.

"Just stopping by to get a few things," Cade rasped, pushing up on his elbows. "Rachel said I could."

Billy smirked. "I very much doubt that."

CHAPTER FORTY-FOUR

NOX SLIPPED past the doors to the employee lounge, hoping to get an estimate of how many men he was dealing with. He had one gun and reserves of ammo, but once the semis started going off, all hell was going to break loose.

He needed to know where Sam was.

The stairwell door rattled. Nox lifted his gun as it pushed open.

Rachel again.

He kept the gun trained on her forehead, jaw clenched.

Upstairs, she whispered. *I found him. Monarch Suite. That's where Sam is.*

Nox blinked in surprise. She gestured past her as if urging him on. He took a cautious step, refusing to trust her completely.

She looked past him, a question in her eyes.

Cade.

The choice froze him for a moment.

Rachel gestured again toward the stairs, then stepped past him.

Good luck, she mouthed before disappearing around the corner.

It made him sick, but he let her go to Cade while he ran up the stairs toward his son.

Nox knew the way well enough. The irony of Sam being held where he and Cade first… almost…. It fucked with his head as he raced up the stairs. When he came to the door, he had time for a deep breath and then into the breach.

The floor was very purposely empty; he could tell by the absolute and unnatural silence. It was a trap, clearly—he'd always known that. Sam was the bait he could never walk away from.

Not for Cade. Not for anything.

Down the hall sat the Monarch Room, the door slightly ajar.

Nox pulled the hood up over his head, then lifted the Sig, leading with it as he walked toward the room. Calm sank down to his bones. He would save Sam or they would go out together.

He thought of Cade's fierce anger and devotion, felt a pang of regret.

Sorry.

CHAPTER FORTY-FIVE

BILLY DRAGGED Cade down the hall on his ass, his meaty hand wrapped around Cade's neck. Cade struggled, choking as his windpipe was crushed under the abuse. When the edges of his sight began to fade, Billy tossed him against another wall.

Spots danced in front of his eyes.

"Mr. Z?" Billy was yelling for their boss. Cade shook his head until his sight cleared.

Zed's private quarters.

"Mr. Z?"

Cade pushed himself up onto all fours, then stood, panting and trying to keep his wits about him. He was close to the front door. Billy had disappeared down the long hall to Zed's bedroom. Maybe he had a few minutes....

No, no time at all. Because Billy came lumbering back, a look of shock on his face. It took him a second to register Cade was standing— and then he charged.

Billy might be built like a fucking wrestler, but Cade had an older brother. He knew how to dodge low and to the side, moving outside of the security guard's wide reach. He ran around the semicircle arrangement of couches, staying low, then dashed down the hallway.

There was a back entrance for the cleaning staff. If he could just get there....

He went flying suddenly, his feet caught up on something on the floor.

Scrambling to his feet, Cade turned.

Zed lay sprawled on the rug, a pool of blood seeping out from underneath him. Half his face was gone.

"Fuck." Cade didn't waste any time. He turned and ran, aware that Billy was on his tail, aware that his boss was dead and unknown horrors awaited him around the corner.

The darkness didn't impede him—Cade knew this suite all too well from those nights when Zed liked to sample his way through the staff. And bless Zed's paranoia for the hidden door—and the gossips who knew it was there. He ducked into the bedroom, listening as Billy thundered in pursuit. Around the bed, through the bathroom, into the walk-in closet. He was so close, his hand on the knob that would take him into the back stairwell—

—when Billy grabbed the back of his sweater and yanked.

Cade didn't go down. He slammed back into Billy's massive bulk, twisting before Billy could get a grip. He fought for his life, crashing his head back in an estimation of where Billy's nose might be.

He saw stars as the back of his head connected with Billy's face. The grunt of pain told him he'd hit the right spot. Then he dropped to the floor, using his full weight to force Billy to let go of him. Cade scrambled for the door again, and again his fingers closed on the knob.

Cade felt Billy coming, the displaced air warning him of the impact. He went to his knees, reaching blindly into the dark recess of the closet. His hand closed around—something—an umbrella, he realized. He scooted to the side, catching Billy's weight against his hip. With all his might, Cade slammed the umbrella into whatever part of Billy was closest, twice in rapid succession. Momentarily stunned, Billy rolled off Cade.

Cade didn't calculate the move or plan anything. He jumped to his feet and brought the umbrella down on Billy's body. He went into a zone of furious fear, whacking the metal and nylon again and again until Billy made no move to defend himself.

Panting, Cade stopped, umbrella raised over his head for another blow if necessary.

Nothing.

Not even a wheeze.

"Oh shit," Cade choked out. He dropped his makeshift weapon, breathing heavily. He tried to skirt around Billy's body, but his size made it impossible; they were crammed into the narrow opening, the door blocked.

Cade took a breath and reached down, grabbed Billy's shirt, and pulled.

It took him forever, but he got the man far enough away to open the door. He tried to pretend Billy wasn't dead, but his hands came away from his shirt wet and tacky, and he knew.

He'd killed him.

Bloody and shaking, Cade got into the stairwell. He leaned against the wall and shook, rubbing his hands against his jeans, trying to get the evidence off of them. *Self-defense*, he thought. *I killed him in self-defense.*

He tried not to be sick on his shoes.

Above him, the door rattled.

CHAPTER FORTY-SIX

NOX EASED into the Monarch Suite, gun preceding him, breath held.

The suite was dark, so Nox dropped to the ground, keeping close to the furniture as he made his way toward the bedroom. He fully expected this to be Rachel's—Jenny's—trap, a final act of revenge, a final coda to the job she'd botched so many years ago. He made it to the bedroom door.

No sounds from inside. Nothing around him.

Nox opened the door a sliver and peered inside.

Someone was on the bed.

Steeling himself, Nox pushed a little farther and crawled into the second room. Someone was trussed up on the bed, a slender figure.

Sam.

Nox rose slowly, gun raised as he scoped the room. Nothing.

Just his son, laid out like an offering.

He knew they didn't have much time left.

After tucking the gun in his waistband, Nox grabbed Sam's legs and pulled him down to the rug. Sam was limp but breathing—thank God—ankles and wrists bound, a cloth in his mouth.

"Sam?" Nox whispered, cradling him in his lap. "Come on." The gag went, then the ropes around his wrists. "Come on, I need you to wake up." He could smell the blood on Sam's clothes, feel the tackiness on his face. The broken sound he made as Nox began to work on his ankles let Nox know they'd hurt him.

Fuckers were going to pay.

Once Sam was free, Nox maneuvered him over his shoulder in a fireman's carry. The lack of guards told him that if they were right about the bomb, it would be happening soon. Maybe he still had time to find Cade.

Nox carried Sam through the suite and back out into the hallway. He drew his gun, knowing he might have to shoot his way out. Back down to the stairwell, panting with the exertion of Sam over his shoulder.

Down below, he heard someone coming.

Gun drawn, he went down to the next landing, catching sight of someone in black moving around below.

Slowly, he went down step by step. Sam was making small sounds of discomfort against his back. "Shhh," he whispered.

Below, something clanged.

"Shit," he heard echoing up. Footsteps got closer.

Then Cade came into view.

Relief flooded through Nox's body.

"Hurry up," he called.

Cade looked up; he was stark white and covered in streaks of blood.

"What—"

"Nothing. Oh Christ, Sam—is he okay?" Cade rushed up; he grabbed Nox's arm, then touched Sam's face. "I heard a bunch of people in the stairwell. They're leaving."

"The bomb," Nox said.

He took off down the stairs then, willing Cade to follow. Twenty-six fucking floors to get down—and he knew the countdown had already started.

"Wait, wait, Nox!" Cade called hoarsely after him. "We have to hit an alarm or something—the fire alarm. All those people."

Fuck.

"When we get downstairs."

"It'll be too late. You keep going down—I'll set off the alarms and meet you at the bottom."

Fuck.

No.

Nox stopped on the next landing. Cade skidded to a halt next to him.

"Can you carry him?" Nox laid Sam down gently on the ground. "Get him out of here. I'm going to hit the fire alarm and people are going to flood these stairs."

"I can...."

"You know this building better than I do, which means you can get Sam out of here quicker," Nox said smoothly. "I need you to do that."

"Right, okay." Cade didn't hesitate. He pushed past Nox, quick to pull Sam into his arms. "There are alarms on each floor—hit the one by the elevators and it'll set off the sprinklers."

Nox brushed his hand across Sam's bruised cheek. He leaned over and touched his forehead to Cade's. His lover looked just as terrified and determined as he felt—like it didn't matter if death was waiting around the next corner. They weren't going to stop until someone stopped them.

A calm he didn't expect fell over Nox. He pulled back, flashed Cade a smile, then ran down the steps to the next floor.

CHAPTER FORTY-SEVEN

LIKE THE fucking devil was on his heels, Cade ran. Sam slung over his shoulder, dead weight, bruised and scared shitless, Cade ran. He skidded a few times, rammed into walls and railings, nearly pitched down to both their certain deaths more than once, but he ran.

Above him he heard the shriek of the alarm, saw red lights flashing. He could hear doors slamming open, frantic screams and the buzz of frightened partiers streaming into the stairwell.

Cade ran.

He reached the street level doors and pushed.

Nothing.

Locked.

"No, no, no," he whispered, banging his fist on the metal. "Open the door."

Nothing.

He fumbled for the access card in his pocket and swiped it frantically in the nearby reader.

It flashed red.

Fuck no.

All the way, all of this, for nothing. The sounds of the evacuation got closer; they would all get down here and panic, crushing him and Sam to death as they tried to escape.

He went back up to the first-floor landing, panting at the strain. That door opened.

Cade stepped into the hallway that connected the upper lobby and maintenance rooms. He hesitated—he was still a full story up, and they couldn't jump. There had to be another exit, maybe one that wasn't locked.

He'd gotten twenty feet, thirty, headed for the back of the building, when it shook violently, throwing him to the ground. Sam flew out of his grasp as the Iron Butterfly screamed and groaned around them.

Cade choked on the dust, and debris filled the air. He staggered to his feet, pulling a moaning Sam into his arms once again. He couldn't manage to get him over his shoulder; instead he dragged him along as they made their way to the back stairs.

Another explosion rocked the Butterfly. Behind him, Cade heard the ceiling fall in, the crash of the giant chandeliers from the upper lobby. The door was twenty feet away. Ten. Five.

Cade shoved at the door and it mercifully flew open under the force of his weight.

They tumbled down the metal stairs into the security room near the back door.

He smelled freedom.

Chapter Forty-eight

Nox hit the alarm, then ran back into the stairwell. He shot at a security camera on the next floor, shorting out the line. The sparks tripped the sprinklers on that floor as well, as the alarms blared and red lights flashed. He ran down the stairwell, each lower floor filling with more and more patrons and staff in various states of undress.

Damian, the business manager he'd met on his first visit, stood in the center of the hallway, frantically directing guests toward both sets of stairs. His eyes got wide when he saw Nox hurry past him. They exchanged terse nods and Nox was gone again.

He needed to make sure Cade and Sam were out.

At floor twenty, in the thick of people in fancy dress tripping down the stairs, Nox felt the first rumble.

"Hurry up!" he screamed. "Hurry!"

He ducked out on nineteen and ran to the back stairwell. Fewer people were evacuating that way, mostly staff and maintenance workers who knew about it. He dodged through them, jumped over the railing, and slid down twice as fast.

Another strong explosion nearly knocked him off-balance.

Smoke filled the stairwell, panicking the crowd. People started falling and were trampled as flight took priority over one's fellow man. Nox grabbed a tiny woman in a housekeeping uniform as she skidded near the edge of the stairs, nearly toppling over.

"Come on, come on, on your feet," he urged her. A man in a bartending uniform grabbed her around the waist and carried her off before Nox could react.

Nox kept moving, trying to keep order even as he scanned farther down for signs of Cade and Sam.

They came to the main floor—and the crowd stopped.

"The door is locked!" someone screamed, and hysteria rose like a storm.

"Shit." Nox pushed his way down through the crying and wailing to the bottom and grabbed at a man in a tuxedo who was frantically pulling on the handle.

"Stand back. Get everyone back." Nox pulled the Sig out and fired at the lock until it broke.

"Try it again. One, two, three." The row of people closest to the door threw themselves at it—it shook under their weight but it didn't budge. Behind them, some of the crowd began running back upstairs to the next landing. Screams told him that wasn't working either. The smoke thickened and Nox kicked at the door in a fury.

A faint scraping sound from the other side caught his attention; he leaned closer to hear through the commotion.

"Hang on!" someone said. "Just wait."

More scraping and then the blessed sound of the door being yanked open.

The flood of frantic people pushed past, shoving Nox along like a leaf caught in a storm. He broke free and ran ahead, pushed open the security door, the final barrier to the street.

He saw Cade then, a few feet down the alleyway, directing people away from the building as it fell apart. Nox pushed the crowd forward, shoving bodies through the door.

"Run! Get as far away as you can!"

Another explosion, this one higher up. The Iron Butterfly rained down glass and steel and fire from its top floors as the survivors ran into the night. As the trickle of people slowed, Nox followed, headed for Cade.

Who saw him a second later.

"Thank God," he gasped, grabbing Nox's arm and pulling him farther away from the building. "Sam's over here." They ran down the alley and around the corner. A block up, Nox saw Sam tucked into the entrance of a tiny Italian restaurant.

They were steps away from Sam when a massive crash turned them around.

The Iron Butterfly collapsed in on itself with a shriek, showering a two-block radius with its destruction.

Chapter Forty-nine

CADE WASHED his hands again, still trying to erase the blood he imagined clung to his skin. He knew it was a little crazy, and he knew the red hue of his skin was from the harsh chemical soap, but he didn't care.

He killed someone last night, and it wasn't any easier to stomach in the morning light.

The tiny bathroom of an abandoned restaurant on the edge of the District smelled rank. A few months ago it was a happening Spanish eatery, but the owner had fallen prey to the gambling right down the street and lost it. It was the first thing they came to, as they raced from the scene of the explosion, that was easy to break into.

It was safe for now.

The running water in the employee bathroom was a miracle, the still working light in the manager's office a gift from God he actually said a thank-you prayer for.

On the floor of the office lay Sam, wrapped in blankets and spare coats, everything Cade had taken from his apartment to keep the teenager warm. Nox had been in and out for hours, back to the printing place to get their things, breaking into businesses to get the supplies they needed. Cade walked back slowly, using the trail of sunlight from the broken windows to maneuver through the overturned tables and chairs, coated in dust. In the distance, he caught Nox's profile, and his heart twisted.

They were in so much fucking trouble, and Cade didn't have a single suggestion of how to get out of it.

He dragged his boots over the dirt—and what he was pretending was more dirt—and God knew what else, and stepped through the doorway. Nox didn't look away from where Sam was curled in that nest of warmth, didn't acknowledge Cade's presence.

Does he blame me? Cade thought. *I blame myself for starting all this in the first place.*

"I need to get some supplies," Nox said finally, shattering the silence.

Cade looked up and nodded. "I can—"

"I'll be back in about an hour," he continued as if Cade hadn't spoken. "You still have the gun."

It wasn't a question, so Cade just nodded.

Nox left without ever meeting his eyes.

Sig in hand, Cade leaned against the wall and watched Sam sleep. Every few minutes Sam's rasping breathing would turn into a wet cough, and every time, Cade's chest tightened in sympathy. Smoke inhalation. Bruised ribs from the beating. So much damage and they couldn't go to the hospital.

They couldn't go anywhere.

The Iron Butterfly was a crime scene, police tape fluttering around the rubble. The body count was 264—from the bomb, mostly. At least another six hundred managed to escape thanks to the early warning. Zed and Billy were another matter entirely, but Cade wasn't sure if the police knew what—or who—killed them yet.

All they were sure of was that the Vigilante had blown the shit out of the biggest casino in the District during Anniversary Weekend, aided and abetted by Cade Creel and Sam Mullens. All the news cycles were saying it, so it must be true.

There was evidence, according to Mason, who'd been frantically calling Sam's cell, which they'd found at the bottom of his backpack. Nox finally put him out of his misery and got valuable information in return. The police chief had been to the City Hall complex twice in the past three days, and the news reported arrests were imminent.

Cade wondered if his friends had gotten out in time.

He wished he knew where Alec was.

What he really wanted? Was to go the fuck home.

CADE STAYED awake until Nox returned, bags of stolen food in his hand. He didn't say anything, just pushed the gun on the floor toward his lover's boots and then lay down to sleep.

CHAPTER FIFTY

NOX SAT on the floor, Sig in his lap, knife in his boot, the sleeping forms of the two people he cared about most in the world a foot in either direction.

He was waiting for sounds of the police, or whoever it was that set the bomb at the Iron Butterfly. He didn't even know for sure who was after him—them. All he knew was that he was waiting for cocked guns and the stomp of feet against the concrete floor.

In his mind, he knew what he should do if that happened.

Three bullets and then oblivion. Three bullets and they would be free.

Except....

What if there was still a chance they could survive? He'd cheated death before. Maybe he could do it again.

The sun shifted as the hours passed. Sam's breathing continued to labor, Cade didn't stir from his tightly wound cocoon. Nox felt the weight of the past few weeks sucking his energy, draining him of his mental process. His hope.

Protecting Sam and Cade was his priority right now. He couldn't do anything until they were gone, until they were safe. It clouded his mind to worry about them, and he couldn't find his anger—couldn't peel away his love to find the fire that had kept him moving and surviving for seventeen years.

He just wanted them to be safe.

When it was dark, hunger pulled Nox off the floor. He ate a few slices of bread and drank two bottles of water before patrolling the perimeter. Still no police, no one canvassing the area. How convenient that the cops weren't sweeping the abandoned buildings closest to the Iron Butterfly.

Convenient.

Maybe too convenient.

ANOTHER HOUR.

Nox stared at a blank wall, cataloguing each tab of wrinkled and filthy paint until something switched on in his mind's eye. Clarity. Space to think.

He traveled through everything that had happened in the past forty-eight hours. He went back two weeks, then two more. He replayed conversations, always waylaid by a memory of Cade under him, splayed out in his bed and absorbing each stroke and thrust….

No. Two weeks. Two more. Conversations. Moments.

What was he missing?

The man in the darkness—the one who told him to back off. Was he the person behind all of this? Was he Rachel's boss? He knew her to be too good of a liar to take anything she said at face value, but Mr. White's reaction to her name….

Who else could have been sending him those messages?

He went over each of the words, each of the nuances, his surroundings.

He was missing something. Something big.

HALF PAST nine and a flashlight beam swung past the opening over the back door. Nox had been waiting there, ready with his blackjack, just in case.

But a quiet creak of the door revealed only Mason Todd, wide-eyed and trailing the tang of fear and sweat.

"No one followed you," Nox said, giving the rookie a long look.

He shook his head. "No. I followed your directions." He pulled a knapsack from behind his back. "I got what you asked for."

Trusting Mason wasn't the easiest decision Nox had ever made, but he resolved he could snap the cop's neck if he betrayed them—it wouldn't be hard, because right now every person with a badge had earned his absolute derision.

They were raping this city as much as the drug dealers, and the blood of thousands of people dripped off their hands.

Mason better be different or he would be floating in the East River by dawn.

BACK IN the office, Nox found Cade awake and sitting up. He didn't say anything, didn't acknowledge him or Mason. The pull to walk to him, the need to touch him, swamped Nox's senses for a moment, but his son's thin cough directed him elsewhere.

The feeling of being divided—take care of Sam, take and give comfort to Cade—was frightening.

From the knapsack Mason pulled medical supplies: little vials of medication and sterile needles, a small machine to ease his breathing, even a portable IV drip with several bags of antibiotics.

"It'll help him faster if we do it that way," Mason said, gently pushing back the covers to reach Sam's arm. He stirred, blinking and moving into wakefulness.

"Dad?" he rasped, eyes unfocused as he looked around.

"Right here. I'm here." Nox sat on the ground next to his son, reassuring him as Mason continued his prepping. Alcohol rub to the inside of his elbow. The careful insertion of the IV into his vein.

Sam whined as Nox rubbed his shoulder.

"Shhh, it's okay. It's medicine. Just breathe." Nox watched every move Mason made, catalogued the way his hands stayed steady even as sweat beaded on his hairline, his gaze trained intently on Sam.

"Where did you learn that?" Nox asked as Sam settled back to sleep.

Mason didn't look up, fully focused on holding the bag and watching the medicine begin to flow. "My father was an EMT in Boston. I started volunteering when I was sixteen."

"Why didn't you become a Boston cop, then?"

"New York seemed to need me more," he said absently, adjusting the line until he seemed satisfied.

Nox felt a sliver of relief then—the smallest possible amount, but still. He'd take it.

"Here's the list," Mason said once they'd gotten Sam resettled, the IV hooked to a portable stand and the blankets once again tucked around him.

Nox took Mason's tablet and scrolled down the list of properties owned by the proprietor of the printing company. When he reached Morningside Sanitarium, he didn't even blink. The Iron Butterfly was next. All the properties attached to a name and address Nox knew would turn out to be a dummy corporation. It was like he knew. The person pulling strings was bigger than he could have imagined.

"I NEED to go out for a few hours," Nox said, startling Mason out of a snooze. The young cop had been sitting at Sam's side since he arrived, barely looking away. Nox was starting to think Mason's help wasn't just about doing the right thing.

"What?"

"I'll be back soon."

Mason nodded, his gaze flickering up to Nox's face. "Okay."

"You armed?"

The rookie nodded.

"Shoot anyone who isn't me." He hesitated, chancing a look in Cade's direction. "If I'm not back by dawn, I want you to go to your captain and tell him everything."

Mason started to say something, but Cade sprung from his makeshift bed in a flurry of movement, interrupting them.

"No."

Nox braced himself. "Yes."

"You can't make that decision for me," Cade snapped, throwing off the coat as he stalked over to Nox. "I'm not a fucking child."

"No—but he is. He's my son, and I'm going to make sure he's alive for his eighteenth birthday," Nox said, calm and unfazed as Cade pressed into him. He could read the frantic movements, could see the wild fear in his lover's eyes as clear as day.

"Where are you going?" Cade demanded. Nox saw the dawning realization in his eyes.

"To get some information."

CHAPTER FIFTY-ONE

CADE HAD to do something, so he folded blankets and coats and sorted through Mason's knapsack of medical wonders. He went through their food supplies, then paced around the room reciting Bible verses in his head.

Yet those who wait for the Lord will gain new strength; they will mount up with wings like eagles; they will run and not get tired; they will walk and not become weary.

He thought about his mom and dad. He thought about his brother Lee and how pissed he'd be if he were here. A guy who didn't do waiting all that well, he would be the one picking up a pipe and rushing out the door, trying to find someone to thump.

Cade was the peacemaker. Cade would say, "Put that down before you get your ass kicked."

He wished his brother were here right now. And he wouldn't tell him to put the pipe down, not at all.

In the corner, Mason continued his vigil. There wasn't much mystery to the way the kid looked at Sam, and somehow that made Cade sad and grateful at once. Sad because they'd probably all be dead or in jail by morning, and grateful because he knew he could trust him.

At the very least trust him to protect Sam.

"I wish we could get him to my parents' farm," Cade said, realizing a second later it was out loud.

Mason looked up. "Where do they live?"

"South Carolina."

Checking Sam's IV, Mason said, "If we could find a boat, that'd take us down the coast."

"We? You leaving your post, Officer?" Cade sat down on the edge of the bruised surface of the metal desk.

"I'm pretty sure I don't have a job anymore. I mean—harboring fugitives, collusion, stealing medical supplies...." A sickly smile bloomed. "I'll be lucky if they don't send me to prison for life."

"We'll get out of here." Cade tapped his boot against the floor. Get down to the farm—if they could do that.

The clanging sound again. Cade got up, made his way over to the door. Behind him, Mason scrambled up.

They stood in the doorway, Mason drawing his gun.

"Cade?" a tremulous voice called.

"Rachel?" Cade ran out into the dining room, making his way toward the sound of her voice.

She was standing by the back door, decked out in black from head to toe like a fashionista ninja. And she wasn't alone.

"Damian's with me." She indicated the stark white-faced terror that was Zed's money man.

"How the hell did you find us?"

Damian blanched. "You sent us a text. To meet you here."

Cade stopped in midstride, fear gripping him. "Someone texted you. And gave you this address."

"Yeah—I was hiding in the residence and then Rachel came," Damian rambled, his voice cracking. "Mr. Z is dead and we didn't know what to do and then we got the texts." He was carrying bags—both shoulders, each hand—looking crumpled and terrified in his overcoat.

Cade ran a hand through his hair. "I didn't send those texts."

"Shit," Rachel spit out.

"We have to get out of here," Mason said from somewhere behind him.

"Come on."

They packed up what little was there—Rachel took the backpacks while Cade and Mason gathered Sam in a makeshift stretcher made from one of the heavy blankets. They moved with agonizing slowness across the restaurant floor, through the back entrance, and down a rickety set of metal stairs.

The air smelled like snow; already icy flakes intermittently hit Cade's skin as they headed for the back alley. The plan was to find a hiding place, then send Mason to commandeer a vehicle.

Not their best work, but it was all they could come up with in the middle of their panic.

Home resounded again and again in Cade's mind.

His mother would be able to help Sam. His father and Lee were exactly the kind of people to have at your back. They were mostly off the grid, self-sufficient.

"We need a boat," he murmured, straining at the weight of Sam and the sloppiness of the blankets holding him. Mason grunted something that sounded like an affirmation.

"A boat?" Damian caught up to them, struggling with the bags. "Are we leaving?"

"Over here," Rachel called—on the other side of a split chain-link fence, she stood beside a garage, its door broken in.

They maneuvered through, the snow falling harder with each passing minute. Inside, there wasn't much room; two trucks sat in all their rusted glory beside tables filled with debris. Rachel was all the way in the back, rooting around.

"There's a breakroom or something," she called. "Empty."

The narrow alley of space between the trucks was a challenge; Sam thrashed a bit as Mason called out to soothe him. Damian brought up the rear, muttering to himself.

They settled back down in the dusty former breakroom. Damian sank into a corner, knees up to his forehead. Rachel knelt next to Sam, fussing with his covers as Mason checked his IV.

"It's almost dawn," Mason said finally, not looking at Cade.

Rachel sat back on her heels and turned to give Cade a long look. "Where's your friend?"

"Out. He'll be back soon." Cade crossed his arms over his chest, feeling defiant. And afraid. "I'll be right back."

Cade went to stand at the opening, hidden behind the partial wall. He watched the abandoned restaurant, the empty street. He breathed shallow, praying in his head, thinking about home like it was the Holy Land. It would solve all their problems. Everything would be all right if he got home.

Thing was, he wasn't going without Nox.

DAWN BLUSHED over the horizon, shades of gray and pink as the snow fell.

Rachel came out to see if Cade wanted another jacket, some gloves, which he accepted with only a murmured thank-you.

Mason came out next. "He said…."

"No."

The sun rose high in the sky. Everyone left him alone.

His stomach rumbled with hunger; he was thirsty, he had to pee, and yet he didn't move. He needed to come up with another plan—talk to Damian, use Rachel's connections, Mason's knowledge of the city. He needed to get Sam to safety, because if Nox didn't come back, Cade could at least give him that.

Then he saw someone moving at the back door of the restaurant, near the delivery door.

Nox.

CHAPTER FIFTY-THREE

NOTHING IN the world was as beautiful as Cade running toward the stairs.

"You were supposed to leave," he said, his voice rough from yelling, his hands aching from the violence he'd wrought at the Habanos club house. "Why don't you listen?"

"Screw you, asshole. I'm not Lois Lane." Cade paused a second before bodychecking him into the wall. "No, actually, I *am* Lois Lane—she wouldn't put up with that sort of shit request either."

Nox put his arms around Cade and held on tight.

"I wasn't going to leave without you," Cade murmured, pressing his face against Nox's shoulder. "I'm on your side, you know that, right? I just want to help you and Sam."

Nox exhaled, shuddering as he pulled Cade tighter.

"You're crazy to hook yourself up in this mess," he whispered, holding on for dear life. "But Jesus, I'm so glad you're here."

Cade was beaming, his pale eyes bright when he pulled back. "Thank you. Also I'm a fucking genius, because I have a plan."

"A plan for what?"

"To get the fuck out of the city. Damian has a line on a boat we can use...."

"A boat?" Nox rubbed his hands up and down Cade's back, relieved and overwhelmed.

"Damian thinks he can get us a boat to take us down the coast." Cade tipped his head back, and Nox saw everything—this terrible situation and the hope flaring in his eyes.

"Down...."

"South Carolina. My parents' farm." Cade was talking fast, so Nox just nodded. "I could get word to them and they'd take us in—all of us. My mom could help Sam—my dad and my brother." He stopped to take a breath. "They could help us."

Nox wanted to refuse him, to veto this plan, but the truth was, he didn't have another solution to their problems at this moment. They were wanted, Sam was hurt—hiding in the city meant always risking being found. He didn't have the security of the shadows anymore. Worse, he didn't have any answers. The mystery man's identity was buried under layers of security he couldn't seem to penetrate. The gang leader didn't know; Brownigan—well, whatever he knew got him killed before Nox even got a chance to ask.

They'd be safe at the farm, at least for a while.

"Okay, let's do this," he said.

Cade slumped against him in relief. "Thank you," he whispered. He pushed up to lay a gentle kiss on Nox's mouth, the sweetness of the gesture making Nox weak in the knees. He cupped his hand against Cade's cheek, bringing him back in to deepen the kiss. They stood there in each other's arms, exchanging soft kisses, until someone cleared their throat.

Damian.

"I need a cell phone and access to a computer network that isn't connected to the city," he announced, hands in his pockets as he stood at the bottom of the stairs. "And probably a lot of money."

NOX AND Cade, arms around each other, walked back to where the rest of them were hiding. Rachel stood defiantly in the corner, a tiny smirk on her face.

Nox's back went up like a pissed-off cat's.

"She's not coming," Nox said, letting go of Cade reluctantly. Damian trailed behind, twisting his hands nervously in front of him.

"Yes, she is." Cade grabbed at his hand, but Nox didn't stop. He walked right up to her.

His gaze met Rachel's—and she didn't even blink.

"I'm not leaving without her," Cade said.

"You don't owe her anything," he said, low and angry, fists tight against his thighs. Rachel's chin went up and she looked at him with accusing eyes.

Cade's words seemed to come from her. "No, but you do."

She'd alerted them to Sam's whereabouts. More than that, she'd kept his secret for all these years.

Cade didn't blink, didn't look away. There was anger in his expression, but oh, the pleading in his pale eyes.

Please. Do this for me. Do this for Sam.

"I won't tell him," Rachel murmured. "Jenny's dead. I just want to be away from here. I just need a way off the island," she whispered, the façade dropping for a moment as she leaned in closer. "This wasn't me, Nox. It wasn't. The only reason I'm alive right now is because Zed was kind enough to warn me."

The implication, the echo of what she was saying, sat thick in the air between them.

"Why should I believe you?"

"Because I found your kid. Because I let you live all those years ago," she hissed. "I almost died on that fucking ferry and I still kept your secret! I stayed away from you so even if they figured out it was me, I couldn't lead them to you!"

Nox stared at her. Of all the faces Rachel—and Jenny—had worn in front of him, this was the closest thing to human he could remember.

"You're a murderer and I don't trust you. But if I take you along, at least I know you aren't running to your friends to come after us."

Rachel's eyes flashed something, and his gut told him to throw her in the river and get the hell out of here. But then she nodded, putting her hands up in supplication.

"Thank you," Cade was saying behind him; Nox felt a soft touch against his shoulder. "Thank you."

"If you compromise us in any way, I'll kill you."

Cade froze beside him.

Rachel went pale, but he saw the respect in her eyes. *Understood,* she mouthed.

EPILOGUE

NOX LEFT Sam on the bottom deck of the yacht, sleeping in the master bedroom under a pile of blankets, under the watchful eye of a nearby Mason, who couldn't—wouldn't—be budged.

He tried not to dwell on what was going on there.

Up top, Damian nervously paced the aft deck as the rays of sunrise poked out from behind the New Jersey skyline.

Outwardly calm, Nox walked the boards of the *S.S. Miriam*, sharing quick glances with the three crew members. He'd vetted them, menaced them, and then laid some serious cash in their hands.

Only the captain knew where they were going; the rest only needed to know betrayal equaled a bullet.

THE MAIN space was well-kept, all gleaming wood paneling, stainless steel appliances, and expensive fabric on the couches. A narrow staircase led Cade to the bottom deck, where doors to three bedrooms and a bathroom beckoned. Only one light was lit, though—the master bedroom.

Voices drew him to the doorway.

In the center of the seventies-chic bed, Sam lay wrapped in a blanket, only his hair peeking out. Mason, dressed in a pair of Cade's jeans and a sweater, was next to him, leaning against the headboard. They barely touched, but there was no mistaking the intimacy between them.

"Hey," he said, calling their attention. Cade noted the way Mason put another few inches between his body and Sam's but didn't jump off the bed. So feeling cautious but not ashamed, Cade guessed.

Mason nodded. Sam poked his head up so Cade could see his rheumy eyes.

"I think we're leaving in a few minutes." Cade smiled. "Just wanted to warn you against sudden lurches." He stepped into the room, dropped his bag near the door. "How are you feeling?"

"Okay," Sam croaked through the blanket. His voice cracked, a wheeze punctuating the sound. "Better."

Cade patted the blanket, assuming it was Sam's knee or close to it. "Yeah, I can hear that," he said without sarcasm. "Looks like you're in good hands."

Mason caught his eye, flushing under Cade's smile.

"Need anything?" Cade included them both—in response, Sam shrugged as he lay back down, as if he'd used up his energy in thirty seconds of conversation. Mason watched him, a frown teasing at his mouth.

"Maybe some water," Mason said, gaze never leaving Sam.

"Good idea." Another pat, pat, pat on Sam's leg and Cade straightened up. "Give me a few minutes."

They didn't seem to notice him leave, nor did they look up as Cade backed into Nox, who was standing right outside the stateroom door.

"Sorry," Cade murmured.

Nox put his hand on Cade's hip to steady him—gentle, possessive—and they stood for a moment, back to chest, watching Sam and Mason.

"You doing okay?" Nox whispered in his ear.

Cade pushed back, needing more of his lover's warmth. They were leaving, they were going to be safe—and yet Cade felt like cold tendrils from the island were twining around his ankles, determined to keep them here.

"Yeah—just... impatient to get moving," he said softly. In the room, Mason fussed with Sam's blankets, his expression devoted.

"Hmm," Nox said, clearly distracted.

Cade swallowed a tired laugh. "He's old enough to date, and Mason's not so old that it's creepy," he whispered, turning his head to give Nox a grin.

"I'm not dealing with this right now." Nox sighed, keeping his arm around Cade as they walked back toward the galley.

THE YACHT sailed under the skeleton of the Verrazano Bridge, around the rusted pylons, and headed south. The captain and crew moved in perfect tandem; Nox leaned against the port railing, welcoming the sun on his face and shoulders after being in that dark restaurant for so long.

He watched the horizon, not the disappearing skyline behind him. He would rather think about the future.

Except....

A noise alerted him to the presence of someone else on the deck. He turned his head to find Rachel, a blanket wrapped around her shoulders, coming to stand next to him. They hadn't seen her for dinner, nor the quick head count Nox insisted on.

His back stiffened; despite her seeming change of heart, Nox still couldn't relax around Jenny.

Rachel.

"I meant what I said," Nox said, staring at the choppy water below.

Rachel turned slowly; in the scant light, he saw one eyebrow raised and a smirk of amusement on her face. "My word wasn't good enough the first time?"

"I don't trust you," he murmured, low and urgent. Sam slept below deck, with Mason keeping watch. The crew, sleeping in shifts, were nowhere near. Cade had been in the shower when Nox had said he needed some air.

"You should learn to let go of the past, Nox. It was a long time ago and we're all different people," she said, steely and calm.

"You're still a murderer."

Rachel laughed. "So are you, my darling."

They stood in silence, streaming through the water and out to sea.

"I'm curious—is Mr. White dead?" Rachel asked, breaking the quiet as the sun set completely in the distance.

Nox tightened his grip on the railing. "Yes."

"You know, then?"

"Yes."

"Mmm." Rachel tightened the blanket around her shoulders. "Another thing to keep from young Sam."

"He's never going to know." Finality in every syllable.

"About Mr. White? About your shared lineage?" Rachel tipped her head to one side, that smirk still dancing around her mouth. Behind them, a light went on, bathing them both.

"None of it." He reached out and grabbed her upper arm, squeezed it tightly. "They're all dead—my mother and father, that piece-of-shit rapist." Nox paused. "Jenny."

Rachel stared at him long and hard, then—smiled. "True," she said softly. "And Rachel is just some nice woman who helped you and Sam in your time of need. A friend of Cade's. You're his devoted father, who would do anything to protect him. All is right in his world."

Nox's stomach tightened. Every instinct reminded him Rachel could not be trusted. He didn't answer her, just kept their gazes locked until she looked away and he dropped his hand from her arm.

"Change of subject?" Rachel asked.

He was just about to turn away, eager to check on Sam. Eager to crawl into bed with Cade. He paused a moment, though, his muscles tightening as he waited. "What?"

"We got away pretty easily," she said, head tilted to one side. "No one's after us so far."

Nox frowned. "I made sure...."

"Someone knew you were at the restaurant. They sent Damian and I there, but not the cops," she mused. "Damian got a boat, found the only trustworthy crew in the city, apparently. Got an injured teenager, a cop, and several people with warrants out for their arrest all the way here without even a tail. For suspect number one, you sure didn't attract attention." At the end of her little speech, she paused. "Ever wonder—why didn't they just kill you?"

It took him aback.

It moved him a literal step back; then he turned on his heel and let his surprise and anger fuel him down below deck. They directed him physically even as his mind bounced around.

Sam being let out of jail.

The warning when they could have easily put a bullet in his head.

Getting out of the Iron Butterfly before the bomb went off.

In the master stateroom, Sam lay curled up under the blankets, Mason's upper body spooned around him, one leg on the floor, his sidearm visible. Protecting Sam.

Nox felt gratitude and a pang of sadness at the same time.

He closed the door quietly and made his way to the smaller bedroom on the opposite side of the deck.

Nox moved in the darkness, making his way around the tiny stateroom. Their gear was stashed on top of a dresser in the corner, moonlight creating patterns as it shone through the round window over the bed. He stripped down to his underwear, silent and stealthy.

Clad only in boxers, Cade slept on, flat on his back, arms akimbo.

A spike of relief shot through Nox as he settled next to Cade. The mattress dipping roused Cade; he turned his head with a quiet sound of confusion.

"Shhh, go back to sleep," Nox whispered, but Cade struggled to open his eyes even as he pulled Nox closer.

"Everything okay?"

"Fine." Nox pressed a kiss against Cade's ear. "Everything's fine."

Cade sighed, winding around him until Nox was a prisoner in the bed, trapped by the bulk of his lover's body. Cade used him like a mattress, pressing him down as he got comfortable.

"Go to sleep," Cade murmured into Nox's chest. "We're safe. Go to sleep."

Nox didn't argue, didn't share the turmoil burning through his brain. They weren't yet safe—they'd gotten away. Nox's main concern was elevating their circumstances so Sam would be all right. So Cade was safe. They were going to South Carolina, and maybe everything would be okay.

Even as Nox's heart steadied, with Cade in his arms, his brain refused to quiet.

Why didn't they just kill you?

Why?

TERE MICHAELS unofficially began her writing career at the age of four when she learned that people got paid to write stories. It seemed the most perfect and logical job in the world and after that, her path was never in question. (The romance writer part was written in the stars—she was born on Valentine's Day.)

It took thirty-six years of "research" and "life experience" and well... life... before her first book was published but there are no regrets (she doesn't believe in them). Along the way, she had some interesting jobs in television, animation, arts education, PR and a national magazine—but she never stopped believing she would eventually earn her living writing stories about love.

She is a member of RWA, Rainbow Romance Writers, and Liberty States Fiction Writers. Her home base is a small town in New Jersey, very near NYC, a city she dearly loves. She shares her life with her husband, her teenaged son—who will just not stop growing—and three exceedingly spoiled cats. Her spare time is spent watching way too much sports programming, going to the movies and for long walks/runs in the park, reading her book club's current selection, and volunteering.

Nothing makes her happier than knowing she made a reader laugh or smile or cry. It's the purpose of sharing her work with people. She loves hearing from fans and fellow writers, and is always available for speaking engagements, visits and workshops. Find her at http://www.teremichaels.com and on Twitter (@TereMichaels), and Facebook (https://www.facebook.com/tere.michaels).

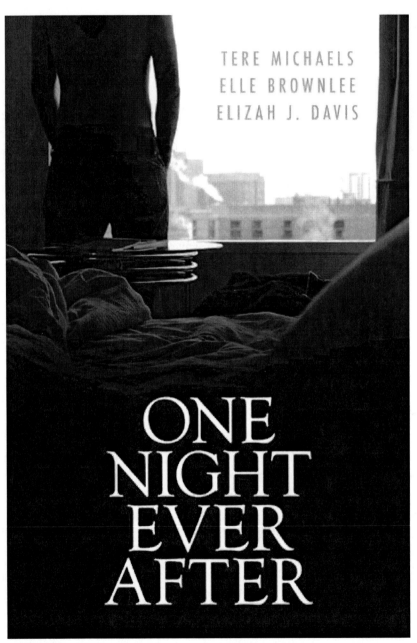

TERE MICHAELS
ELLE BROWNLEE
ELIZAH J. DAVIS

ONE
NIGHT
EVER
AFTER

http://www.dreamspinnerpress.com

PAWN TAKES ROOK

LEX CHASE

http://www.dreamspinnerpress.com

http://www.dreamspinnerpress.com

CPSIA information can be obtained at www.ICGtesting.com
Printed in the USA
LVOW08s0200190215

427262LV00001B/33/P

9 781632 162168